# The ARCANA

## BOOK THREE

## JACI MILLER

*The Arcana: Book 3*

The Scrying Trilogy

Copyright © 2019 by Jaci Miller

Solitary Pen Press

Cover design and interior formatting by Streetlight Graphics

Print ISBN: 978-0-9988069-4-5

Ebook ISBN: 978-0-9988069-5-2

First Edition 2019

www.jacimiller.com

www.solitarypenpress.com

# ALSO BY JACI MILLER

## THE SCRYING TRILOGY

*The Scrying*
*The Hallowed*

## ANTHOLOGIES

Realms of Magic, A Spellcasters Story
Collection: *The Dark Season*

# DEDICATION

To all those who love to write,
and those who love to read.

*"Walk into the darkness but do not
be seduced by the illusion.*

*For if you cannot see your way through
to the light within, all will be lost."*

-Adaridge, the last Druid of Thanissia

# CHAPTER 1

*Christmas 2014*

THE PARTY WAS IN FULL swing when Lucien Beck exited the elevator from the thirteenth floor. An energized buzz drifted toward him. The second-floor gallery, a wide-open space with a grand balcony overlooking the main lobby, echoed with laughter and shouts.

Holiday decorations highlighted the revelry as the guests unwound from the workday. The forty-foot Christmas tree stood at the center of the lobby the top visible over the wrought iron and glass railing. An impressive silver star sat atop the crown twinkling as the joyous sound of holiday music filled the air. Tiny fairy lights illuminated a gold banner that read *Beck Holdings Annual Christmas Party*.

*She outdid herself,* Lucien thought.

His eyes searched for her in the crowd finding her standing by the staircase laughing with the other guests. Sensing the familiar gaze, she turned and smiled giving him a subtle wave. Lucien nodded in response and moved through the throng of holiday revelers, shaking hands and acknowledging guests, until he reached the makeshift bar at the back of the gallery.

"The usual Mr. Beck?" The bubbly blonde bartender

said, batting her eyelashes as she flashed him a pearly-white smile.

"Yes, thank you. Jenny, isn't it?"

She blushed, nodding and handing him an iced champagne flute of sparkling Perrier. Her fingers brushed his hand, and she smiled coyly before flitting away to help another guest.

"Does it ever get tiring?"

"What, throwing holiday parties for my employees and clients?" He turned to address the statuesque woman beside him.

Dressed in white, her pantsuit was a stunning off-set to her rich caramel skin and amber eyes. With her graying hair pulled back into a perfect chignon, she was both stylish and classic.

"Hello, Celeste. I'm glad you could make it."

She ignored his pleasantries. "You know what I mean Lucien. The endless parade of faceless women."

He shrugged, indifferent to Celeste's astute observation.

At thirty-four Lucien Beck was New York City's most influential and eligible bachelor. CEO and sole shareholder of Beck Holdings, the multi-million-dollar company he built from the ground up. In the past decade Lucien had amassed a commercial real estate empire but in the past few years had branched out, buying failing businesses and re-energizing them or liquidating their assets. Today his portfolio included commercial properties, a news organization, and a five-star restaurant. His charitable organizations comprised of two animal shelters, a youth center, and a small medical facility located in the Bronx and aiding low-income individuals.

Lucien scanned the familiar faces in the room. Besides his employees, many of the guests in attendance at this year's annual holiday party were charitable donors. Celeste, one of the most important.

She cast a pitiful look toward the young bartender who still couldn't take her eyes off Lucien. "They will never learn."

"Learn what?"

"That you have no interest in any of them, past a night in their bed."

"Don't be so crass Celeste, it's beneath you," Lucien said in a teasing manner.

He and Celeste Winslow had been friends and colleagues for the better part of a decade. They had a strong business relationship and a comfortable friendship. Lucien admired her tenacity even though sometimes her tact lacked.

He glanced at the stunning woman beside him and smiled. She'd done well for herself.

Celeste grew up poor, married rich, and became a widow twenty years later. Although many called her a gold-digger, she liked to think of herself as an opportunist.

Growing up in the heart of the Louisiana bayou Celeste was a poor black girl with no future, but she refused to become a statistic. The first in her family to graduate high school and the valedictorian of her college class, Celeste flourished. After graduation, she got a job at one of New York City's premier financial institutions specializing in multi-million-dollar portfolios. Her natural beauty and talent for numbers soon elicited the attention of the owner. Despite their thirty-eight-year age difference, they married within months. After his untimely death, Celeste thrived rising in the ranks of New York society and becoming a respected power broker. As the CEO of the most prominent financial institution in the city, Celeste took her late husband's significant estate and tripled it. Her business prowess silenced her critics.

"Are you having a nice time?" Lucien inquired. His eyes drifted, searching the crowd.

Celeste noticed the redheaded woman who drew his attention. "Have you slept with her, yet?"

"Who?"

"Don't play games, Lucien. Your assistant that's who."

His eyes clouded over, and his jaw clenched. "Lilith is off-limits."

Lucien's strange obsession with the redhead was so unlike him but Celeste knew better than to push. "Is Lilith ready to come to our little group?" she asked moving the conversation toward a more acceptable topic.

"Soon."

Celeste mused. Lucien had found Lilith on the streets a little more than a year ago. Taking her in, he'd gifted her a small apartment in one of his buildings and hired her as his personal assistant at Beck Holdings. He was incongruously overprotective yet kept her at arms-length personally, a dynamic that didn't fit the Lucien Beck she knew.

"We will be ready when you are, Lucien."

He nodded curtly his eyes flicking back to the redhead weaving her way through the crowd, greeting guests. Lilith had come into his life unexpectedly but at an essential time and now was part of a very specific future. Lucien needed Lilith to be guided by Celeste and the others, but he didn't want to scare her. His plans required her to trust him completely so when the time came, she would do as asked without hesitation. "Give her a few more months, and you can introduce her to the group."

She nodded. "The Coven will be waiting."

Celeste Winslow was not only one of the most influential women in New York City but also the High Priestess of a secular group who lived in its shadows. Practicing the magical arts in seclusion, the Coven would help cultivate a side of Lilith locked too deep for Lucien to access.

"I must make the rounds," Lucien said, kissing Celeste chastely on the cheek. "We will talk soon. I have something important I need to discuss with you after the holidays."

"Of course. Merry Christmas, Lucien," she said as he walked away.

Even though they'd been friends for a long time another side of Lucien Beck existed, one he didn't want anyone to know—a dark side. Obsessively private Lucien rarely let others get close. Celeste knew he hid secrets but never dared to ask. He'd only ever trusted her with one and even then, it was because she could help him keep it.

Celeste sighed as he took Lilith by the elbow and whispered something in her ear. She found his interest in her curious. His philanthropic nature drove him to help those in need, but Lilith was different. Whatever Lucien Beck wanted with the little redheaded waif Celeste would probably never be privy to—and her instincts told her it was probably for the best.

He stood staring out his office window at the city far below.

The executive suite, encased in a deathly quiet this time of night, soothed his frayed nerves. The last of the partygoers had left about thirty minutes ago, and he relished the silence.

Lucien loved this time of night when the office was his alone and the lights of the city stretched out before him. Darkness lay beneath the acres of concrete, a hunger morphing the city into something primal, something he desired to be a part of.

Taking the key from around his neck, Lucien unlocked the door at the back of his spacious office and stepped inside. Pushing aside suits and coats he slid a hand down the back wall until he found the hidden panel. Mechanisms clicked and whirred as he turned the key, and a section of the wall slid open to reveal a small elevator within.

Lucien stepped in and opened a second panel. A red beam flickered from the high-tech retina scanner hidden inside. A series of electronic beeps sounded as he leaned forward and placed his eye close to the panel. In response, the elevator began to descend.

The doors opened revealing a dimly lit room. It flooded with a soft white light as his presence initiated the motion sensors. The stainless steel walls reflected the glow. The single room had a king-size bed against the far wall and a small kitchen near the elevator. Located to the right of the bed, on the other side of a protruding half wall was a full bathroom.

The one access to this room was the elevator.

It was not only a fortress but a prison.

Lucien walked to the kitchen and pulled out a small bottle of Perrier, taking a long sip before proceeding to the office area.

He turned on the electronic panel embedded into the wall and a bank of video screens lit up. Images of the lobby, both elevators, the gallery, and his personal office appeared. Lucien studied the silent images before opening the top drawer in the desk and pulling out a bulky manila folder.

Pouring the contents of the envelope on the desktop, Lucien shifted through the numerous private investigator's reports and notes until he found the grainy photo. The piercing green eyes of the woman staring back at him were intense severing deep into his soul. He didn't know who she was or where to find her, he just knew he must. Someday their paths would cross but until that time something urgent required his attention.

Lucien put down the photo and picked up the Offer to Purchase waiting for his signature. It took him years to discover its identity and its whereabouts but to think it was in such a mundane place—*an old flour mill in Brighton Hill.*

The town had no intention of selling and he knew he was in for a fight, but he needed this property for it was a place that would ensure the future his lost legacy had intended.

# CHAPTER 2

*March 1, 2016, 3:32 am*

AFTER DANE LEFT, STEVIE STOOD in the cold darkness numb with grief and shock. Paralyzed by the overwhelming horror inside the house and the haunting change in Dane's eyes the hours ticked by unnoticed. She remembered dialing the phone and hearing the concern resonating in his voice before everything went black.

Huddled in the back corner of the yard she managed to get as far from the house as possible while still staying close enough to ensure Ella Watts wasn't alone. The images of that room, the smell and fear haunted her memories as the cold fingers of death reached out toward her from the house's darkened bulk.

The night air sunk deep into her bones as she remained transfixed in the backyard for hours, Diego by her side, until *he* arrived. Now Mr. Callan stood above her, his face ashen, his voice tense as bright green, worried eyes bore deep into her own.

"Stevie. Are you alright?"

Flinching at the sound of his voice she shut her eyes and thought back to the phone call, the conversation itself still murky in her memory.

*How long has it been?*

Her hand shook as she grasped the hand he extended and got to her feet. "Yes, I'm fine," she answered. The sorrow buried deep within his bright green eyes was evident and her bottom lip quivered. "I'm so sorry."

Mr. Callan's strong arms encircled her, his chin resting on top of her head. The warmth penetrating through his wool coat soothed her, and she leaned into the soft fabric and his fatherly embrace.

A sorrowful shudder ran through his chest as Nathan Callan swallowed his pain and grief.

Breathing in his comforting scent, her aching fear diminished somewhat. No longer alone and no tears left to cry her body slumped, grief and fear had emptied her completely.

"We have to hurry," he said, releasing her from his embrace. "There is much to be done before the sun rises."

The sadness pooling in his jade eyes betrayed the confidence his firm voice conveyed, but she knew Mr. Callan would not let it paralyze him. There was too much at stake.

"Are you sure you're fine?"

Nodding her assurances Stevie glanced around the dark yard. Shadowy figures appeared moving wordlessly toward where they stood.

Mr. Callan had come to her aid, but he hadn't come alone.

Five individuals moved in behind him, three men and two women. They didn't speak just gazed at her with curious eyes. Dressed in black they wore matching pendants hanging from a thin leather string around their necks—a simple silver Celtic cross. Crudely etched lines marred the smooth metal reminding her of tally marks.

"Stevie, these are members of The Syndicate."

She looked from one solemn face to the next. "The Syndicate?"

Mr. Callan nodded. "An elite group of gifted witches that ensure magic remains unseen by mortals."

He turned to a young man, whose eyes shone gold in the muted moonlight. "See what remnants remain, but don't disturb the scene. I will be up in a moment."

The young man nodded. His yellow eyes flicked toward her before he turned and vanished into the dark house.

Mr. Callan addressed the others with a solemn nod. Without a word they turned and disappeared back into the shadows.

"What's going on?" She motioned toward the gloom. "Why are they here?"

Mr. Callan sighed. "The sun will be up in a few hours and at that time I will come home from a business trip and find that my wife has passed in her sleep from an apparent heart attack. The Syndicate will make that a reality before I call the police and an ambulance."

An image of the bloody horror in the bedroom rose in her mind. "How?" Her voice barely a whisper, cracked with emotion.

"Each member, including myself, possesses a particular skill set. I'm unable to get into it as time is short. You must trust me when I say, this is for the best." His gaze trailed to the dark house. "Alistair will confirm my suspicions, but I am confident this is the work of dark magic. Dane's mother was killed for a specific reason."

His voice cracked with emotion as the last sentence fell from his lips. He slighted, then pulled his shoulders back, pushing the emotions inside where they would not be outwardly seen.

Stevie noticed the way Mr. Callan never let his vulnerabilities show for too long. Dane was a lot like her father in this way.

"But, why Mrs. Watts?"

Mr. Callan shook his head. "It's unclear. Hopefully, Alistair can discover something that will be helpful."

"What can I do?"

"I need you to come back inside with me. You have to tell me exactly what you and my daughter witnessed."

Involuntarily she took a step back as the Callan's home drew her gaze. Her hands began to shake, and her eyes widened.

"What I ask is difficult Stevie, but necessary."

Diego pushed his head into her leg in reassurance. "OK," she muttered, her fingers grazing his bushy fur.

Mr. Callan reached out and squeezed her hand. "You must also tell me the rest of what you and Dane came here to disclose."

"The rest?" She rubbed her aching head. *What had she told him during their frantic phone call?*

"I'm aware of the prophecy Stevie, and your connection to the ancient bloodlines of Thanissia. Although much of what you told me on the phone was incoherent, I connected the dots enough to recognize that my father's suspicions, at least about Dane, were correct. How far has the prophecy progressed?"

"Enough to understand we are involved—me, Dane, Kai, Gabby, Elyse, and Marlee."

Mr. Callan's attention shifted towards the dark sky. "And the old worlds, are they awakening? Is the ancient magic getting stronger?"

"I believe so. All the Druidstones except one has been reignited. The others have gone with the immortals to the Air realm. Dane and I are supposed to meet them."

"Immortals?"

Her shoulders sagged. "It's a long story but there are others from the realms. Survivors who've been waiting for the prophecy to pass."

Callan nodded. "Interesting, I would never have guessed any of the ancients would have survived this long."

"A few did." Stevie shuffled the snow with the toe of her boot. "There's something else."

"What is it?"

"Dane. She's bound to one of them."

Mr. Callan's green eyes widened. "Bound?"

"A magical intertwining of emotions that connect two people, I mean immortals together. It's an intense experience and apparently exceedingly rare."

His face paled, and she wondered if she'd divulged too much. "I thought you should know."

"Have you met this person."

"I have. His name is Rafe and he is very interesting. He's an ancient warrior, a Warlician."

Mr. Callan's breath hitched. "A Warlician warrior from the ancient realms bound to the ancestor of the Warlician line. That *is* interesting. I'm sure even my father couldn't predicate that."

"Dane's grandfather?"

His eyes softened noticing Stevie's confusion. "Yes. It seems my father knew of this prophecy and Dane's connection to it. He'd been researching it for years. Connecting our family lineage with the myths passed down through generations. I suspect he intended to pass on the information gathered to Dane, but never got the chance."

The edges of the night sky began to brighten, an indication that dawn was not far off.

"You will need to go to the Air realm."

"I can't. The portal key is with Dane."

"How did the others get there?"

"Through the portal in Braemore Woods. A tree. An Elder Oak."

"Then that is your answer."

"What about Dane?"

His green eyes flashed once again with the sorrow he desperately tried to hide from her. "Only Dane has the power to change her destiny."

Nathan Callan scrutinized the brightening sky. "Dawn will break in a few hours, we must hurry."

As if on command the others appeared from the shadows and walked without pause toward the dark house. A muscular blonde man with pale skin and ice-blue eyes waved his hand and a ripple interrupted the dim. He pulled the hoodie of his black jacket over his head and knelt on the snow-covered ground.

As they passed him, the soft-spoken words of an incantation drifted toward her ears. "What's he doing?"

"Jon is what we call a visualist. His ability allows him to create illusions and make people see something that isn't real by physically altering the energy around an object. Jon will ensure the house looks normal and empty while we work. Just in case any of my neighbors pass by."

Stevie followed Mr. Callan and the others into the dark house. The metallic scent of blood wafted down the stairs, suffocating them in its appalling odor. Bile rose in her throat, and she choked it down willing herself to ascend the stairs.

Steeling her nerves, she entered the master suite after Mr. Callan. His shoulders sagged at the scene inside—his wife butchered and left to bleed out like a slaughtered animal. The room spun as she tried to quash the overwhelming feeling of horror rampaging through her. Blood pounded in her ears. Her eyes drifted to the corner of the room where the young man, Dane's father had sent in earlier, knelt his fingers sliding across the bloodied floor.

"What did you find, Alistair?" Mr. Callan asked, clearing his throat.

"Traces of the usual ritualism powders and dark alchemy are present but no hint of daemonic energy. This atrocity wasn't committed by someone or something not of this world. Whoever killed your wife, was human."

"Are you sure?" His voice deepened, stress and grief straining his attempt at calm.

Alistair shook his head. "Regrettably, yes."

"So, one of our own broke the covenant."

"It would appear so."

"Can you track them?"

"It will be difficult, but I think I can." He hesitated. "Nathan, there is something else."

"What is it?"

"Some of Ella's blood is missing."

Nathan flinched and a somberness surrounded him. "He took it."

Alistair's golden gaze flashed, and he nodded.

Stevie scanned the macabre scene in front of her. Blood spatter coated the walls and saturated the bedding. "How can you be sure of such a thing?"

Alistair cocked his head. Narrowing his eyes, he looked at her as if bored. His nostrils flared. "Call it a gift or a curse, whatever you like. I know things. I can sense anomalies in others."

He walked to where they stood and kindly placed

his hand on Mr. Callan's shoulder. "I'm sorry Nathan we all loved Ella. If it's of any solace, she didn't suffer."

Alistair's eyes locked on Nathan Callan's, and something unsaid passed between them. "I'll be downstairs if you need me."

"Thank you."

"When would you like the cleaners to come up?"

Mr. Callan sighed. "Send them up in ten."

Alistair's golden eyes pierced the room's dimness as he eyed Stevie.

Shivers crept across the back of her neck as his eyebrow raised and he mouthed *FIRE* as he passed her and exited the bedroom.

The echo of his footsteps followed him as he retreated to the floor below. Confused by their interaction and perturbed by his insolence she shifted uncomfortably. His piercing gaze left her unsettled. Pushing the image of Alistair's face out of her mind she stepped toward Mr. Callan. "What is Alistair going to track?"

Nathan Callan's sad green eyes turned toward her. "Alistair is a hunter and is most effective in tracking daemons. In the right circumstances, he can track almost any type of magic. Alistair is part witch and part daemon, so his senses project on multiple levels making him highly intuitive—an effective tool in our line of work."

"Daemon?" Stevie gasped.

He smiled. "You're new to this world and there's much you don't understand. For now, you will have to accept it as is as I don't have the time to explain. Alistair may be a little brash, but he is a talented hunter and loyal friend."

Mr. Callan's lips quirked, and his green eyes flashed.

"So, you're the ancestor from the fire realm." He

saw the confusion shadow her face. "Alistair is percep-
tive and sensed your energy when he brushed by you. I
can feel a difference as well. Immortality suits you, my
dear. Knowing your current family, it doesn't come as
a surprise that you're born from the Dragon Gypsies of
old."

Stevie forced a smile. "You seem to know a lot about
the ancient realms."

Mr. Callan's green eyes softened. "Myths told to me
by my father. Bedtime stories of make-believe lands.
Or so I thought." He pulled his shoulders back. "I am
sorry you have to carry this burden. Destiny is not always kind."

I He brushed her cheek affectionately then turned
and walked toward his wife. His hands shook as he
placed them on either side of her head and bent over
her grazing his lips across her pallid ones.

The tenderness of the moment left Stevie feeling uncomfortable, and she averted her gaze.

He pulled back. A frown deepened his brow as his
tongue swept over his lips. He lifted his fingers to his
mouth running them over the skin and then sniffed the
tips—concern evident on his face.

"Do you recognize anything specific about this
ritual?" Nathan Callan turned abruptly back to where
she stood.

Her hands trembled and her mouth went dry as
tears began to sting her eyes. "No, how would I?"

"Your ancestors were great alchemists. It's in your
blood. Look beyond the obvious. What do you see?"

A wave of nausea battered her stomach, and she
rubbed her clammy hands on her jeans trying to calm
her nerves.

Mr. Callan motioned for her to stand beside him.
"Use your gift."

Stevie moved on unsteady feet toward the bed unsure of what exactly he meant for her to do. The acidic aroma of dried blood engulfed her, and she held her breath against its pungent scent. Her hand shook as she moved it toward Ella Watts' lifeless body. A tingle crept through her fingertips as they touched cold skin. Her magic surged, the ancient energy flowing through her. Like in the old mill, when she'd first encountered the daemon pods, her blood began to race. It pounded in her ears, the roar deafening, as its curiosity came forth.

"Belladonna," she whispered.

"Yes, and plenty of it. I can taste the bitterness of the poisonous plant on her lips."

"What does it mean?"

"It means Alistair's correct; my wife didn't suffer through a torturous death. Her assailant gave her a peaceful one prior to desecrating her body."

"Why?"

"My guess would be they genuinely didn't want her to suffer. Her death was one of necessity; to make a statement."

"For what purpose?"

"I'm not sure. The timing suggests it might have everything to do with the prophecy and possibly all of you. Someone wanted to send a message."

Stevie cringed as she stared at the wall, where the word WRATH, written in blood, had begun to dry and crack. The word obviously meant something to the killer and defined this horrific act.

Whatever message they tried to send it was personal and directed at Dane—*but to what end?*

# CHAPTER 3

ASH SWIRLED LANGUIDLY AROUND HER and Diego as they sat atop the massive ethereal beast. The wings of the smoke dragon flapped noiselessly, propelling them through the dissipating night sky. The cold air bit cruelly at her cheek before the warmth of the whispering smoke vanquished it back into the darkness.

Diego lifted his head, glancing at her before he shifted his weight and returned to a comfortable sleep. Her eyes had grown accustomed to the bleak gloom enshrouding the world prior to the break of dawn. The dark houses dotting the landscape below were visible in the muted light. They sailed silent overhead; their presence oblivious to the mortals still asleep within those dim structures.

The emerging sun began coloring the distant horizon in a palette of morning hues. A subtle rainbow of purple, deep oranges and mottled blues appeared as the dawn heralded the beginning of another day. The waking daybreak calmed her frazzled nerves, and she closed her eyes allowing her mind to wander back through the last few hours.

Naomi and Stella, the cleaners, had used a specific type of old-world magic to ensure the bedroom no longer looked like a crime scene. Miraculously, they put

Ella Watts' mutilated corpse back together, leaving her with a belly scar that could certainly pass as a cesarean incision.

Eli, the third male in the group of five was nicknamed 'the doctor,' because of his unique abilities. He could manipulate the bodies organs, blood, chemistry, even DNA to replicate any disease he desired. After the cleaners finished, Eli simply changed Mrs. Watt's symptoms so the medical examiner would, during the autopsy, conclude she had indeed succumbed to a heart attack.

From the time Nathan Callan and the others arrived, everything had happened so fast. By the time he told her to leave, minutes before the emergency responders came, absolutely nothing looked unusual. The Syndicate ensured everyone involved would concur, Mrs. Watts died of natural causes. As the flashing lights from the emergency vehicles woke up the neighborhood, the witches disappeared into the shadows of the fading night. Mr. Callan remained—the grieving widower.

Stevie opened her eyes as a shift in their trajectory drew her mind away from the grisly happenings of the night.

The smoke dragon began to descend on Brighton Hill. It glided soundlessly through the twilight, staying on the shadowed side of the rising sun as it made its way to the Elder Oak.

As they flew toward the clearing, she wondered again where Dane had gone. Her calls and texts remained unanswered and the deafening silence from her best friend concerned her. She'd never seen such visceral anger like that from Dane and Stevie was apprehensive about what she might do—*and to whom.*

The bulky shadow of the old mill stretched upward into the early morning sky, a stalwart silhouette standing in contrast against the rising color heralding in a new day. Its interior loomed dark and forlorn as Dane stood with her back against a tree, watching the first strands of light creep over the horizon. Her hands shook as the rage churning through her blood caused her magic to behave erratically. She flexed them trying to gain control.

Her eyes searched the darkness trapped inside the old mill, but no visible light penetrated any of its windows. Her eyes scanned the façade, searching for any indication that the redhead dwelt somewhere inside the mill's depths.

Dane had come here for one reason—*revenge.*

Lilith mercilessly slaughtered her mother and now must pay for her sins. The empathy Dane once had for the young woman was now consumed by grief and hate. The ancient dark would no longer have its puppet. Lilith may be under its control, but it didn't matter her death was imminent and as a result, the dark witch would finally be free of its daemonic clutches.

Dane couldn't save Lilith in life but maybe in death, she would find some peace.

"The stillness of the breaking dawn is hauntingly beautiful, is it not?"

Dane whirled at the sound of the voice, energy balls bursting from her palms at the unexpected intrusion.

"Easy."

The voice echoed from the dark still unaffected by

the early morning light. Her eyes searched the gloom behind the tree looking for its source, but the shadows exposed nothing.

"Reveal yourself," she demanded, lifting her magic-laden hands higher. Shadows shifted as something in their midst moved within them. The snow crunched underfoot breaking the stifling silence surrounding the mill as a man emerged from the darkness, his pace tentative. He was tall and well-dressed. His dark blue suit and polished brown shoes oddly out of place in the snowy field.

"I mean you no harm," the man said lifting his hands in a nonthreatening gesture.

"And who exactly are *you*?" Dane hissed. Green energy spit from her palms as her powers reacted to the change in her emotions.

With profound confidence, the stranger moved seductively toward her until he stood mere inches away. Like a snake stalking its unwitting prey, his mannerisms were poised and unabashed. He looked down at the energy churning in her palms, but no indication he feared her power reflected in his blue eyes—only curiosity.

His lips quirked, as the cold night air dissipated around him. The subdued light of dawn flickered across his perfect features. His piercing eyes locked on her own as a smug smile played on his lips.

"Someone who's been looking forward to meeting you for a long time," he replied.

A strange sensation spread with his words. A serenity that extinguished her rage, lulling her into a sense of euphoria. His proximity disarmed her, and Dane lowered her hands. Her mind whirled at the sudden retreat of her fierce emotions as she unwillingly submitted to the tranquility emanating around him.

Her eyes drifted over his features, studying the stranger standing before her. An intentional unkempt shave highlighted his square jaw and his hair was cut short on the sides but kept longer on top. It swept upward off his forehead and away from its perfect side part. Thick dark brows lifted in amusement.

"And does *someone* have a name?" Her voice tightened as she frowned at his insolence. Her body tensed a reaction to the bizarre energy wafting around them.

He smiled again; his lips parted. Lifting his hand, he caressed her cheek. Flinching, Dane glared at him. She wanted to retreat, to step away from this stranger, but her ability to break from the provocative trance holding her in its grip did not seem important.

She waited for his response, seething at his brazen attitude.

"Lucien. Lucien Beck."

"Is that supposed to mean something to me?"

"Not yet." Lucien lowered his hand and took a step back. His aqua eyes flashed as he continued to stare, his head tilting as he studied her. "So, I finally get to meet the incomparable Dane Watts-Callan."

"How do you know who I am?" She questioned, the unease creeping back.

"Let's just say, I've done my homework."

"What does that mean?"

His eyes penetrated hers. "Do you believe in destiny, Dane?"

Her breath hitched as the beating of her heart increased.

"I assume you are here for Lilith," he continued, not waiting for a response.

"What do you know of Lilith?"

The tranquility encapsulating her dispersed and an intense rage surged inside her.

Lucien put his hands in his pants pockets and nonchalantly looked toward the old mill. "She's my sister."

The silence of the dawn lay heavy over the grounds. The winter air prickled at her skin. Blood pulsed chaotically through her veins as Dane made the connection. "You're a Tierney."

"I was." Lucien turned back toward her. "A long time ago."

"I didn't realize Lilith had a sibling."

A dark shadow passed over his features. "Lilith has no knowledge of our family ties. We were separated when she was an infant and have led very distinct lives. The Lucien she knows is a different man."

A faint whisper caressed the edges of Dane's mind, as his words faded on the night breeze. The energy pulsing around him seemed strangely familiar. A memory tugged at her conscious mind and Dane met his eyes as she grasped at it. "The shadow evident in Lilith's memories—it was you."

His face remained impassive except for a slight twitch appearing in his upper lip. He said nothing continuing instead to stare stoically into her eyes.

"You are in her memories but without clarity like a haze weaving itself in and out of her subconscious." Dane's mind reeled. "How? If you never had a relationship with Lilith how is it possible you are in her memories?"

An eyebrow raised as he shook his head. "I never said I didn't have a relationship with my sister. I said she didn't know we were family."

"But her memories of you are blurred like someone no longer wanted them to exist."

"I showed you what I wanted you to see. Call it a subtle introduction."

"Why?"

"Because I can." Lucien's eyes darkened as his demeanor shifted and the tone in his voice changed. "Lilith is weak," he said, glancing back at the mill. "Incapable of carrying the power of the Tierney name and for that she's expendable. But I found her weakness to be useful in another way."

"To link the ancient dark to this world."

Lucien nodded. "Is that what you refer to it as? Interesting."

"What do you call it?"

"The beast." Lucien sighed. "Sadly, my sister is even too weak to be a reliable conduit. Her mind cannot handle the beast's dark energy for much longer."

Dane thought about Lilith's madness, the way she'd attacked both her and Rafe with that vacant, crazed look in her eyes. Lilith was confused, unhinged even, but was she capable of performing the level of violence her mother had endured. While her body had been horrifically mutilated, there was a precision to the act. The wounds were deliberate and measured as if her attacker had a purpose.

Did Lilith have the capacity for such precise violence or was her mother's death perpetrated by someone saner and in control?

Dane scowled at Lucien Beck accusingly. "You sacrificed your own sister to the ancient dark and now it's killing her."

Lucien nodded. "An unfortunate consequence."

"That's rather cold."

"Why do you care? After all, Lilith killed your mother, did she not?"

Her voice lowered as grief and rage wrapped around her words. "How do you know about my mother?"

His bright blue eyes darkened as a shadow passed over them.

Dane flinched. *What was that—deception?* She couldn't tell it happened so fast. Lucien's cool exterior had slipped for a moment providing her with a brief glimpse of something else existing within this man.

"Did Lilith kill my mother?" A tightness wrapped itself around her chest. Her breathing became restricted as she waited for his response.

Lucien ignored the question. "A darkness is coming, Dane and inevitably the world as it is now will end. It's only a matter of time."

His remark was casual, unapologetic. Lucien spoke of the evil from another realm as if he was conversing about the weather. It didn't seem to affect him in the least that this beast was destined to invade and decimate mankind.

Her hands began to shake as the rage once again pounded through her. She so badly wanted to unleash her magic on someone providing a release from the anger and grief consuming her—to lose control.

"The ancient dark will be destroyed. It's been foretold," she said through clenched teeth.

Lucien chuckled. "Darkness will take over this world because the prophecy will never come to pass."

"You appear quite confident in your assessment, Mr. Beck."

He nodded. "This world is nothing. It represents the worst of humanity and requires a cleansing, a new direction. A magical rebirth will ensure our survival because humans have become the plaque that litters the earth and are intent on destroying it. A reclamation is necessary."

"By whom, you?"

"There is always one who must carry the burden for all."

"And the ancient dark. You think you can control it?"

Lucien scoffed. "I already do."

Icy fingers of dread wrapped themselves around Dane. "How?"

Lucien leaned against the trunk of the tree, his hand caressing the bark. "It's not the how that is important but the why."

"Then why?"

"To change the prophecy and restore my family name. My ancestor's name. A Tierney will rule this world when all is done."

"A Tierney will rule nothing but the ashes of an ancient evil," Dane spat. "The Arcanists have all risen. The prophecy can't be stopped. The ancient dark will be destroyed." Defiance shone in her eyes as she glared at Lucien.

He chuckled as he moved in to once again stand in front of her. His eyes flicked to the dark bulk of the mill. A kaleidoscope of bright colors broke over the horizon lighting up his handsome features with the brilliant dawn of a new day.

"Prophecies are meaningless, Dane. They rarely lie in truth and can change over time. Depending on the circumstances, one can easily be unraveled." His bright blue eyes turned back toward her as a slight sneer played at the corners of his mouth. He grasped her by the back of the neck pulling her toward him until their lips almost touched.

She gasped.

Lucien held her gaze as tension seethed around them. Brushing his lips across her cheek he whispered in her ear.

"You just need to pull the right thread and the whole thing will unravel."

Dane shivered. "And you believe I'm that thread." Her voice was heavy with loathing.

His eyes flickered with something dark as he pulled back. "I'm counting on it."

Releasing her Lucien glanced once again at the old mill, his demeanor reverting to relaxed confidence. "You just need a little help in understanding that this age-old prophecy is irrelevant. You can't save everyone, Dane. Sometimes destiny is irrevocable."

A sinister spark flashed in his eyes leaving her feeling there was much more to Lucien Beck than he was ready for her to uncover.

"What are you doing here?"

Dane was curious why a man like Lucien Beck wandered the grounds of an abandoned mill before the light of dawn had even made its appearance?

"Checking on my investment." He smiled confidently, pointing to a bulky sign she hadn't noticed.

'SOLD—Future site of Beck Holdings Inc.'

"You bought the old flour mill."

"As of a few days ago, I own this property."

"I didn't realize the city had decided to sell."

"It took a while but I'm very persuasive."

"And everything in the mill?" Dane winced thinking about the daemon pods throbbing inside.

"All mine." Lucien acknowledged. "I'll see you soon," he said disappearing into the fading dim.

# CHAPTER 4

A CHILL BLEW UNIMPEDED ACROSS THE open field, its icy tendrils wrapping around her skin. Dane shivered as Lucien's final words disappeared on the winter wind, an echo swallowed up by the howl. She pulled up her collar and huddled closer to the trunk of the tree.

Their interaction had left her both confused and curious. Dane didn't like feeling anymore out of control than she already did, but something drew her to him. *Why?* She shook away the afterthought of Lucien Beck, her attention returning to the mill.

Daybreak began to warm the air as the sun rose above the horizon. The mill stood dark and silent, no sign of Lilith present. Its emptiness leeched across the field toward her as she returned to the jeep. Exhaustion seeped into her muscles as she climbed into the driver's seat.

Overwhelmed by her mother's senseless death she gripped the steering wheel as tears began to surface. The memory of her parent's bedroom flooded to the front of her mind leaving her feeling defeated and alone. Choking back a sob she pushed the image and the emotions down. Weakness was not an option. Dane needed her mind to be clear to figure out what to do next.

Three missed call notifications and six text messages filled her screen, all from Stevie asking her whereabouts. Needing to get away, she'd left her stranded knowing her father would have been the first person, Stevie called. Nathan Callan would take care of everything. There would be no need for him to keep his powers or his connection to the Syndicate a secret anymore, so he would explain what Dane could not.

She scrolled through the messages and read the most recent text.

> *"Where are you? I'm worried. Heading to the Elder Oak. Meet me there. We need to find the others."*

As Dane stared at the words, relief flooded through her—Stevie was back in Brighton Hill and safe.

The sudden ring of the phone startled her. Her father's number filled the screen. The rush of blood pounded in her ears as she pressed the button to ignore the call. Now wasn't the time to speak with him. It was too painful, too fresh, too real. A few moments later her phone beeped, indicating a voicemail. She clicked it off and put it in her jacket pocket. Speaking with her father would have to wait. He would try to soothe her and take away the pain, but she didn't want that, she wanted to live inside the anger and drown in her grief. She wanted the ache to feed the rage surging inside her because it fueled her strength and her thirst for revenge.

Dane started up the jeep and backed down the long drive, heading home to shower and get some rest. After a few hours of sleep, her mind would be refreshed, and she could decide what to do next.

A twinge sparked in her chest as she drove through the early morning dawn. A very specific ancient magic pulsed in her blood reminding her of something, someone special—Rafe. Her heart quickened as his face drifted through her mind before fading away, lost in the rage festering inside.

"What is it?" Kai asked as Rafe's face paled. A slick film of sweat covered his brow, and he winced. They had just reached the edge of the fae city when his strangled cry alerted her to his troubles sending her running to his side.

Rafe's brow furrowed in pain as his hand flew to his heart, fingers clawing at the shirt covering his chest.

"Rafe, are you OK?" The worry tingeing her voice made Sebastian and the others turn as well.

"What do you feel?" Sebastian questioned, closing the distance between him and the warrior without hesitation.

"Something is wrong. The rage is overwhelming." Rafe's voice rattled in the back of his throat, and he heaved trying to gulp air. Irrepressible emotions surged through him as he collapsed before Sebastian could make it to his side. One hand clutched the damp earth, the other clawed at his chest.

"Dane," he gasped.

"What can we do for him?" Kai inquired as she bent over Rafe, a hand on his back.

Sebastian's green eyes flashed with concern. "I am afraid, nothing. The binding Rafe and Dane share is a connection only the two of them control. Rafe must find it within himself not to yield to the overwhelming emotions Dane is obviously experiencing."

"Dane? What do you think is happening to her?"

"There is no way for us to know, but do not worry, Stevie is with her."

Helpless to provide relief as he fought the onslaught of emotions surging through him, they stood at his side. Finally, his breathing leveled out and color rose in his cheeks.

He lifted his eyes to Sebastian.

"Something has happened." Wiping the sweat from his pallid brow Sebastian helped him stand. Worry etched his face. "Dane. She is out of control. The rage erupting within her is consuming the light inside. It's like a black river winding through her soul swallowing everything that's good. I must go back."

Sebastian's eyes softened, and he lifted his hand placing it on Rafe's shoulder.

"I understand your concern my friend but alas there is nothing you can do. Until we know more, we must continue with the task at hand."

His voice lowered, and he leaned in looking Rafe directly in the eyes. "You must trust in her. Dane is strong and quite capable. She does not need you to save her. Learn from the past."

Rafe nodded, understanding what Sebastian referred to.

Wiping his drenched brow, he picked up his fallen pack and eyed the others, a forced smile on his face. "Let us continue to the Druidstone."

Kai squeezed his hand as the others walked away. "Dane will be fine." She forced a smile, but her voice betrayed her.

Ignoring the shiver creeping over his skin he nodded and turned to address Marlee. "These gates lead to Tariedrelle, the city of your ancestors."

Marlee's eyes scanned the gilded iron gates towering above them. Her skin prickled as she gazed at their opulence. The gate stood about twenty feet high. Gold iron, twisted into intricate scroll and filigree details, adorned the wrought iron bars. At the top, vicious points gleamed in the rays of the late day sun. Bright green vines, dripping with dewdrops and covered in enormous plum-colored flowers, entwined themselves around the gilded fence and obscured the view of what lay beyond. The scent wafting from the flora had a pungent sweetness.

*"Fae blood is scented. It is sickly sweet, reminiscent of the strange flora that grows on your lands."* Gabby's words echoed through her memory, and she wondered if this was what the celestial referred to.

"Are you coming, Marlee?" asked Elyse breaking the spell. She nodded and followed her friend and the others through the city gates.

A shallow canal lay inside the gilded fence, circling the outer edges of the city. A delicate tinkling sound rose from the depths of the water as a lazy breeze ruffled its surface. The water sparkled brightly at the bottom and every so often twinkling pins of light floated lazily upward. After breaking the surface, they continued to ascend into the air until the golden haze swallowed them up, reminding Marlee of tiny fireflies, their abdomens flickering in the dusk.

"Twilight is the part of the day when you can see the sparks of elemental magic ascending into the mist," Rafe said indicating the tiny pinpoints of light as they disappeared overhead. "As the sun sets and the moons rise it will once again be invisible." A thoughtful look appeared on his face as he reminisced. "Fae magic moves through the environment constantly. Even in stasis, it is in constant flux. Its power may be minimized but its visual effervescence is still noticeably apparent. The beauty of Athir cannot be stifled."

The setting sun in the distance cast out its brilliant colors.

"When the triple moon rises, you will see how majestic fae elemental magic is."

He smiled at her sensing her hesitation to accept what her eyes witnessed. Marlee's caution meant she didn't trust her instincts the way the others did, and Rafe knew well enough not to push. Marlee would find her own way through her destiny, in time.

Brannon and Killenn stopped at the water's edge to fill the canteens.

"Can we drink that water?"

They both looked at Marlee strangely, forgetting she was a mortal with no knowledge of the land of the fae.

Killenn grinned, "We can until the fae in you is reborn and you decide we are not worthy." Brannon replied with a chuckle, but a stern look from Sebastian silenced them both.

"What Killenn is trying to convey, although clumsily, is the fae are rather protective of their territory. Since the air element infuses every part of this world, they have been known to guard the resources within their domain carefully. The water in this canal possesses specific magical properties that when ingested gives a person the ability to walk with ease, making foot travel much less strenuous. Fae water was a popular commodity in our time and sold quite liberally at market. You ancestors would not take kindly to us taking it without purchase."

The heat of embarrassment tinged Marlee's cheeks

as she digested Sebastian's words. "Wouldn't the elves have the same water?"

Sebastian shook his head. "Both races use the elemental magic of this world differently. The fae used to reside in an elemental plane above this one but after the war tore Athir apart, they descended here. Their use of the air element has always been more carefree than that of the elves, the fae have a propensity to infuse everything with its essence."

"That's putting it one way," Gabby said haughtily.

Ignoring her Sebastian continued. "Your ancestors are what we refer to as, tricksters. They are impish and enjoy games and tricks. Often, they use their magic to amuse themselves which is sometimes detrimental to those who are the recipient of their mischievous ways."

"Are fairies dangerous?"

"Maddening is a word better suited to your kind." Gabby rolled her eyes as Sebastian silenced her with a look.

"No Marlee, the race of fae are not dangerous. While they have been known to be spiteful, they never intentionally cause harm to another," he assured her.

"They don't sound very nice." Marlee lowered her eyes.

Kai's heart clenched as her friend's face fell. Marlee Lynch was kind and caring and would never treat anyone with disrespect for her own amusement. Would Marlee change after receiving her birthright? Kai certainly hoped not. Gabby's new personality is change enough.

Elyse moved toward Marlee protectively, sensing her unease. "Apparently my ancestors are even worse. I am told the elves were standoffish and rigidly disciplined lending to their reputation as perfectionists."

Rafe interjected, "Neither race is as bad as the celestials. Both the fae and the elves were always much more popular in the Five Realms than Gabriella and her sentinels."

Gabby glowered at Rafe but shrugged in agreement which set the other ancient immortals to laughing, easing the tension somewhat.

"Shall we go take a look at your ancestor's city?"

A small white-washed wooden bridge spanned the width of the canal giving them access to the wooded area beyond. On the other side, a stone path wound its way through the forest toward the city located on its northern border. Enormous hardwood trees, whose trunks stretched hundreds of feet into the sky before bursting into perfect umbrella-shaped canopies, provided the forest with cooling shade. The trunks, covered with the same flowering vines as the outer fence, acted as a natural garden for the foliage and wildlife.

Small, pale blue, and green birds flitted from flower to flower seemingly unconcerned by the presence of strangers in their world.

The late-day sun sent beams through the tall canopy, lighting the surrounding air with golden-hued rays. Gilded flecks floated in the beams twinkling unhindered before drifting away into the shadows. A soft mat of moss covered the forest floor, and small white and purple flowers dotted its surface. A white fox-looking animal scurried from its den, chasing a butterfly as it zigzagged out of reach.

"It's like a storybook," Elyse said amazed at the peacefulness of their surroundings.

"Yes, the fae are good at disarming any who wander into their domain. They are masters of illusion and deception." Sebastian noted. "But do not make the mistake of being lulled by its tranquility—the fae and their city are not born from a fairy tale. They are as formidable as any of the Thanissia races."

Continuing down the path, the sound of their footfalls echoed off the massive tree trunks. Kai could sense the magic below the surface of the calming beauty. It observed them, taking note of their presence as it hid behind its visual charade. It was tinged with darkness, not malevolent, but roguish as if it would jump out at any moment and then laugh at their terrified reaction. The wariness of the other immortals indicated to her that they too detected the energy simmering beneath the forest's ethereal beauty.

"The path ends just ahead," Tauria said pulling Brannon toward a gap in the forest.

The sun had begun its descent when they reached the opening. Red and gold rays splashed brilliantly across the rooftops of the city towering before them, lighting it up with an enchanting glow. Like the outskirts of the city limits, a gilded fence surrounded the city of Tariedrelle. Winged gargoyles sat atop the fence, their blank eyes staring straight ahead toward the bordering woods. The same flowering vine covered this fence. Dark plum flowers glistened in the fading sun. From somewhere in the city Marlee could hear a thundering sound, one which could only come from a waterfall.

Rafe signaled to the group to approach the gates with caution not sure if, like Kaizi, there would be anyone left waiting in this realm. He did not enjoy surprises and this time would take no chances. Drawing his sword, he put his finger to his lips, then motioned for Brannon, Drow, and Killenn to move to the open gates.

Flanking either side, they waited, weapons drawn, for Rafe to enter the city.

The silence escaping from behind the city walls did not imply a threat as much as it echoed loneliness. Marlee was enthralled by the comforting silence, totally unaware of the darker fae magic swirling underneath—waiting.

Rafe signaled to the others to join him.

Tauria followed her brother into the city, shadowed by Sebastian and Drow. Other than the haunting silence, no sign of life existed in this world. Nothing to indicate there was anyone else here but them.

"This is impressive," Kai said as she scrutinized the city.

A massive wading pool stood at the center. An aqueduct, raised on an arcade by tall arches, spilled water into it from a stone chute. Like the canal, the water twinkled with a light underneath its surface. The spray sparkled as water streamed down from the aqueduct above. Kai could see a thunderous waterfall in the distance. The arched arcade stretched from the wading pool upward to the waterfall where the aqueduct collected water; dispersing it throughout the city along a spiderweb of smaller aqueducts built high above the buildings. To the right of the waterfall, on a pristine moss-covered cliff, numerous small white buildings sat. To the left a massive tree. Its sweeping foliage swayed in the evening breeze.

Tauria sensed her awe.

"That is the tree of Tariedrelle," she said. "It is the life force of the fae people. It collects all the elemental magic flowing from the ether and stores it until it is needed. They revered that tree like no other, even more so than the Elder Oak which as you know grows on fae land."

Tauria gestured to the surrounding courtyard, where Elder Oaks grew with abandon, their twisted limbs stretching out across the mossy green earth.

"The sun is setting quicker than anticipated," said Rafe, as the last of the beams disappeared behind the rooftops. "Perhaps we should stay in Tariedrelle for the night and trek to the Druidstone early in the morning."

"I agree," said Drow. "With the fae water, it will not be difficult to make it there swiftly. It is always better to travel through these lands with the light of day on your face than to get lost in its shadows." He glanced knowingly at Killenn before turning his attention back to Marlee. "This way it will give you a chance to explore, and we can gather any supplies and weapons we might need."

"What does Drow mean when he says it's better to travel through these lands during the day?" Kai asked Tauria as he conversed quietly with Killenn.

Tauria's eyes darted toward the dark sky rolling in the distance. "I believe he was referring to the Oberon Fen—the cursed lands. The path around the lake comes near the edge of the Fen and if someone strays off the path and into the cursed lands—" Her words trailed off as the dark sky above the Oberon Fen flashed with angry lightning. "It's a treacherous place full of violent memories and lost souls and not somewhere one wants to be after dark."

Before Kai could inquire more about the ominous lands, she walked away.

"Do not worry yourself about the Oberon Fen, Kai," Sebastian said coming to stand beside her.

The menacing sky churned in the distance. "We have no reason to enter those forsaken lands. No reason at all."

# CHAPTER 5

THE SMOKE DRAGON SAILED EFFORTLESSLY through the thick canopy of trees. Its form morphed as it weaved in and around branches. Stevie and Diego sat atop the smoldering air as it shifted beneath them, always keeping them aloft and secure. The clearing was empty and the crisp, frozen leaves blanketing its floor moved as they were caught in the downdraft created by the dragon's descent.

Murky wisps swirled around them as they jumped to the ground. She raised her hands twisting them back and forth. The smoke circled downward, spiraling like water in a drain until the ancient magic creating the dragon disappeared into her hands, leaving a hint of burnt ash to float aimlessly in the air.

The aching silence of dawn saturated the clearing, and the rising sun gave the area a strange filtered glow as light and shadows fought for dominance. Quiet and waiting, the Elder Oak stood in grand opulence in front of her.

Searching for the hidden panel that would reveal the portal stones and open a way into Athir, she circled the trunk. The bark's rough surface, chilled by winter's touch and abrasive under her skin, sent shivers down her spine.

A slight vibration hummed with the belly of the trunk.

Diego whined behind her.

"Just a minute buddy," she said, not taking her eyes off the tree.

His whine deepened as her hand rose to the scar on the trunk's backside. A strange warmth emanated from its depths spreading beneath her palm as the humming increased. Her palm followed the direction of the throbbing pulse until it reached a spot where the throb was undeniable.

Placing her hand flat on the trunk she closed her eyes, allowing her senses to explore. Images flashed through her mind—earth, fire, spirit, water, air. Heat rose from the trunk pulsing faster as the magic recognized her ancestry. Sparks flew as the bark under her palm vibrated. Startled, she pulled her hand away as the surface began to morph. A panel opened to reveal the portal stones, their surfaces glowing with brilliant color.

Diego whined louder and began pawing at the ground. He had grown impatient with this world and wanted to get back to the universe from which he was born.

Stevie patted his head. "Soon, Diego."

His ears perked and his head cocked to one side. His golden eye glistened as he stared, the other burning red with resolve.

Smiling at his impertinence, she reached toward the yellow stone, pressing it deeper into the slot. A buzz filled the clearing. The frozen leaves rustled, levitating upward as a golden mist ascended from its surface. It

40

warmed the air, swirling idly into a shimmering, spar-kling funnel in front of them.

The screen of her cell phone remained blank, there were no texts or missed calls from Dane. Sighing, she looked down at Diego. "I hope we can find the others, or should I say I hope you can."

Diego's eyes gleamed, and he barked, his stance indicating his readiness.

"Let's go then," she said, taking his collar and fol-lowing him through the misty haze of the Athir portal.

They emerged on the other side as the midday sun be-gan to sink below the far horizon. The world, cast in a brilliant yellow and orange haze, glistened in the warm breeze blowing across the beautiful green landscape that stretched out before them. Stevie turned in a cir-cle looking for a clue as to which direction the others had gone. The position of the sun in the sky indicated there was approximately an hour of daylight left. With any luck, she could find them before night smothered this strange land. A path lay to her right and her eyes followed its direction.

"Follow the path," she said, recalling the directions Sebastian had given them. The problem was those di-rections started from the point where they would have emerged using the portal ring—close to the Temple of Air. Without knowing where in this world she'd emerged she decided it still made sense that a path was the best thing to follow.

"Diego, do you know the way?"

The Dragonwolf howled, pawing at the ground, then with a quick glance her way he took off running toward a sparkling lake in the distance. Stevie looked at the setting sun before hurrying after him.

The city of Tariedrelle sparkled in the dusk as the last of the sun's rays fought the dusk threatening to snuff them out. The pin lights Marlee had seen floating upward from the canal were now visible in the darkening sky. A swath of light hovered over the rooftops. Above this layer, the night sky, brightly lit by the triple moon, stretched endlessly.

A sensual, ethereal glow blanketed the entire atmosphere and the land below. Rafe had been correct, you did need to experience the wonder of the triple moon for yourself to truly appreciate its beauty.

"It's pretty amazing, isn't it," noted Elyse as she came to stand beside Marlee at the center of the courtyard.

"It's surreal," Marlee agreed.

The three moons hovered low in the sky, two full and one quarter. Their edges overlapped and where they intersected the glow turned golden. She sensed the moon's essence as it drifted unencumbered through the night sky.

Rafe joined them, his knowing smile acknowledging the wonder shining in Marlee and Elyse's eyes.

"Nothing is more enchanting than an Athirian moon. Your people, both the elves and the fae, are nocturnal. Although the magic of the air element is prevalent in the daylight hours, its essence is on full display when the moon rises in the sky."

He pointed to the blanket of lights hovering overhead.

"Athir's essence is visual. The yellow mist, widespread during the day, is the realm's elemental magic. It stores the moon's light, refracting it back and giving the illusion of a glowing sky at night. It is quite something to behold. The magic of the other realms is much more structured, but here it is amorphous and overt. Its magic and its moons are the reason Athir is known as—the realm of haunting beauty."

Kai called to them from across the courtyard where she was partly hidden under the shade of the aqueduct. "The others have found us a place to sleep for the night and some food. Dinner will be ready in an hour. In the meantime, let's have a look around."

"I will be happy to show you the home of your ancestors, Marlee," Rafe said noting the tension in her face.

"Come on it will be fun, and you have to be curious," Elyse said tugging on Marlee's arm and dragging her toward where Kai waited impatiently.

The sun had lost its battle with the night and the final glimmer of its rays disappeared below the horizon. Rafe's eyes drifted toward the Oberon Fen. The glow from the triple moon did not penetrate the inky blackness bearing down on the dark lands below. No sparkling stars hovered above it; only searing flashes of lightning lit the sky in random patterns. When the lightning ceased flashing, the sky, a vast pitch-black canvas, ached of something ominous. A harbinger of the past; a reminder of the hate that saturated the land so long ago and nearly destroyed it.

Kai's voice penetrated his thoughts. "Let's go, Rafe."

Behind the courtyard, the city of Tariedrelle stretched out before them. While the city wasn't big, it was full of stunning architecture and breathtaking landscaping. They stood at the edge of a luscious garden. Brilliant green moss covered the ground and colorful flowers bloomed everywhere. The scent of their flora imbued the evening air with a delightful aroma.

Marlee inhaled, her nose tingling as it pulled in the magical essence of the garden.

Along the edges, small stone paths wound through the mossy green carpet, leading to a group of small buildings and shops surrounding an expansive cobblestone area. The buildings were white-washed wood, but their gilded doorknobs, hinges, and window grates highlighted the fae's affection for opulence. Leafy green vines, dewdrops glistening on their surfaces, crept up the side of the buildings, wrapping themselves around chimney stacks and window shutters with abandon. Delicate, lacy moss dangled from the rooftops. Long tendrils waved in the warm breeze swirling through what Marlee assumed was a market square.

They followed Rafe as he carefully weaved around the pillars of the arched arcade leading them to an orchard of trees behind the market. The rumble of water intensified the closer they came to the far side of the city. A chill ran up Marlee's arms. As they moved past a grove of fruit trees, the tree of Tariedrelle came into view.

The silver haze seeping from the triple moon lit up the massive tree. Its green canopy dripped with the silver light. Enormous leaves covered the branches and fluttered gracefully in the evening air. Thick vines wrapped themselves tightly around branches. Smooth and without bark, the trunk, its grain a multitude of different brown tones, flickered as the moon's glow ignited the elemental magic embedded under its surface. Tiny pins of light dripped from the foliage, cascading off leaves and branches like raindrops leftover from a passing storm. The tree was the heart of Tariedrelle and the source of their powers. It stood proudly, infused by the ancient magic flowing through the Thanissia universe, and waiting for its people to rise.

"Something is not right," Brannon said to Rafe eyeing the tree suspiciously. "I've seen this tree a dozen times in my life but never has there been a time when I was not enthralled by its stature or its beauty. This is the first."

Rafe frowned. "Maybe it has yet to reach its full power. It has been in stasis for a long time and the Athir Druidstone has not yet been awakened."

Brannon nodded. "Yes, maybe."

They continued around the backside of the tree where a set of wooden steps led up the hillside. The deafening rumble of the waterfall echoed around them. At the top, a small path wove its way through moss-covered boulders. Following it, they came to a ledge behind the curtain of water leading to the other side. The waterfall cascaded furiously from above. A wall of water thundering past them as they walked across the slick rock ledge to the other side. The cool spray from the flow covered them in a fine mist.

Marlee stopped and looked through a crack in the curtain of water.

"I have never seen anything like this."

Between the flow of water, the top of the aqueduct could be seen. A frothy, river flowed down its channel dispersing water to the city. The market, garden, and courtyard glistened in the moonlight as the elemental magic wrapped itself in and around every inch of the city.

A city of elemental light—it was breathtaking.

Outside the gilded gate, Marlee could make out the Dark Forest. The tops of the tall trees swayed delicately in the night breeze.

From the corner of her eye, she saw a flash. The

gloomy sky above the dark lands roiled with volatile lightning. The crackle and sizzle boomed over the din of the pounding water.

Darkness called to her, whispering as the inky blackness inched toward her.

"Marlee?" Elyse said firmly breaking the trance. "Are you alright?"

Marlee's gaze drifted back to her friend.

"Where did you go?" She asked, concern softening the eyes behind her glasses.

"Did you hear that?"

Elyse frowned. "Hear what? I can't hear anything over this waterfall."

"It's nothing. Sorry." Marlee stammered. Her heart pounded in her chest as she peered at the black sky flashing irritably over the Oberon Fen in the distance. The whispering had stopped.

*It must be my imagination playing tricks on me.*

Turning she followed the ledge out to the other side of the waterfall before Elyse could inquire further.

The small white buildings, Marlee had seen from the courtyard were shaped like a beehive, the structures simpler than the ones below and much less ornate. Gossamer fabric blew gracefully from open windows. A knocker at the middle of the door, located below a small window, was the only gilt on the white-washed wood.

"This is where the fae resided," Rafe said rationally. "Their dwellings if you will."

He reached for the doorknob of the house nearest them and turned it. When the door swung open, he gestured for the others to enter.

The dwellings were much grander on the inside than they appeared from the outside. While the gold gilt was minimal on the exterior, the inside gleamed with its presence. Gold wrought-iron chandeliers hung from the ceiling and matching washbasins and jugs sat pristine on gilded trays. Floor to ceiling bookshelves, trimmed with gold-leaf accents, circled the walls. In the bedroom, two four-poster beds sat across from one another. Fluffy white comforters, the edges trimmed with gold braid, were folded neatly at the bottom of each bed. No color existed anywhere in the dwelling, just a palette of white, gold, and wood the same as the rest of the city.

Tariedrelle was simple, yet elegant, tranquil even, nothing revealing the mischievous and deceptive nature of its inhabitants. Maybe that was the point—*misdirection.*

"Come," Rafe said, "It must be time to eat. I can hear Brannon's stomach rumbling from here."

Brannon chuckled. "I could eat."

They left the dwelling and headed down the moss-covered cliff on the backside. The incline at times was steep but wooden steps built into these slopes helped make the trek less treacherous. The warm night breeze rustled the long grass that edged the stone path. Tiny purple flowers dotted the tips of the blades. Like the rest of the foliage in the city, a pleasant fragrance rose from its vividly colored flora.

Marlee ran her fingers through the blades of grass. They tingled.

At the bottom, a small gilded gate gave access to a tunnel which passed under the city walls and back into the courtyard.

As they entered, Rafe sensed they were not alone. His eyes searched the darkened area as he raised his hand motioning to the others for silence. He clasped the grip of his sword and pulled it with ease from its sheath, signaling Brannon to follow. Together, they walked toward the entrance gate.

The woods on the other side darkened the area outside the gilded fence and although nothing was visible, Rafe knew something lurked there. He tightened his grip on his sword as the gate creaked and the shadows hid whatever moved among them.

Rafe glanced at Brannon who nodded and raised his sword, waiting.

The gloom parted as the moonlight lit up the courtyard and Diego trotted into the city of the fae followed closely behind by Stevie.

# CHAPTER 6

**"I** HOPE THAT'S NOT FOR ME." Stevie pointed at the sword still held aloft by Brannon.

He grinned and sheathed his blade.

Rafe's eyes searched the blackness beyond the gate.

She placed her hand on his arm and shook her head as the others surrounded her.

Kai offered to take Diego and get him something to eat, so they could speak in private. The others, taking the hint, made themselves scarce.

"What happened, Stevie? Where is Dane?" He asked the moment the others walked away. "An uncontrollable rage surged through me earlier. It was Dane. Because of the binding, I experience it with her."

His eyes held the worry he tried to mask in his voice, but she understood how intimately their emotions entwined and how devastating that must have been. After seeing Dane's response to her mother's death, she knew her reaction must have brought Rafe just as much suffering.

She explained everything to Rafe, not leaving any details out. At moments, the anguish flooded back, and she stopped to compose herself. No one had any idea where she went, not even Dane's father, who Stevie spoke with before entering the portal.

Rafe remained silent as he listened, worry etching his handsome face. She too was worried, but the prophecy could not be wrong, Dane would find her way back to them.

If nothing else, Stevie must believe in that.

Across the courtyard, Kai observed their interactions with concern. She knew that look. Whatever Stevie was telling Rafe, it wasn't good. Sighing, she walked to the table where Diego lay chewing on a bone and began stroking his head.

Tauria and Gabby had set a big outdoor table for dinner. They prepared the meal with some food they found stored in a pantry in one of the market buildings. It seemed the fae, adept at infusing each part of their world with elemental magic, had managed to keep much of their food from spoiling, even after all this time. Although variety was scarce the plates of greens, wild rice, and loaves of bread were a welcome sight. A flask of wine sat at each end of the long table and Tauria had picked some fragrant flowers for a centerpiece. Kai studied the table. The display was picturesque, normal and strangely of place under the circumstances.

Drow circled the edges of the courtyard. His cabernet eyes never left Stevie as she spoke to Rafe. Kai noted a change in the royal a few days prior. The way he hovered near her friend trying to be inconspicuous and the subtle way his hand brushed against her arm when they spoke. How when she was near, his pale skin seemed to glow with a faint tinge of color. The prince was smitten with her, but Kai was not sure she even noticed.

She grinned at the thought—Stevie royalty. That would be something.

Killenn took a seat at the table beside her. "What are you thinking about?"

"About the past few days." She said not wanting to discuss her observations about Drow. "It's all happening so fast and sometimes it seems we react more than think."

"Many of us have had knowledge of the prophecy for a lifetime, but your destiny has been thrust upon you without warning. It must be daunting. Our worlds are so different from yours."

Kai smiled, nodding in agreement. "It's not been easy, but for me personally it brings me closer to my mom. To the person, you knew."

"Your mother was a warrior. You remind me of her. She would be proud of you, how you are handling your destiny."

"Thanks," she said as Rafe and Stevie joined them.

"Shall I gather everyone?"

"Yes. I think it will be easier if I tell them all at once."

Kai and Killenn left to find the others and within moments, they had assembled around the fountain.

Stevie repeated her story, glancing at Rafe every so often. He stayed silent, his face a hardened and unemotional mask. Kai and Elyse had numerous questions, which she did her best to answer. Unfortunately, she had no answers for why Dane left or where she was now.

"What do we do?" Elyse asked.

"We continue on as planned," Sebastian answered. "Dane will find her way back to us."

"And if she doesn't?" Kai's eyes welled with tears.

"She will." Stevie's voice broke and Drow put his arm around her.

"It's been a long day for everyone. We can sort this out in the morning after we have rested," he said.

Thanking him, she smiled her eyes shining with something Kai had never seen before. Maybe she was wrong. Maybe Stevie did know how he felt about her and maybe she felt the same. Her eye caught Killenn's who grinned and winked in return. A silent acknowledgment that he too had observed Drow's growing affection for the newest member of their clan.

Tauria and Brannon brought out the food and placed it on the long table motioning for the others to join them. Taking their places, they spoke amongst themselves until the conversation lulled and each became lost in their thoughts about the past and what was to come.

After a few hours, empty wine bottles littered the table, and many were yawning. A full belly and a long day of travel were taking its toll.

Moonlight cast the courtyard in a silver hue. Dancing sparks floated amongst the beams like tiny fireflies; small, flashing pins of light weaving lazy patterns above. A peaceful serenity began to lull some of them into a false sense of well-being. Sebastian recognized the effects of fae magic, infiltrating the senses and disarming those not from this world. It was simple yet intoxicating and no one used it better than the fae. Although they were skilled on the battlefield, they preferred using their powers without provocation and prided themselves on their ability to gain an advantage without overt bloodshed.

Even in stasis the magic still defended the city.

As the others cleaned up and headed to their respective dwellings for the night, Sebastian pulled Rafe and Gabby aside.

"I do not believe the death of Dane's mother is a coincidence. I believe it was a way to push Dane toward the darkness."

"For what reason?" Gabby asked.

"To interfere with the ancient prophecy. To change the course of her destiny." His bright jade eyes narrowed. "We must not let it. Darkness cannot consume her, or the future will be lost. For the prophecy to unfold the way it is meant we must find Dane, otherwise I'm afraid fate will not be kind."

He turned to Gabby. "You are the only one who can find her."

Gabby agreed. Only she could track the ancient bloodlines.

"I will return to the new world in the morning."

She met Rafe's gaze. "I will find her."

He nodded, a simple gesture of gratitude.

"You must continue to the Druidstone, activate it and then go straight to the Druid sanctuary. When I find Dane, I will meet you there. Find out as much as you can from the old texts. The Druids had their secrets. Maybe they too had some answers."

Marlee tossed and turned, unable to sleep. There was a murmur on the wind filtering into the city, beckoning to her. She tried to ignore it, but it had a way of luring her mind. The whispering ebbed and flowed, drawing her into its cadence, enticing her to listen.

She sat up as it suddenly disappeared.

Glancing across the room she noticed Elyse was still fast asleep, her face peaceful under the moon's glow. She got out of bed and tiptoed from the room, moving through the shadowy fae house toward the door. Stepping into the warm night air she looked up at the star-laden sky. They twinkled in the inky blackness. A serenity surrounded her as a warm breeze tickled her cheek, but it rapidly diminished as a prickly shiver crept over her skin.

Her heartbeat quickened as the whispering returned beckoning to her as it floated through the city on the evening breeze. It pulled her attention toward the thunderous sky off to the east, where lightning continued to flash over the dark lands known as the Oberon Fen.

She cocked her head and listened. The whispering was coming from those cursed lands—calling to her.

"Can't sleep?" Elyse asked, startling Marlee by her sudden appearance.

"Did I wake you?"

The whispering had ceased immediately upon Elyse's arrival as if it did not want to be heard by anyone but Marlee.

Elyse shook her head. "I think there's too much going on to sleep well, if at all." She gazed at the night sky. "It's so quiet here."

Marlee frowned realizing maybe Elyse couldn't hear the strange whispering. "I never got a chance to talk to you before we came here. Have you spoken with Cal?"

Elyse smiled at the mention of her husband. "I called him before we left. He is good. Work is keeping him busy, which helps. He doesn't ask a lot of questions."

A sadness edged her words. Marlee knew what she was thinking. Unlike the others, she and Elyse had families not connected in any way to magic. Their destiny would create a huge problem for them back home.

Although Elyse seemed confident and sure about her immortal future, Marlee could sense there was uncertainty below the surface. But like everything else in her life, Elyse Simms would deal with those hurdles when she had to.

"Let's go back to bed. We have quite the day tomorrow." Elyse yawned, stretching her arms above her head.

"I'll be in shortly," Marlee said, smiling as her friend squeezed her hand and disappear back inside the house.

Her eyes turned back toward the flashing sky in the distance. It was quiet. There was no longer any whispering floating across the breeze, calling to her. The occasional rumble of thunder accompanied the bright flashes of light as the two danced in the night sky above the Oberon Fen. The silence surrounding the city of Tariedrelle was unsettling.

It left her feeling anxious like something terrible was about to happen.

# CHAPTER 7

THE TEMPLE OF AIR STOOD upon a tall pillar of rock, the spire on its roof partly hidden by a bank of swirling golden clouds. It looked like a small marble gazebo; the base surrounded by five round pillars holding up the thatched roof. Sturdy vines curled around the columns, weaving their way up toward the roof where they blossomed into a multitude of orange and purple flowers. The effect caused the thatched roof to look as if it wore a crown of blooms. A staircase of bleached wooden steps led up the side of the rock to the temple. Moss griped the slopes, the rock wet from rivulets of water running across their surfaces.

Marlee could sense a shift in the air around the gazebo as she and Elyse ascended toward it. Sebastian and Drow accompanied them to the top while the others stayed at the foot of the staircase.

Kai shifted uncomfortably her eyes darting to Tauria. "Can you feel that?"

"The Temple recognizes the blood of its people. The air is awakening."

Goosebumps appeared on her arms, and she rubbed at them absently. The sun, still low in the sky, provided the morning with plenty of warmth but a cool chill crept across her skin.

"Why does it make me feel anxious?"

Tauria's green eyes narrowed. "Air magic affects people in different ways. We breathe it in, so it is difficult for us to control how our chemistry reacts to it. It is at its most potent near the temple because the realm is in stasis. The temple holds the magic in condensed form. Once the Druidstone has been activated and your friends have received their birthright, it will disperse across this world evenly. Your body will be able to absorb it better and the feeling of malaise should fade."

Kai's eyes shifted to where Brannon, Rafe, and Killenn stood. Like Tauria they did not seem affected by the concentrated magic swirling in the air around the temple. Stevie, on the other hand, looked a little sweaty and pale.

Another wave of nausea rolled through her. She wiped her brow and lowered herself to the ground, thankful Gabby had left earlier to go back to Etheriem. Otherwise, Kai would have to endure smart-ass comments about how weak her race was. The sun blazed in the sky, and she shielded her eyes watching Marlee and Elyse scale the pillar of rock, silently wishing they would hurry.

As they neared the top, Elyse could see the gazebo clearly. There was nothing of interest inside. The floor was made from the same bleached wood planks as the stairs. At the center stood a small basin atop a pedestal. Golden water filled the basin. It shimmered in the bright morning light that found its way into the shade of the gazebo. Flecks of light danced on its surface.

"How do we activate the Druidstone?" she inquired as they stood gazing at the stone basin.

"It requires mixing the blood of both races," Drow

said picking up the small silver athame laying on the lip of the basin and holding it out toward Sebastian. The gold water rippled in response, as if it anticipated what was to come. He took the blade and reached for Marlee's hand. Instinctively she pulled away, her blue eyes full of doubt.

"It must be done," he said, his face softening.

Trembling she lifted her hand placing it palm up in his outstretched one. Sebastian raised the knife and sliced into her index finger. She winced at the sting as the blade cut her skin. Bright red blood rose from the open gash. He lowered her hand until the bleeding wound was inches above the basin's golden water. Tilting her finger, a single drop fell into the water and disappeared under its depths. Sebastian drew the sharp blade of the athame across Elyse's outstretched finger. A single drop of her blood fell into the fountain and vanished.

The basin stilled and the ripples on the surface faded. In mirrored symmetry, the golden water reflected their faces back to them. The breeze whispering through the gazebo also faded. Everything in the gazebo was calm, silent.

Minutes passed before the golden water began to bubble. It churned, its direction becoming deliberate as it funneled at its center as if swirling down an unseen drain. The golden hue also began to change, darkening until the water in the basin became blood-red. It sloshed recklessly over the side as the churning increased, becoming more violent. A crescendo of voices filled the air as the golden clouds descended on the gazebo wrapping it in a golden fog. The air swirled funneling around Elyse and Marlee and trapping them in its midst until they were swallowed up by the golden vortex.

Drow and Sebastian stepped from the gazebo back into the sunlit day. Away from the roar of the whirlwind, all was peaceful. They glanced down at the others who waited patiently below both concern and awe etched on their faces.

The vortex inside the gazebo continued to swirl, a chorus of voices, rising and falling with each rotation.

There was nothing to do now but wait.

Elyse saw the fear in Marlee's eyes as the golden mist closed in around them. She reached for her hand but grasped air.

Marlee was gone.

She heard a song in the distance and turned toward the sound. Reaching blindly in front of her, she moved through the mist. After a few steps it thinned, and she emerged into a ravine. Stone cliffs, the shade of a stormy sky, banked a crystal blue river. Sparkling lights of gold danced upon its surface. At the far end embedded into the rock, was a door. The song she heard was coming from behind it.

She walked along the bank of the river lulled by the melody. The water also seemed to echo the strange song as the surface shimmered in unison. As she drew closer, the voice grew louder, the lyrics clearer. Although she did not recognize the words, it reminded her of the Gaelic records Dane's grandfather used to play.

A guitar accompanied the shrill pitch of a flute as the beautiful female voice sang in harmony.

The melody was slow, the notes evocative.

Elyse was drawn to the haunting song.

When she reached the door and placed her hand

on the iron handle, the music stopped. A gust of wind whistled down the ravine, ruffling her hair.

She shivered.

The heavy stone scraped along the ground as it yawned open.

Elyse peered inside.

Beyond the door, a dark green forest waited. Lanterns, hanging from the branches, lit a path through its density. The music sprang up again, the voice floating toward her, the haunting melody enticing her to follow the sound. A lantern-lit path guided her way, small dots of throbbing light winding through the forest. She followed it until she emerged into a secluded hollow.

Soft green moss covered the ground and trees. Long tendrils hung from the branches swaying in the warm air. More lanterns circled the outskirts casting a soft yellow glow across the hollow. At the center, dancing on a bed of white flowers was a bare-footed woman. Her body swayed to the music as she sang, and she wore a long green gown of gossamer fabric that flowed in waves around her as she moved. A crown of flowers and thorns adorned her head and her long red hair swept across her lower back. The woman did not seem to notice Elyse as she continued singing the haunting song.

She stepped closer to the center of the hollow. The woman's eyes were closed and as she threw back her head to sing, Elyse noticed the tips of pointed ears peeking through her long, thick hair.

Mesmerized by this woman and her song, Elyse watched in awe, enchanted by the spectacle.

Music echoed off the trees. The woman's voice was clear and beautiful and the longer she sang the more spellbound Elyse became.

*Far away from the land you know*
*Upon thy shores, you found your home*
*Worlds apart and down below*
*The dawn of night doth call you*
*On this sacred ground, you rise*
*Blood doth make you kin to I*
*Bear the mark of thy old and wise*
*I will take you home*

The spellbinding melody lulled Elyse as she gazed upon the woman, her slow methodical movement hypnotic. Lantern fire flared and the hollow began to sway and spin as a fuzziness draped itself over her mind.

The refrain echoed around her, a soothing sound enticing her to sleep.

Heaviness pulled at her eyelids and her body went limp as the hollow swam around her. The lantern light disappeared into blackness. Ancient magic flowed under her skin taking her back to the world from which she'd come.

Marlee observed them from inside the golden fog, hidden behind a thin layer of mist separating her world from that of the elves. She wasn't alone on this plane there were others, and they giggled as they murmured in her ear, unseen voices of a long-forgotten past.

She watched as Elyse returned, as concern morphed her features when Sebastian and Drow told her Marlee had not, and then discussed what to do, finally deciding to split up. Drow and Sebastian would escort Elyse to Niramyst, the others would take Diego and search for Marlee.

A scowl furrowed her brow at the thought of the elvish city, its sprawling size dwarfing her own home. The ancient city was hidden deep inside the Dark Forest. Full of archaic beings and creatures, the forest was a solemn place where time stood still. If one did not know the right path to take, one could get lost for days—*it was a place she hated.*

The whispering behind her increased as those hidden in the dark clamored to be heard. A restless echo from the past. They'd existed in the fog for a very long time and ached to taste freedom again. To help them find a way out of the entombing darkness they needed her to unlock the Fen and link what was left of their world to this plane. They needed her to guide them.

After the war, the elves had begrudgingly agreed to the peace treaty including providing the surviving fae sanctuary on the elven plane of Athir. Over time old wounds healed and their differences became less conflicting. The races stabilized into a unity of sorts but the fae always harbored a secret. The Oberon Fen, once a gateway between the two planes, still provided them with an escape to a small portion of their original home, which had survived the war. They never revealed this to any of the other races, allowing them instead to think the gateway destroyed.

Because of the sheer brutality of the war, the bloodshed had stained the Oberon Fen and it became a dark scar; a mar on this realm. A reminder of a violent past. The cursed lands leeched fear and death making it easy for the fae to guard their secret.

The Oberon Fen, like the rest of the realm, had submitted to stasis. Purged of its dark magic it fell into silence, but now it called to her. It recognized the blood of her ancestors and the dark past it represented.

As the others departed the Temple of Air, the whisperers retreated into the dark leaving her alone in comforting silence. She detested the world below and didn't want to go back to the plane of the elves, she wanted to follow the whisperers.

Darkness called to her and she smiled.

The elves would no longer dictate the rules of this plane after the gateway had been opened.

Her ancestors would come home and once again rule the Oberon Fen.

# CHAPTER 8

THE TRIPLE MOON BEGAN TO rise over the cursed land as they trekked toward it. They stopped as the pebbled path split in two, meandering off in different directions. As it wound left, the path followed the western side of the sparkling lake, while the right headed northwest through a tangle of thorny bushes, their withered leaves rustling in the breeze.

"This is the outer edge of the Oberon Fen. The hand of death has reached out much further than I had anticipated." Rafe's fingers grazed the dead leaves. "We must be aware of our surroundings from this point," he said as Brannon swung a thick bladed knife, cutting the unruly bushes to broaden the path.

As they moved further into the tangled field of thorns and away from the sun-soaked flatlands, the air chilled. Long shadows crept like dark fingers of dread in on them.

Stevie shivered "Why is it so chilly?"

"I think it is wonderful," Kai chuckled. "Athir was proving to be a bit warm for my liking."

Raising an eyebrow, she tilted her head toward her friend. "You know it's disturbing to hear you say things like that. I'm not the one normally whining about the cold."

"It is quite a change," she agreed.

Pushing through the last of the barbed bushes, they

stood before a set of iron gates. Ropes of weighty vines wrapped themselves around the metal but any foliage that used to thrive from the stalks was now shriveled and lifeless. Tall rock pillars flanked the gate. The rock, covered with black moss, dripped with an oozing liquid the color of rust. Stone gargoyles sat atop the pillars, their blank stares adding to the menacing design. Long, tails slithered around their moss-covered bodies. Sharp fangs protruded from snarling lips, and curved horns jutted from their heads. Claws gripped the sides of the pillar as their vacant eyes gazed upon the strangers who stood before them. Although they were carved from stone, their appearance was very unsettling.

Killenn approached the gates, yanking on the thick chain and padlock securing them. He bent and picked up a sizable rock, attempting to break the latch with force. Neither the chain nor lock budged. The metal, unfettered by corrosion or weakness normally apparent on aged iron, held fast. Sheepishly he looked back and shrugged.

"Let me try," Kai said, pulling a water bottle from her backpack. Unscrewing the cap, she filled the key-hole, splashing water over the lock mechanisms. Icy vapors rose from her hand as she wrapped it around the padlock and began muttering an incantation. Ice crystals appeared on the metal and as she exhaled misty puffs of air appeared.

Seconds later a crunching sound echoed around them as the padlock began to bend and crack under the extreme cold, shattering into a pile of shards and dust in Kai's hand.

"Very imaginative of you," Rafe acknowledged, nodding his thanks as he unwound the heavy chain and wrenched open the metal gates. The hinges creaked in protest, shuddering as they swung open, shaking off years of stationary existence.

A stagnant wind blew out of the cursed lands as it was released from its confines. Rafe coughed at the stench riding its wake—a musty, moldy odor ripe with decay. The others gagged and held their breath until the stench seeped into the thorny bushes behind them and dissipated.

"Welcome to the Oberon Fen," Killenn joked.

"What was that awful smell?" Stevie's nose wrinkled in disgust.

Diego growled, his hackles flaring as he shook his mane.

"Death," Brannon said, his hand tightening around the hilt of his sword as he peered into the shadowy land lying just beyond the iron gate.

A desolate orchard stretched before them. There was no color, no vibrancy, only a depressing palate of gray and black and the aching silence of emptiness.

Dense fog rolled across the ground toward where they stood, swirling in and out of the charred trees. Gnarled branches, mostly void of vegetation except for a few derelict leaves and rotten fruit clinging to the decayed wood, creaked and groaned. Twigs and debris littered the ground as the stale wind shook them loose.

They entered the Oberon Fen cautiously, unsure of what to expect or where to go. The place was a graveyard of the past, void of life except for the maggots and beetles crawling in and out of the rotting fruit and scuttling across the moist earth.

Weaving through the orchard they followed Brannon and Rafe. The warriors were the only ones who had traversed the lands of the Oberon Fen, although that was long before war tainted the lands with the blood of the dead.

"What happened to this place?" Kai asked, touching a piece of fruit that clung to a vine. It quivered and fell to the ground splitting open on impact with a loud squishing noise. The black flesh of the fruit released a horde of small green ants from its innards.

"Gross." A breathy gasp escaped Kai's mouth as she took a step back.

Killenn came to her side, looking down at the rotten fruit and the scurrying insects. "This is what happens when elemental magic dies. When land, which relies on it to exist is starved—it rots from the inside out."

Kai shook her head. "Why the heck do we think Marlee is here? Why would anyone want to come here?"

"The Oberon Fen was once the gateway to the fae plane. Air magic was siphoned from these orchards to make a funnel connecting the two planes. They had an agreement with the elves that these fields, with its lush, fertile earth would act as the grow lands for their specialty crops."

His hand swept through the air indicating the forlorn orchard. "These trees once grew an apple-like fruit known as a Maeb."

With the toe of her boot, Kai nudged the one laying demolished on the ground.

"They had a crisp, salty exterior with a soft, sweet fleshy center," he said. "The Maeb was prized for its unique flavors and was a popular ingredient in many dishes made throughout the five realms."

His eyes tracked toward the back half of the Fen where the lightning flashed, and the rumbling echoed. "Farther west, near the gateway, is the vineyard where the sacred Eddinberry grew. The fae used to make exceptional spirits with the berry as their key ingredient." His mouth quirked up at the side, and he lowered his voice. "I have on many occasions partaken in a glass or two of their Eddinberry Firewater and the next morning wished I had not."

Kai laughed at the warrior's memory. She suspected most of the men in her company had done the same.

Thunder rumbled in the distance.

"Come, let us catch up to the others," he said.

As they moved away from the dead Maeb tree, it began to quiver. Twisted branches shook as if chilled by the cold wind. Kai and Killenn disappeared into the trees lining the orchard unaware of the tree's movement or the soft giggle that arose to drift on the surrounding air.

The whispers surrounded her, echoing in the gloom as Kai and Killenn discussed her homeland.

She sneered at their words. *As if they know anything about the real Athir.*

Marlee purse her lips as the chorus of whispers became chaotic.

She tilted her head, listening to their commands.

The air in the orchard was weak but it had enough magic left for her to make mischief.

As they walked away, she breathed in deeply, sucking air into her lungs and blowing it back out. It was enough to animate the dead Maeb tree.

The whispers turned to giggles.

Marlee smiled—they were pleased.

When they activated the Druidstone, the golden mist had brought her here to the darkness. An archaic plane, hidden from sight. A place where she could look down on the world below. The whisperers resided here, hiding, never revealing themselves. She sensed their presence and knew without question they were her blood, the imprints of her ancestors—ancient fae who faded into history long before the war commenced and destroyed these lands. A primordial race. The beginnings of her bloodline and the ones whose power she would inherit.

The ones who would, in time, rule these lands.

Marlee floated unseen behind the group of immortals as they crept through the Oberon Fen. Hidden behind the veil of the dark plane they were oblivious to how close she was to them and how futile their search for her would be. She would only be found if she wanted to be. Saving the mortal world was no longer of concern to her—*she was fae and the Oberon Fen was now her home.*

The whispering intensified as the group reached the end of the orchard and crossed the dry riverbed. Marlee sensed the whisperer's excitement as the immortals drew nearer the field of battle.

During the war, the herb fields had seen the bulk of the carnage. The blood-soaked fields became a silent witness as the elves slaughtered the fae in droves. The lush acres of red clover and pilewort had been trampled underfoot. Their leaves dripped with blood as the bodies of the dead lay amongst them.

The whisperers had not forgotten and now their time had come. With Marlee here, they would rise once again and take back what had been taken from them so long ago. She was their portal, a way out of the plane they were trapped in and into the realm below—the Oberon Fen, full of violent memories and lost souls.

Giggles echoed through the darkness behind her.

It was time—time for the ancient fae to make their return.

Diego had kept his nose to the ground as they walked, stopping occasionally to sniff the air and shake out his fur but now, he stared impatiently down at them from the top of the river embankment.

Stevie glared at him as she scaled the steep sides, pulling herself up using the woody vines hanging over the rocky shelf. "Lose the attitude, Diego."

He shook out his fur and trotted off.

Killenn chuckled behind her. "The Dragonwolf is not one for patience."

"Remind me again why my ancestors revered them so much," she asked as she reached the top.

"They are much like the Dragon Gypsies in temperament," he said, pulling himself over the embankment to stand beside her.

Her dark red eyes squinted, and she frowned ignoring his quip.

Acres of open land stretched out in front of them— the herb fields. Once lush and full of color, they were now caked with dried blood and littered with piles of petrified ash where bodies of the dead once lay.

The triple moon had risen to its peak and cast a silvery radiance over the entire realm. Although the sky above them was dark and flashed with angry lightening the glow of the moon breached its density providing enough light for them to travel by.

Stevie scanned the horizon.

To her left, stone mountains rose majestically toward the sinister sky and to the right, the riverbed wound through the desolate lands in the direction of the vineyards near the horizon.

Long evaporated, the parched bed was cracked and dusty. Like the rest of the world, nothing of substance grew. The vegetation that did find its way up through the cracks perished the moment it encountered the stale air.

The Oberon Fen was truly the land of death.

As the others joined them at the top, a dense fog rolled hastily toward them from the mountains. Its movement seemed deliberate, spreading out and covering the field in a dense mist until everything disappeared behind a hazy wall.

"That was strange," Stevie said.

Diego crouched.

A shiver ran down her spine as his lips curled back baring his teeth. Hackles raised he let out a threatening growl.

The fog swirled in response and Stevie and Killenn took a step back as it drifted closer.

A heavy, dampness saturated the haze as it thickened, soupy and dense like the kind found in a small seaport town on a wet, autumn night. There was also something different about this fog. Unlike the one rolling over the orchard, this one was unnatural and moved with purpose as if guided by an unseen hand.

Chilled, damp air surrounded them and Tauria shivered.

The fields no longer felt empty, there was something hidden in the fog, waiting.

"What is it?" Rafe asked noticing his sister's unease.

Her face crumpled in thought. "I'm not sure but the fog conceals something."

"Maybe we should wait until daylight to continue searching for Marlee," Kai said. "It's difficult to see and Tauria did say this wasn't a place we want to be after dark."

Tauria did not respond instead she crouched down

and placed a hand flat on the cold earth and closed her eyes.

A whisper drifted toward them through the mist. It was faint, but it was there. Behind that was another sound. Shuffling? Slow methodical scraping as if something was being dragged across the ground.

"Can you see anything?" Brannon probed.

"How can she see anything through this fog?" The hair on the back of Stevie's neck prickled, and goosebumps rose on her forearms. Another serious growl rattled through Diego's throat, and she grasped his collar tighter just in case he decided to charge.

Brannon turned toward her. "Tauria has the gift of witchsight. Her vision is quite precise when she focuses. It gives her the ability to separate things in her field of vision. It is like peeling back the layers of what you see to visualize what is hiding beneath."

"Quiet," Rafe hissed, watching as she opened her eyes and stood. Slowly, her pupils expanded until most of the green of her irises disappeared behind round black globes.

Flashes of lightning scorched the sky followed by a crashing rumble of thunder. The fog, a ghostly gray under the silver haze of the moon, shifted as if something moved within it.

Moments later her head twitched, a gasp escaped her lips, her legs buckled, and she fell into the waiting arms of Brannon who tenderly lowered her to the ground.

"I'm fine," she said squeezing his hand. He pulled her to her feet and affectionately touched her cheek.

"Are you sure?"

Tauria nodded. "There is definitely something hiding in there, but I was unable to see it clearly. Silhouettes move within the mist, but something blocks them from my sight."

Stevie rubbed her arms as fingers of dread crept over her skin. "What is it?"

"An energy unlike any I have experienced before. Whatever it is it knows we are here and it's not alone. There are others, and they wait for *us.*"

# CHAPTER 9

**M**OONLIGHT GLINTED OFF THE BLADE of his sword as Rafe pulled it from the sheath at his hip. The powerful beams from the triple moon lit up the dark fields enough to see. He was thankful it was harvest season on Athir for the normal Athirian moon would be no match for the dark, angry skies of the Oberon Fen.

Lightning bolted through the sky overhead as his eyes scanned the wall of fog stretching out before them. It reached at least sixty hands above the herb fields, covering its full width.

There was no way around it, they would have to go through.

"Do you think I can freeze it?" Kai asked readying her hands. "Then you could just break it with your sword."

Rafe shook his head. "Although it feels damp to the skin, it is not vaporous water. It is something else entirely. Magic has created it, of that I am sure, but for what reason I do not know. I do know your powers will not affect it."

He reached out his blade, pushing it into the swirling mist. There was a hiss as the metal touched the fog but when he withdrew it the blade was untouched by any damage or substance.

Running a finger down the flat side of the blade he showed Kai the dry tip. "No moisture."

This time he reached toward the haze with his bare hand. Again, it hissed as it curled around his fingers and swept up his arm but nothing more egregious happened. Certain it would not harm them, Rafe turned toward the others.

"Stay together. Be aware of your surroundings. Arm yourselves and be ready for anything. If we can stay away from whatever lurks in there, we shall. If not, we fight. Stevie, I am afraid the smoke dragon will be ineffective as you will not be able to see your target. These fields are nothing more than dirt and decay. There is no fire for you to manipulate so you will have to rely solely on your instincts and your fighting abilities, as will you Kai."

In response, she pulled the katana from her back, arcing the blade smoothly through the air. It hummed as she picked up speed, her movements precise and elegant.

Kai drew the dual Scimitar short blades from the sheaths at her waist. The curved blades, thicker at the point than the hilt, glinted in the muted moonlight. She too swung the blades effortlessly through the air crossing her body in a figure eight motion.

"Ready?" Rafe's eyes narrowed as he glanced at the others.

Tauria held her bow in one hand while the other adjusted the quiver on her back giving her quick access to her arrows.

"A good fight is what I've been missing." Brannon's grin widened as he unsheathed his sword and winked at Killenn.

"The daemons in the Dead Lands were not enough for you?" Killenn teased loading an intimidating bolt into the flight groove of his crossbow and heaving the weapon across his shoulder.

"That, my friend, was just a warm-up."

"Then you should have no problem with shadows."

"Let's go." Rafe lowered his voice as he signaled to Stevie to release Diego. As she let go of the Dragonwolf's collar he darted into the heavy fog, emitting a long aching howl as he disappeared into the churning mist.

Cautiously they moved forward followed by the others.

The fog swirled around them, hissing as it touched their skin. Its density made it difficult to see and Rafe used the faint glow of the triple moon penetrating the fogbank to guide them.

As they ventured further into the forsaken fields the air began to move as if gusts of wind propelled it. One minute the fog was thick and stagnant, the next it thinned into a hazy veil. At these moments the field of vision extended to yards instead of inches.

Shapes darkened the fog and Tauria lifted her bow, aiming toward the right side of the field. Her head tilted as if listening to something the others could not hear. "Something is heading this way," she mouthed, pulling back the bowstring.

The others turned, weapons raised, waiting.

A scraping noise broke the strange silence followed by a wailing moan. The mist swirled as a dark figure moved toward them through the mist.

Rafe tightened his grip on the sword as the fog parted, revealing a corpse. Not the rotting daemon corpses like the ones buried beneath the underground caverns of the Dead Lands but a reanimated corpse of a long-dead warrior.

Dressed in a tarnished gold and white breastplate

the corpse lumbered toward him. The orange stone of Niramyst embedded in the front of the helm glinted.

Rafe recognized the armor immediately.

"Elves," he shouted to the others.

The moment the word left his lips the corpse lifted the weapon it dragged behind itself—a long glaive with a very sharp blade at its end. It swung the glaive outward almost slicing into Rafe's arm before he raised his own weapon in defense.

Metal struck metal as the blades connected. The elf was surprisingly strong and fast and Rafe could do little more than block its swings.

Brannon joined in matching his blade stroke with Rafe's.

The blade of the glaive gleamed in the silvery haze as it crashed down on Brannon's sword. At the same moment, Rafe thrust his blade upward under the lower tips of its helm and straight into the elf's throat.

The glaive fell as the elf swayed. The small glitter embedded deep within its black eyes extinguished and it collapsed to its knees.

Rafe pulled the blade from its neck and the body crumpled, hissing as it hit the arid earth.

The fog churned around them as multiple figures appeared in its depths.

"There are more coming," Rafe said. "Get ready."

The others moved outward creating a broad circle, readying themselves for the emergence of corpses of long-dead elves cursed by dark magic to walk the battlefield on which they died.

The mist darkened as more shadows moved toward them.

Tauria circled the area, firing arrows.

"You are shooting blind, Tauria. Wait until they are close, and you can see their dead eyes," Brannon said.

Elves began to emerge with weapons drawn—bows, swords, polearms, and knives gleaming.

Killenn fired, his bolt piercing the helm's thick armor. Cocking the crossbow, he loaded another into the flight groove. Elves dropped to the ground with a hiss as his bolts hit their mark. Tauria stood with her back to him, shooting at the elves that emerged on the other side of the field. With nimble fingers and a precise shot, she too felled one reanimated corpse after another.

Bone-chilling cold sank into her skin as Stevie found herself pushed back into the fog and away from the others by a rather sizable elf corpse. The air pressed down on her until it was difficult to breathe or see. Magic surged in her blood as it pumped uncontrollably through her veins looking for a way to escape, but without fire, it was useless—she would have to fight.

Swinging her katana, she connected multiple times with the elf, but its armor repelled each blow. It carried a battle-ax almost half its size with two curved blades like an executioner's ax. It grunted as it raised the massive ax over its head with intent.

As the blade began to swing down the fog parted, and a snarling Diego jumped on the elf's back sinking his incisors into its fleshy neck. His momentum sent them both sprawling to the ground. The elf tried to right itself, but Diego pounced again, ripping decomposed flesh off the bone.

A shriek shattered the dense night as the elf howled in fury grabbing Diego around the body and squeezing.

Diego yelped in pain.

Hastened by her Dragonwolf's predicament Stevie ran and jumped on the elf's back. She plunged her katana through the eye hole of its helm with such force the point of the blade exited through the back of its skull, knocking the helm to the ground. The elf staggered backward and fell to its knees, the sword still lodged in its head.

Echoes of a raging battle drifted through the fog from her left, the sound of blades and cries carried on the night air. Grabbing Diego's collar and the katana she rushed toward the sound of clashing metal. As she neared, she saw her friends fighting the hordes of elves surrounding them.

Kai swung her blades, loping heads off bodies in one motion. Black blood squirted from the headless corpses. Tauria and Killenn fired arrows at such a quick pace and with such agility, she was sure they must be using magic. Blood gushed through Brannon's fingers as he gripped his forearm and rushed headfirst into a corpse who had Rafe pinned to the ground.

Stevie let go of Diego and raised her sword as he darted into the foray snarling and snapping at the corpses.

*There's too many!*

As her blade connected with the end of a glaive a flash of glittering light exploded around them sweeping across the battlefield and disappearing into nothingness.

The elves instantly stopped attacking, turned, and marched to the far side, falling into formation with their weapons at their sides.

Tittering laughter and a soft fluttering sound echoed from the outer edges of the fog. The luminosity of the triple moon washed over the battlefield as the mist rolled away to the far edges of thc field.

On a pile of bones and skulls, a few yards from where they stood, sat Marlee. She was dressed in black leather pants, the slim legs tucked neatly into brown leather boots. Under a maroon velvet vest cinched at the waist by gold rope, she wore a white peasant blouse, intricately embroidered with green leaves and vines. Her blond shoulder-length hair was perfectly straight ending in a blunt edge and her skin glowed with ethereal gold light. Beneath the moon's rays, her pale blue eyes shone silver as she gazed intently upon them.

Stevie had never seen Marlee look more beautiful. An unfamiliar regalness and self-assurance exuded from her. Blue eyes turned her way and a malicious smile crept over her face as if she knew exactly what she was thinking.

*"Ahrund silvar no-mirith,"* Marlee uttered.

The elves stamped their feet, turned in unison, and disappeared in a cloud of shadowy smoke.

"That was so much fun, wasn't it?" she squealed jumping to her feet and clapping her hands together.

Kai and Stevie glanced at one another confusion marring their expressions.

"Don't be upset. My friends and I just wanted to have a little fun. They've been so lonely of late."

Anger flashed in his jade eyes as Rafe stepped toward her. "I don't think the dead get lonely, and I am sure the elvish warriors would rather not have their corpses desecrated for your amusement."

Marlee's glee vanished, her expression turning vapid.

*"Mar-o ven sindafall,"* she said waving her hand dismissively at Rafe. "The elvish brethren are nothing more than a pile of ashes—a memory of a past long lost. Do not mourn the dead warrior for they do not deserve your pity."

A chorus of giggles sprung from the fog still hovering at the edges of the field. As the heavy air began to swirl into funnel clouds, the tittering morphed to whispers and floated toward them on the cool breeze.

Something hid behind the curtain of mist; Stevie could feel its presence.

She turned to Marlee. "Who are 'they,' your friends?"

Marlee's eyes darted toward the fog, and she tilted her head as if she listened to something that only she could hear.

"They will introduce themselves," she said twisting her hand around in the air as the mist behind her began to swirl. Individual funnels formed spinning faster as they moved toward her.

An eerie silence fell over the herb fields and the funnel clouds dissipated revealing a dozen or more phantom beings floating in the air behind Marlee.

Stevie gasped.

The phantom beings resembled the gargoyles guarding the front gate. White eyes stared vacantly from bald, swollen heads. Long pointed ears twitched at the slightest noise and large wings, the membrane tattered, fluttered. Their mouths were lipless slits, but sharp fangs protruded glistening with dripping saliva. The beings wore no garments, yet no indication of gender could be detected, their androgyny unambiguous. Blue veins crisscrossed the pale skin covering their gangly limbs—skin so translucent a faint outline of the stone mountains in the distance could be seen through them.

An incoherent whispering reverberated between them.

Clasping her hands in front of her Marlee said. "I'm sorry we must leave you now, there is so much to do. Please don't be angry over our little game, it was all in fun."

Her eyes locked on Brannon, and she licked her lips seductively. "You are very skilled with a blade. I wonder what else you're skilled at."

Enraged, Tauria raised her bow but Killenn pushed it back down as the beings behind Marlee became restless.

Ignoring the act of defiance, Marlee absently twisted the hefty silver ring on her middle finger. "Well I'm bored with you," she said waving her hand dismissively. "I must be off—unfinished business with an elf."

The whispering intensified as the beings behind her stirred again.

Her voice echoed through the night as the mist crept across the field engulfing Marlee and the strange beings.

"Until we meet again," she called out, her eyes sparkling with mischief.

When the fog dissipated moments later, they were gone.

# CHAPTER 10

THE HERB FIELD LAY SILENT.

The corpses of the warrior elves had vanished.

A strong odor of damp earth permeated the air, but the field was just as it was before, desolate and empty. They stood at its center, eyes searching the distance for any sign of Marlee or those entities, but they were gone.

The menacing sky above them thundered, lightning scorching the night. The Oberon Fen had settled back into its comfortable, cursed existence.

"Did you see her ears?" Killenn said.

Rafe's jade eyes darkened as he thought about the long points stretching upward from between the strands of Marlee's blonde hair, the tips slightly folded. "Yes, they were unusual."

"And those things in the fog behind her? What were they?"

"They looked like the Kelties of old. They remain the last fae species with wings but the ones with Marlee were translucent not flesh and bone. An aberration of the past, maybe."

"Many species after transcending do not resemble their physical form in its entirety. Imprints possibly?" Tauria said.

Stevie frowned. "What's an imprint?"

"An energy of sorts or the essence of what is left behind after a being transcends into the afterlife," Tauria explained. "An imprint can manifest in many ways. It can be of visual form, a whisper in the conscious mind, or a cold chill wrapping itself around objects in the living plane."

"But the Keltie was almost extinct long before the Great War. There hasn't been a sighting of one on Athir since the peace treaty reached its hundredth signing cycle. It's not possible they have returned, is it?" Brannon asked.

Tauria moved in beside her brother and in a low voice said, "We need to get to the gateway."

Hearing her words Kai stiffened. "Why? I thought the gateway was no longer viable, and we don't know where Marlee's gone. Should we not try to find the others first?"

Tauria turned her green eyes toward Kai. "We must confirm if the gateway is open. If those winged creatures are Kelties, they must have come from the plane beyond. Which means it was not destroyed in its entirety during the elven/fae war as previously thought."

"And Marlee? Has she been taken by them?"

Rafe sheathed his sword. "She was speaking Fa'delhan. It seems as if she may *be* one of them."

Uncomfortable silence hovered over the group at the idea that Marlee's birthright may have come from a long, lost primordial race.

"What's Fa'delhan?" Stevie asked breaking the tension as she wiped the blood from her dirt-stained face.

"It's the language of the Keltie. An olden language, spoken long before the elven/fae war. A dead language. Fa'delhan had not been spoken for centuries even before our time. I know of its existence because my brother had an interest in the history of our realms."

Rafe looked at Killenn who nodded in agreement.

"One thing seems certain, Marlee's birthright did not come from the Athir tribe but from one much more primordial."

Kai sensed there was something more ominous. "These Kelties, what do you know of them?"

"Killenn can speak to their race better than I," Rafe said. "Dragon Gypsies are much more familiar with the primordial races of Thanissia."

When Killenn spoke the tone of his voice turned somber, his eyes narrowed, and his jaw clenched. "The Keltie was the first of their kind. The birth of their race. *Pureborns*. They existed on the plane between the ether and Thanissia for centuries before many of our races even existed. Unique from the fae that in time would evolve on Athir, the Kelties were bloodthirsty, vindictive, and evil. They wanted for nothing and cared for no one. In the Keltie culture weakness was a trait relevant to other species and punishment for it in theirs was severe. They would clip the wings of the feeble, grounding them."

"I was unaware the fae ever had wings," Brannon said.

Killenn shrugged. "It has been a very long time since any did. By the time the war broke out the pureborns had died off leaving a new generation of wingless fae. The race had adapted to their new conditions and over time, thrived. Although they lost their ability to fly and the power to glamour they still morphed into a formidable race. They found other ways to gain respect without drawing blood."

"Glamour?!" Kai said. "There was nothing glamorous about those creatures."

"It is not a physical trait but a mental one. To glamour, is to manipulate the mind of another." Rafe said.

"To make one see what is not there. To bend one's will to your own desires. It was this power that made the Keltie so malicious."

Killenn agreed. "Yes, the Keltie did not fight in the war. They had all but disappeared by that time. Unlike the familial line, the Athir fae did not prescribe to violence, nor were they skilled in warfare like their ancestors. Although quick with a knife and bow, they did not spend much time perfecting fighting tactics. They evolved into tricksters; cunning in their deceptive techniques and masters of illusion, which is why the vicious bloodshed during the war nearly wiped them out. If the Keltie still existed, the elvish kind would never have started a war, of that I am sure."

"I think Tauria is correct," Rafe said. "The sun will be up soon. We must go to the gateway and see what we are up against. If the Keltie fae is still in existence, we can be sure they will not care about the ancient darks return nor what it could mean for your world or ours. They will only care about what they desire. Make no mistake, they will not be allies in this battle."

As the others followed Tauria and Killenn toward the vineyards Brannon pulled Rafe aside. "If the Keltie have come back to this plane, the prophecy could be in jeopardy."

Rafe clasped his friend's shoulder. "Then we must hope Gabriella can find Dane without issue. The powers of all six races are more vital to our success now than ever before."

"And Marlee."

"We must find a way to reason with her. To make her understand what is at stake. She needs to return to the mortal world with us. It is the only way to stop the ancient dark's rise."

"And if we can't make her see reason. If she refuses to come willingly?"

"Then we take her by force."

# CHAPTER 11

THE SKY SHIMMERED A PERFECT shade of lilac as Gabriella walked toward the Hall of Elders. Etheriem pulsed with energy, the Druidstone once again providing her homeland with its unique magic, an essence long absent from these lands.

Her boot heels echoed down the hallowed halls as she hurried toward the courtyard. Her skin pricked as she emerged into the quiet sanctuary—*something was different.*

Silence greeted her. The beacon no longer beckoned to another plane of existence within the ether. Its call had been answered.

White weeping trees shook as she entered, their long flowery foliage sweeping back and forth across the ground. The scent of jasmine filled the air but underneath its sweet fragrance the essence of something unusual throbbed.

She sniffed, her eyes shifting toward the shadows near the far side of the courtyard. The presence she sensed was ancient, formidable energy that no longer belonged in this realm, yet one she was very familiar with.

Walking into the murk she felt a familiar pull, a ghost from her past. Black wings stretched out behind her in defiance as she moved, feathers ruffling in the breeze.

He stood in a dim corner of the courtyard, waiting. Iridescent eyes penetrated her own and an all too familiar feeling of inferiority washed over her as his steely stare assessed her. He didn't speak, but his jaw clenched as she moved. Determined not to surrender to past insecurities she straightened to her full height.

"Gabriel," she said, saying his name more like a statement than a greeting.

Massive wings shuddered as he stepped from the shadows, his gray armor glinting as it caught the light.

His continued silence intimidated her, and she groaned inwardly at her weakness as she waited for him to speak.

Finally, his face relaxed. "It is good to see you again Gabriella."

Unaccustomed to any sort of familiarity from her twin, she shifted uncomfortably. There was a time long before their stations had been established in the celestial hierarchy when they had been close. He had taught her to fight and trained her in the precision and dedication required of the sentinels. He was also the reason she rose to lead the sentinel army. But as his responsibilities and stature as a Seraph increased, their relationship fractured. His importance in their ethos outweighed the familial connection. Seraphs were marked from birth, making them exceptional and distinct from other celestials—including a *twin* and therefore their destinies would never be equal.

"I apologize for activating the beacon," she said, choosing to ignore his comment. "I would have understood if you did not heed the call."

"I know you would not activate the beacon without just cause."

Gabby's eyes flashed as she searched his face looking for something that would make his statement less hollow, but his gaze stayed steady.

"The ancient dark is back," she blurted out.

A shadow crossed his handsome face, but he didn't seem surprised by her statement. "And the prophecy? Has it come to pass?"

Confused by his apathy but unwilling to show her frustration she answered. "Those prophesied as the ancestors of Thanissia have all been found and three have already accepted their birthright. The remaining two are currently in Athir, their destinies imminent."

Gabriel's eyes narrowed. "What is troubling you?"

She winced. Regardless of the distance between them, she could never hide anything from her brother. "Dane, the daughter of Seri and ancestor of Claaven Callathian seems to be missing."

"And this is a problem?"

"Very much so. She is the key to the prophecy. The cornerstone. Without her powers, the others will not be able to defeat the ancient dark. The new world will fall to the same fate as ours."

Her voice cracked as her frustration built.

"And this is the reason you ignited the beacon?"

Gabby glared at him. "No, this problem has just transpired. I signaled to inform you of the others, ancient immortals trapped between time and space, but her disappearance has incited concern."

The haunting silence of Etheriem pressed in around her as she waited.

"These immortals you speak of our known to us. The gatekeeper, in light stasis who the Guardian tasked with guarding the portal and the Dywen warrior protecting the Book of Realms."

"Their names are Sebastian and Rafe and while both have joined us in this quest, there are others."

THE ARCANA

Gabriel's head tilted with interest, but he stayed silent allowing her to continue.

She had his attention now.

"The realms were not abandoned by all when the time of the immortals ended. The Warlician warrior destined to protect the Book of Realms was not the only one left behind when our worlds fell into stasis."

"How many?" Gabriel inquired, his voice even.

"Four. Another Warlician, a female witch, and two Dragon Gypsies."

"Dragon Gypsies?"

Gabby nodded. "One is a royal. He calls himself Drow."

A shadow crossed Gabriel's features as he digested the information.

"This is an interesting turn of events. The prophecy did not foretell of ancient beings crossing through the fabric of time."

He paused briefly his brow furrowing in thought.

"Including yourself and the two Warlician warriors tasked by the Guardian, there are in total seven immortal purebloods who have transcended into this time?"

"Correct."

He began to pace; his long leather coat and the tips of his folded wings swept the top of the grass. Unseen energy stirred in the courtyard, ancient magic responding to his sudden movement. Magic swirled around Gabriel, enticing yet dangerous—an essence only the Seraph's invoked—raw, intimidating power infused with a specific primordial energy. It was disarming.

As her brother paced, Gabriella sensed a shift in his essence. He was troubled.

Moments passed in silence until finally, he stopped. "This is worrisome," he said more to himself than her.

91

"While it stands to reason the powers of immortals may well help in the battle to come, the possibility of a significant ripple in time initiated by their presence cannot be ignored. It could cause the prophecy to be disrupted in ways we are unable to foresee."

His wings, still perfectly folded behind him, lifted. A gloved hand tightened around the grip of the massive sword hanging at his side, and he proceeded to pace once again.

Gabriella took a deep breath, shaking off the unwanted anxiousness rising within her. "There is something else."

Gabriel ceased pacing and turned toward her; his steely gaze fixed.

Averting her eyes, she said. "The last Druid has reached out from the All Souls."

This time her words provoked a reaction. His stoic expression cracked as a dark shadow slipped over his features. "Adaridge."

It wasn't a question, so she remained silent.

Suddenly, she felt his magic surge as his eyes filled with the fury of a thousand storms. Gabriella took a step back. She knew of their tumultuous history but had not anticipated this type of reaction. Her brother never lost his composure.

"How do you know this?" His face contorted as he fought to gain control.

"He has been in contact with the ancestor of Claaven communicating with her through the ether."

A calmness surrounded him as Gabriel gained back control and the apathetic Seraph once again stood before her.

Iridescent eyes met her own. "If this is the truth and the last Druid is making his presence known, then there is something about the prophecy we do not understand, something relevant to its outcome. For the Druid's spirit to risk leaving the All Souls, the need must be dire."

Gabby shuddered in anticipation knowing he was correct. "The others are heading to the Galenvale Grove. They are hoping they will find answers within the Druid sanctuary."

"That is the most reasonable place to start but the answers they seek may very well be those they do not want."

Shivers crept over her skin at her brother's words, their double meaning not lost on her.

"And what of the one who is missing?"

"Her name is Dane." There was a coolness in her voice, and she flinched.

Gabriel did not react, but she noticed the slight twitch in the tips of his wings. Her insubordination was beginning to try his patience. Before the Great War, she frequently found herself caught between the hierarchy of her world and the twin brother she longed to be closer too. As a Seraph, Gabriel demanded respect from the sentinels beneath him, including her. At times, she found it difficult to remember her place which often caused tension between them. And like now his silence was more of a scolding than his ire.

Ignoring the flash of disappointment in his eyes she continued. "I am heading back to the new world to search for Dane. Every moment the ancient dark grows stronger and it will not be long before its powers can manifest on earth. Once that happens, it will break free of its prison. Its rise will be upon us soon."

Gabriel nodded. "I must return to the ether to tell the others what you have learned."

There was a hint of sadness in his words that left Gabby with an ache in her heart.

"Will I see you again?" The words left her mouth before she could stop them, and she cringed at how needy she sounded.

He diverted his eyes from her gaze. "I came because you called, but I was also instructed to deliver a message. The Guardian of Deities has forbidden the Seraphs from interfering. The mortal world can never know of our existence, there is too much at stake. If this world is to survive, we must allow those whose destinies are tied to it be the ones to save it."

"But what of those who belong to our time and are here now? Should they not fight? Should I not?" As her anger swelled, she glared at her brother. "This world is born from ours. Is it not our destiny, our responsibility to protect it?"

His face softened as he backed into the gloom. "I am sorry Gabriella, but we will not intervene. If this world is fated to perish, then that is the way it must be."

The Guardian of Deities was abandoning them to their fate and her brother to hers.

As she entered the armory, anger seethed under her skin, not because the Guardian and Seraphs had deserted them but because her brother was right. There was too much at risk. While the Seraphs power would be an asset in the battle to come, it would entail showing their existence to mortals. A mortal seeing a Seraph would trigger fear but witnessing their battle magic would be utter chaos.

Gabby shuddered at the thought.

The power wielded by a Seraph is unlike anything other immortals possess. Awe-inspiring in its strength yet terrifying in its violence. It is a sight that would surely change the way mortals viewed their strange religious beliefs. A Seraph's magic and the carnage it inflicts would certainly shift the world's thinking into an unhealthy population of nonbelievers.

Mortals needed to trust in something and find hope in something bigger than themselves. It was in their nature to believe. They created an entire doctrine based on the unknown—God, angels, heaven, and hell. For them faith provided a sense of security, guiding them through turbulent times, and answering the questions they themselves cannot. By showing them the harsh reality hiding behind their perceptions it would surely be the beginning of their end. Mortals were a fragile species, easily led astray and easily broken.

While she may not like it, she understood the Guardian's reasoning, but it did not leave her feeling any less resentful, empty, or abandoned.

Brushing aside her anger, she hurriedly filled two sacks with the weapons that remained on Etheriem and left the armory.

Exiting onto the balcony of the highest tower of the Hall of Elders, she gazed across the Leylands. The perfect lilac sky rippled with silver threads as the ether funneled its magic to the other realms. Static flowed through the air igniting a slight prickle on her skin.

From this vantage point, Gabby could see to the far horizon. She thought back to a time before the ancient dark invaded her home, before she fell to earth, and before her life as a celestial ended.

A sadness clenched her heart as she gazed across the lands of her beloved home knowing this may be the last time, she saw Etheriem again.

Making her way back to the portal her fingers caressed the white stone walls of the sacred halls but as she stepped through, leaving the past behind, she knew what she had to do—find Dane.

Her time in this world may be ending but the new world still breathed of life and hope. She would not let their world perish as hers had.

The ancient dark would not win again.

# CHAPTER 12

I T DIDN'T TAKE THEM LONG to reach the vineyards; a maze of wooden slats from which hung brown, fruitless, shriveled vines feasted on by fat, slimy, white slugs. The air reeked with an earthy acidic smell, like the tart odor of a good wine gone bad combined with the suffocating stench of decomposing vegetation.

"Which way?" Tauria inquired.

"To the center," Rafe said. "The vineyard surrounds the well."

"*A well?* The gateway to the fabled fairy plane is a well?"

"Not just any well," Brannon said, nudging her playfully. "This one you have to see to believe."

Rafe and Brannon took the lead, guiding them through the acres of rotten vines. Occasionally, Diego scampered ahead, scouting the area for anything lurking.

After an hour they reached the center of the vineyard, a vast open area with flat stones covering the ground. Each one was placed in a precise pattern, spiraling toward the base of a massive stone structure at the center.

The well towered before them rising skyward sixty or so feet. Its circumference tapered toward the peak. The *well* was not your typical well but an ancient tower of stone and moss, dead flowers, and mud.

"Not as I remembered it," Brannon said frowning.

"You expected something different in these cursed lands?" Tauria teased.

"Yes, the well was the one thing that remained untouched by the war and the destruction of the Oberon Fen. I don't understand what happened."

"Maybe the magic of Athir has not found its way here yet," Killenn suggested walking to the structure.

"Is that where the Keltie emerged from?" she asked directing their attention to a glistening white circle hovering above the top of the well.

"It must be," he said. "Somehow, Marlee's transformation has allowed her to breach the plane beyond, releasing the Keltie fae from their infinite limbo."

A crackling flash lit up the dark sky and a cascade of glittering rain began to fall from the circle. Torrents of water streamed down the well's sides. The cracked and caked mud crumbled and washed away under the torrent of gold water leaving once dusty and dull stones gleaming. The moss, its color changing to a vital green, glistened as its velvety carpet returned. Dead flowers bloomed, covering the entire column in a multitude of brilliant colors. Gold, glittery water seeped through the cracks and spilled into giant gilt bowls protruding at different heights from the sides. Once again, the well shone with the beauty and robustness which had long forsaken it.

Killenn whistled in appreciation as the rain ceased.

"That is how I remember it," Brannon said winking at Tauria.

The well certainly was breathtaking but what caught Killenn's eye was the funnel of gold-dusted air now swirling above it.

"That may tell us something," he said pointing to the churning air.

He stepped to the well and pushed the toe of his boot into a crevice.

Finding a handhold, he began to climb skillfully scaling the tall structure in minutes. At the top, he crouched and closed his eyes. Placing one hand into the swirling dust and the other flat on the well, he uttered an incantation.

Moments later he descended the tower.

"I have no doubt those creatures with Marlee are, in fact, ancient Kelties or the imprints thereof. The golden dust is saturated with archaic dark energy."

"What did you do?" Stevie asked. "Up there."

"I performed a simple yet effective spell. An ancient incantation passed down through generations of Dragon Gypsies. It determines if there is an essence or energy specific to a race in the air. I searched for something primordial."

"And you found what you were looking for in the funnel?"

"I did, plenty of it. Their marker is strong in the dust. The Keltie fae has definitely emerged into this plane."

"Now what?" Kai asked fidgeting with the knife strapped to her thigh.

Killenn gazed across the field at the pink horizon. The sun would rise soon and the Dark Forest surrounding Niramyst would be easier to traverse.

"We head to the ancient city of the elves."

"But what about Marlee?"

Killenn frowned thinking about Marlee's last words. "I have a feeling we might find her there."

"How can you be sure?"

"Because if Marlee is being guided by the Keltie, she will inevitably want to settle an old score. And as there is just one elf left on this realm, she will seek her out."

"Elyse!" Stevie exclaimed. "But they're best friends. Marlee would never hurt her."

"Marlee is no longer the person you know. Her mind is corrupted by a bloodline long extinct and one who thrives on violence. The Keltie was a vicious race and I don't think their endless exile changed that. Trust me when I say Elyse is in danger."

# CHAPTER 13

E LYSE PUT HER GLASSES IN her pocket amazed at the clarity of everything since receiving her birthright. Shimmering dust coated the leaves on the trees and each blade of grass swayed methodically in the floral-scented breeze. Ripples on the water's surface gleamed like a bed of diamonds. Athir was coming alive and it was extraordinarily lovely.

Her hand went to her cheek, fingers caressing the raised skin. Besides exceptional vision, her birthright left her marked. A filigree of scaring followed the line of her right cheekbone curling at each end with two raised dots at the top and a lone leaf branching off the bottom. Sebastian said it was the mark of her people, a sect among the elvish population known as the Elves of the Wood.

As they came to the edge of the forest, Sebastian said. "The Dark Forest surrounding Niramyst is very old and full of magical beings. The Elves of the Wood were its guardians, protecting the entities within."

"And now it's my turn."

He placed a gentle hand on her forearm. "You will do well to listen closely as we pass through the Dark Forest. What you learn may be beneficial to our cause."

"What am I listening for?"

He smiled. "What lies hidden."

As they left the sunny flatlands and entered the

shadowy forest the scent of pine and damp bark assaulted her nostrils. The air was cooler here, not an uncomfortable chill but rather a caressing freshness that slithered up and down her skin awakening her magic.

Needles crunching underfoot echoed around them as they went deeper into the quiet forest. Air magic saturated the woods. Wisps caught in the air drifted aimlessly through the trees causing the entire forest to sparkle. The bark of the trees shimmered with a golden sheen and moss-covered boulders shone without the aid of sunlight. Even the shadows caught in the recesses of the thick woods were less ominous than when they'd first entered.

As they made their way toward Niramyst, Elyse became acutely aware of multiple entities hidden in the shadowy forest.

*What lies hidden,* she thought as the energy of these beings reached toward her. Whispers rose in her mind as the hidden spoke amongst themselves—curious of her presence.

Branches on a large tree began to shudder as she neared stretching outward as if waking from a deep sleep. The leaves rustled as she placed her palm flat on its large trunk.

Closing her eyes, the scar on her cheek began to glow with glittering light. "I can hear the tree spirit it speaks to me in tongue, but I understand what it's trying to convey."

Sebastian and Drow glanced at one another. Neither had ever witnessed a guardian of the forest interacting with one of the most ancient of creatures. The tree spirits were legendary entities. They communicated using a long-dead language only the Elves of the Wood understood.

The tree continued to move. Its leaves and branches swayed even though the evening air was calm. Other trees joined in. A chorus of nature filled the air as the tree spirits awoke. The raised mark on Elyse's cheek throbbed with pale golden light in response.

After a few minutes, the trees calmed.

Brushing her hand lightly across the tree's rough bark she murmured something in elvish. The tree groaned as its branches shook.

She turned to Sebastian and Drow.

"There's a darkness coming. The tree spirits feel the tainted energy. It's primordial but it's not the ancient dark but rather a darkness specific to this realm, and one which no longer exists on this plane. Its intentions are unknown, but the tree spirits are restless."

"We must get to Niramyst at once. To the elvish fortress." Drow said.

Sebastian agreed, and they set off again but this time at a hurried pace.

After exiting the Dark Forest, they entered a small stone tunnel in the side of a hill. On the other side was Niramyst—a sprawling city of waterfalls, bridges, gazebo-like structures, and towers, all built around a gaping chasm.

As they passed over the bridge, Elyse leaned over the side. Hundreds of feet down at the bottom of the canyon, white-tipped water rushed toward the far end. Numerous waterfalls flowed down the chasm's rock walls spilling into the furious waters of the river below. Warm steam rose from its depths dispersing a strangely dry mist into the air that tickled her skin as it drifted by.

"The fortress is the best place for us to wait out the night." Sebastian pointed to a tall stone structure in the distance. Its twin towers stretched skyward. "This is where we will find the elvish weapon cache, and we can rest in the sleeping quarters on the upper echelon. The fortress also houses a tower that overlooks the entire city, including the only way in."

Elyse nodded knowing Sebastian was attempting to reassure her that whatever the tree spirits were warning her about they would be prepared.

The main gate stood ajar and a cooing echoed from the courtyard beyond.

Drow unsheathed his sword.

Elyse cocked her head listening. Soon, a smile spread over her face, and she began to laugh. "Put your swords away they won't hurt you."

"They?" Drow asked sheathing his sword as requested.

Placing her index finger on her lips she motioned for them to follow. She peered around the gate visually confirming what she already knew. At the center of the courtyard, jumping playfully on the fountain, were six furry creatures no bigger than a rabbit. Snow-white fur glowed in the sunlight. They had small heads accented by big pointed ears and long, slender bodies ending in a hairless, stubby, black tail. Their tiny feet had no toes making them look like fluffy white pancakes.

"What are they?" whispered Drow.

Sebastian's face lit up. "Those wonderful little creatures are Zibits."

"Whatever is a Zibit?"

"Did you ever venture off Kaizi?"

Drow looked taken aback. "The Velkia royals leave the realm of our people for diplomatic reasons and no other. Athir is the only realm I never had dealings with, therefore had no reason to learn of their culture or their strange inhabitants."

Sebastian rolled his eyes. "Then you are missing out on one of the most amazing creatures in this universe, my friend"

"It's a rodent. What is so appealing about it?"

"Watch." Elyse picked up a pebble and threw it at the group of cuddly creatures.

The moment it hit the fountain, the Zibits reacted. Tiny gossamer wings, the shade of night, unfolded from their furry backs, and they scattered. Zipping back and forth they searched for the threat, their black eyes growing until they were the size of silver dollars. As they flew, a shrill chattering erupted from their throats, and they pulled back their gums to display razor-sharp teeth.

"Not so cute anymore, are they," she laughed.

Walking around the gate she made sure the Zibits spotted her before she continued toward them. They flitted like hummingbirds over the fountain their bulbous eyes never leaving her. Their back paws smacked together in warning, but Elyse was already using her ancestor's powers to communicate with the ancient creatures.

She cooed at the furry animals as she stepped carefully toward them, a sing-song tone to her voice. The Zibits reacted. A couple stopped flying and came back to the ground. Tucking their wings back inside their fur they padded at the earth with their front paws. The braver ones flitted toward her, circling curiously. One landed on Elyse's shoulder. Its tiny pink nose pushed against the raised mark on her cheek, and then pawed at it friskily.

Drow watched in awe. "What is it doing?"

"Playing," answered Sebastian, a broad smile

spreading across his face. "The Elves of the Wood have such an amazing relationship with the creatures of the Dark Forest. I suspected the tree spirits would still be in existence, but I had no inkling creatures of flesh and blood might be. It's miraculous the Zibits survived stasis. They are such curious little creatures."

Elyse waved for them to follow.

The Zibits black eyes observed them suspiciously as they passed the fountain. A small one thumped its back paw on the dirt drawing Drow's attention. The creature hopped down from the fountain and jumped over to him. Its pink nose twitched, and it began to peep, a slow curious sound. Drow bent down, squatting until he was face to face with the strange little creature. Surprisingly, the Zibit reached out and touched his hair. It peeped again, this time with excitement, thumping its back leg.

Drow remained motionless.

Soon other Zibits joined. Their curiosity at never seeing a royal before stronger than their instinct to stay away from immortals. They tugged at his long white locks. One jumped on his shoulder and curled himself under and through his tresses. Another padded at his cabernet-colored eyes, tilting his head to the left and right methodically.

The childlike joy of these little creatures was intoxicating and Drow found himself beguiled by their presence. He laughed and pet their silky fur as they cooed. Never had he felt such unencumbered freedom.

"Zibits," he said to himself, smiling as the word echoed in the air.

Sebastian glanced at Elyse, his jade eyes sparkling. "I think our Velkia royal just realized what he was missing."

# CHAPTER 14

FROM THE BALCONY OF THE fortress's central tower, Elyse could see the triple waterfalls in the distance. The rushing water plummeted off the top edge, spraying white mist into the air as it thundered into the roiling river below. The late-day sun warmed the sky. During this time of day just before twilight air magic shimmered like dew across the lands. It was breathtaking.

Drawn away from the beauty by a rumble in the distance her eyes flicked to the sinister sky above the Oberon Fen. It had been a few days since their arrival in Niramyst and there still wasn't any sign of the others. Her instincts warned her something was amiss, and she worried about her friends who'd traveled into the cursed lands. Although the tree spirits hadn't been specific, she assumed the darkness they spoke of would find its way from there.

"What has you so thoughtful?" Sebastian asked joining her on the balcony.

"I was thinking about the others. It's been a few days and no word. Should we worry?"

"They will be fine. Rafe, Brannon, and Killenn are fine warriors and very astute when it comes to their surroundings. No harm will come to your friends, I assure you."

Elyse always felt comforted by Sebastian's words

but this time she couldn't shake the menacing feeling simmering inside her. Glancing back at the dark skies on the horizon she thought about Marlee and how afraid she must be alone in a strange world. Wiping a tear from her cheek she silently prayed the others had found her.

"What happened between the elvish and fairy races? What started the race war?"

Sebastian frowned. "Your birthright did not provide you with this knowledge?"

"There's a lot of knowledge that's still fuzzy in my mind."

He patted her hand. "It will become clear in time."

Gesturing to the golden mist sparkling around them he said, "The magic that flows from the air essence is very fluid and therefore can be used in different ways. Being a mischievous race, the fae preferred a more elusive use. They did not flaunt their magic, choosing instead to infuse the environment with it and allowing it to breathe organically. The race of elves was much more structured and aggressive. They used magic to protect the Dark Forest and its inhabitants and maintained strict control over the element. While their differences made Athir unique, it also caused much friction."

Sebastian turned to face her. "However, for a long time, it did not complicate their coexistence. What exactly happened to cause the war, no one really knows. Smaller issues began to rile the populations. Fights broke out among lesser factions. Pettiness grew into mistrust and fear. The sentinels and Warlicians managed the situation for ages but then the uprising happened. The war itself was a surprising escalation. There was no indication it had risen to such an antagonistic level."

Sebastian's eyes clouded over as he remembered a time long past. "After the war ended neither race would explain, and the Guardian of Deities did not demand one. The war was over, the peace treaty signed, and both sides had already lost much. It was time to heal."

"After such a long and bloody war, it must have been difficult for them to forgive."

"It was but the Druids helped with a gesture of unity among all the Thanissia races."

"How so?"

"The Druidstones. They were crafted by the Druid priests and gifted to the races after the war on Athir. A gesture to promote peace and harmony and join the magic of the ether and the Five Realms together as one. It created a symbiotic relationship between the elements and the races they governed. It had long been rumored the stones were equal parts of each realm."

Elyse lifted an eyebrow. "In what way?"

"According to legend, the stones were dug from the deepest parts of the All Souls seas where the magic is the oldest and purest. They were then cut by Kaizi artisans and carved with magical ice knives crafted from the ice glades of Viccinius. Each was washed in the sacred pools of Athir and dried in its golden air before being imbued with the rich earth of Dywen. Although similarly crafted every Druidstone is unique, a symbol of the realm to which it belongs. The Five Realms entered a new age of magic after the creation of the Druidstones, but the power of the stones would ultimately lead to our downfall."

Absently he rubbed the scar on his face.

"The ancient dark," Elyse said softly.

"Yes. The Druidstones pulled directly from the ether, filling the Thanissia Universe with an unimaginable magical essence. The Druids had no idea it would call to such unspeakable evil."

Elyse looked away from Sebastian and back to the threatening skies over the Oberon Fen. "Why do I get the feeling peace and harmony are about to come to an end and history is going to repeat itself?"

From the edge of the Dark Forest Marlee surveyed the city of Niramyst. The elf stood on the tower balcony speaking with the elder Warlician. The moon would rise in a few hours and when it did, she would make her way to the fortress. She knew the tree spirits had awoken; their energy drifted through the treetops, but she paid them no mind. Under the cover of darkness, she would seek her ancestor's revenge.

The whispering of the Keltie surrounded her, a chorus of noise that drowned out the warnings the tree spirits tried to impart.

She cocked her head and listened, a scowl forming on her face.

"I will not be merciful," she said. "The elf must pay with her blood for her ancestors' sins."

The whispering intensified.

Her eyes tracked back to the elf, watching as she made her way back inside the tower.

She nodded in agreement. "Yes, I will cut out her heart."

The whispers giggled.

# CHAPTER 15

THE FORTRESS WAS DEATHLY QUIET.

Elyse tossed and turned unable to sleep. She got out of bed and walked to the balcony. The warm air ruffled her hair and the smell of apple blossoms scented the breeze. Taking a deep breath, she studied her surroundings.

The landscape stretching out before her glistened in the silvery moonlight. The waterfall roared in the distance and its pounding surf blended seamlessly with the other night sounds to create a soothing chorus.

Leaning over the balcony she stared up into the starry sky and listened to Athir's night voice. Puffy white clouds drifted in front of the moon, hiding its glow as they passed.

The world darkened and she shivered.

Leaving the balcony, she closed the doors behind her.

A sudden chill crawled over her skin—a warning.

The clouds moved past the moon and the room was once again cast in a silvery light.

"Hello, Elyse."

She jumped as the familiar voice echoed from the dark.

Marlee sat in the corner of the room, legs thrown casually over the arms of a wing-back chair. Her platinum hair shimmered in the moonlight and her skin glowed a ghostly shade of pale.

"Marlee," Elyse exclaimed. "I've been so worried. Where have you been?"

She flicked her hand upward. "Around." Dropping her legs to the floor she leaned forward. "I see you've made yourself comfortable."

"Strange, isn't it? Being here."

Marlee smiled and shrugged. "Do you remember?"

"Remember what?" She said taking a step back. Marlee's apathetic tone was beginning to make her feel uneasy.

As Marlee leaned back in the chair, her face disappeared behind the shadows. "How you betrayed me."

An echo of whispers filled the room and Elyse tensed. Her eyes searched for the sound, but nothing hid in the murk but Marlee.

"I don't know what you're talking about."

The whispering grew louder, filling the room with a chaotic chorus. Elyse covered her ears.

"It is time for your penance my friend. For elf blood to spill and for your race to finally die. This world belongs to us it always has, and we no longer wish to share."

Marlee stood, walking out of the dim with a look of indignation contorting her pretty face. The blade of a knife glinted in her hand.

The room seemed to grow smaller as Elyse realized—Marlee was no longer her friend. In a twist of fate, she had become the enemy.

Panicked she bolted toward the door but Marlee blocked her path.

She wagged her finger. "No. No. You must stay and face the consequences, elf."

Her blue eyes were wild, feral almost, the irises

filled with cruelty. "You took what wasn't yours and now we want it back."

A surging cacophony of whispers echoed through the room as Marlee casually walked toward her swinging the sharp blade and singing.

*Run, Run, while you can.*
*No one lives on this bloody land*
*You took what was ours once before*
*Now we're back to even the score.*

Elyse's heart thumped in her chest.

She was mocking her.

"Why are you doing this?" she screamed as she searched for a way out. "What do you want?"

Reaching behind her Marlee pulled out a second knife. Moonlight glinted off the blade. "Your life."

Elyse ran for the far wall, sprinting toward the one weapon in the room.

A howl erupted behind her, and she was lifted off her feet by a gust of wind. She writhed in pain as she was slammed to the floor the air knocked from her lungs.

Marlee laughed. "So weak."

She lifted one of the knives, running the pad of her index finger along its sharp edge. *Watch,* she mouthed, extending her finger and showing her the cut, blood dripping from the open gash.

Elyse gasped as the wound miraculously closed. Marlee had healed herself.

An unexpected knock on the door interrupted the moment and drew Marlee's attention. Scrambling toward the wall Elyse pulled the polearm from its display hooks. Curved blades adorned either end. She moved the weapon in small circles as if she were rowing a boat.

It felt good in her hands. Comfortable.

The knocking grew louder.

"Help!" she screamed.

"Elyse?" Sebastian said from the other side of the door. The pounding intensified as he tried to break it down.

Marlee turned to face her. "Playtime is over." Malice ignited her blue eyes as she crossed the distance between them with little effort.

A thrum of whispers filled the room spurring her on.

Marlee lunged. The knives came within inches of her face before she managed to block them with the handle of the polearm and push her away. Swinging the weapon in an arc, she lifted the flat side of the blade connecting with the knife and forcing it from Marlee's grip. It clattered across the stone floor.

A smirk formed at the corner of her mouth. "Impressive for an elf."

Elyse rotated the polearm this time the right blade swung toward Marlee. "I don't want to hurt you."

"Hurt me?" she laughed, twirling around the room in glee. "I'm going to cut you from pelvis to sternum and gut you like the foul filth you are."

She shrieked as she ran at Elyse, her remaining knife gripped in her hand and held high over her head.

Elyse flung herself to one side spinning the blade of the polearm skillfully. The tip caught Marlee's thigh ripping through leather, skin, and flesh.

Blood poured from the gash and the unseen whisperers roared.

The door to the room smashed open and Sebastian burst in sword raised, followed by the others.

Elyse turned in time to see ghostly bleached figures appear over their heads.

"Watch out," she yelled.

Killenn and Sebastian swung their swords, narrowly missing the ghostly fae as they swarmed. The metal of Kai's scimitar sang as she pulled it from its sheath, knocking an entity back with the butt of the hilt. She screamed as it raked its claws across her shoulder.

Marlee stood at the center of the room speaking an unknown tongue. An evil glint shone in her eye as she conjured up a small funnel of air. As it twisted and turned around the room it sucked in furniture and other objects flinging them back out moments later.

Debris rained down around them.

With a command from Stevie, Diego ran at Marlee his large paws and considerable weight knocking her to the floor.

The wind ceased.

She jabbed at the Dragonwolf with her knife cutting him in the muzzle. Yelping he backed off. Saliva dripped from his teeth as he bared them. Another surge of wind erupted picking Diego up and blowing him through the glass doors. He landed with a thud on the balcony as wood and glass shattered around his limp form.

Stevie yelled in fury lunging at Marlee, but a ghostly entity grabbed her in its talons and tossed her sidelong against the far wall.

The entities continued to attack but Tauria and Killenn managed to break away. Placing their backs against the walls they assaulted Marlee and the entities with a barrage of arrows.

Elyse pounced. Her polearm whirled back and forth, blade crashing against blade until Marlee began to fatigue. Her wounds could not heal fast enough before another formed, and she was losing a considerable amount of blood. With a final burst of energy, Elyse twisted to avoid a lethal swing of her knife and got behind her.

Marlee was pinned. One blade of the polearm was against her throat the other dug into the floor. The entities instantly ceased their attack and fled back into the shadows, waiting.

Marlee winced as the sharp blade cut into her skin. Arrows protruded from her body and blood ran in rivulets from the wounds. The barrage from Tauria and Killenn had weakened her. The powers she recently gained from her birthright must not be fully formed yet, and she'd expelled her strength too quickly. She hadn't planned on such an intense and exhaustive battle against a multitude of immortals—only Elyse.

Marlee's anger surged, and she struggled against Elyse's grasp.

"Die, elf."

"Not today thanks."

Sebastian lifted an eyebrow at her words, and she shrugged with satisfaction.

Early morning rays shone through the smashed balcony doors lighting the room in a soft orange luminosity.

The entities' whispering ended replaced by unearthly shrieks as they fled the glistening rays that dissipated the shadows.

"Go," Marlee croaked.

The ghostly figures disappeared, and the room became quiet.

Elyse removed the blade from Marlee's throat, and she staggered backward blood dripping from the corner of her mouth.

"You haven't won," she hissed.

"Haven't I?" Elyse spat.

Kai lit the wick of a candle and held it aloft as Stevie began to mutter. The flame flickered reaching out toward where Marlee and Elyse stood. Like a burning snake, it weaved its way between them stretching upward until they were separated by a wall of fire.

Elyse dropped the polearm, exhausted.

Blue eyes reflected the flames as Marlee backed up the heat pushing her toward the balcony. She spat at the fire as she stepped out into the breaking dawn. The wall of flames blocked her from the other immortals, and she shrieked in frustration. Yanking arrows from her body she tried to douse the fire with air, but the flames fed on the gusts, growing higher.

Enraged, she screamed.

Ambient light flickered across Elyse's face, and she shut her eyes. A warm tingle spread through the mark on her check as it began to glow.

She heard Marlee shriek and she opened her eyes.

Through the flames she could see her flailing as fluffy, white creatures with black wings surrounded her. They dived at her head, razor-sharp teeth digging into her flesh. One after another they attacked unrelentingly until she crumpled to the ground, bloody and unconscious.

Stevie extinguished the wall of flames and hurried to the balcony. She cradled Diego in her arms speaking softly to him. He whimpered and licked her hand.

"Is he alright?" Kai asked.

Rafe bent down and checked Diego over. "He may have some glass in his paws and the breath was knocked from him, but he will be fine. It takes a lot more than this to down a Dragonwolf." He leaned over and checked Marlee's pulse. "I suspect she will be out for a time but let us bind her securely before she awakens."

"The entities that were here. They looked like the Keltie fae of old. How is that possible?" Sebastian asked.

Rafe indicated the unconscious Marlee. "It would seem her birthright is connected to something much older than us."

"So, you are implying the gateway has been reopened."

"It has."

"Remarkable." Sebastian glanced at the rising sun. "They are gone for now but are sure to return. Keltie will not wander in the daylight, so we must make haste and get to the Galenvale Grove before nightfall."

"What about her?" Killenn asked.

"We will have to take her with us. She cannot be left behind for she is part of the prophecy. There may be an answer in the Druid sanctuary that will help."

"What is wrong with her?" Tauria asked, nudging Marlee with the tip of her boot.

Sebastian indicated the creatures who now sat lined up on the balcony railing. "She has been injected with a heavy dose of a serum that induces a deep state of unconsciousness. Their bite is very toxic."

"What are they?" asked Kai.

Sebastian smiled. "They are Zibits—extraordinary little creatures."

# CHAPTER 16

I T HAD BEEN ALMOST TWO weeks since Dane encountered Lucien Beck at the old mill. She hadn't
stopped thinking about him and his cryptic messages since they met. It unnerved her how quickly he
got under her skin.

Lucien Beck the entrepreneur, and philanthropist
was obviously someone used to getting his own way,
but it was Lucien Beck, the Tierney, who interested
her. He clearly had secrets and an agenda but the way
he spoke of the prophecy is what worried her.

Replaying their conversation in her mind she was
convinced Lucien Beck planned to use the ancient dark
to his advantage. He obviously possessed magic—*dark
magic*, for he had managed to link this world to the one
that trapped the ancient dark.

That made him powerful and dangerous.

Lucien Beck was a variable she hadn't counted on.

She turned the corner toward the town hall.
Tonight, she would get answers. Tomorrow she would
join her friends.

Her mother's death had pushed her into an overwhelming destructive rage but over the past weeks,
she'd managed to gain control. Revenge would not
bring her mother back nor would it take away the pain.
Her friends had sacrificed their mortal lives for oth-

ers, and she'd abandoned them. It was time to make it right.

The clock tower struck midnight the chimes echoing through the night sky. With every stroke, the full moon grew closer as did the passing of the prophecy.

She must face her destiny and the Second Coming.

Rounding the side of the municipal building she descended the staircase leading to the back door. Grasping the heavy padlock, she visualized an energy ball seeping through the keyhole. Her warrior magic expanded it as it wove its way through the lock mechanisms.

With a muffled pop the lock broke.

Dane looked around. Nothing but the night's silence greeted her.

She pushed on the door and it swung in on creaky hinges. Pitch black stillness filled the space. The ambient light from the open door scarcely reached a few feet into the building.

Clicking on the small flashlight she swept the beam back and forth. It was a small storage space. Piles of old cardboard file boxes were strewn around the room. Tall bookcases lined the walls their shelves filled with dusty, leather ledgers. Stickers on the spines cataloged the dates and counties to which they referenced. Opening a few of the cardboard boxes she found them full of old city maps and town records. Since there was nothing here dated within the past few decades, she left the room in search of the more recent land records, specifically—city land sales.

Light from the streetlamps trickled through the glass windows casting a muted glow across the tile floor. Dane extinguished her flashlight and looked around. Office doors stood closed on either side of the room each frosted glass insert stenciled with the room's name. Her gaze flitted over the doors seeking the one that read—Land Records Room.

Soundlessly, she turned the doorknob but found the door locked.

A nameplate reading, *Jules Torres, Land Records Clerk,* sat on a desk to the left of the door. Opening the top drawer, she searched through papers, sticky note pads, and paper clips until she found an old brass key tucked under a notebook at the back. As she pulled out the key, she noticed it had a piece of masking tape looped around its bow. In black magic marker were the letters LRR. Assuming, it stood for Land Records Room she walked back to the door and slid the key into the lock.

As the key turned, she heard a faint click and the door swung open.

File cabinets lined the walls, and she scanned the labels looking for the drawer marked G. The drawer opened with a screech making her cringe. Flipping through the interior folders she found one labeled Gristmill Flour Company—Mill Sale.

"There you are," she whispered pulling the file and flipping through its contents.

The sale of the mill finalized about a week ago. The purchaser was Beck Holdings Inc., Lucien Beck CEO.

So, it was true.

She flipped to the final page of the purchase and sale and jotted down the address and phone number of Beck Holdings, New York City. As she rifled through the rest of the documents, she discovered a short-term residential lease agreement. Removing the obscure document from the file she read the two-page agreement. It pertained to a small house on the far side of town. It seemed Lucien Beck was renting a home for two months from the mayor.

Dane added the address of the rental to the notepad and stuffed the file back in the cabinet. On her way out she locked the door and replaced the key back into the clerk's desk. There was nothing she could do about the broken padlock, so she left it on the ground where it fell.

Returning to her jeep Dane put the rental address into her phone mapping system. Potter Circle was a new subdivision, a ten-minute drive from the town hall. She would wait until daybreak and then confront Lucien Beck. Before she sought out the others, she needed to get some answers.

It took a few moments for the door to open in response to her knock. His handsome face didn't register any shock at seeing her on his doorstep in the early morning hours.

"Dane, what a nice surprise."

"Is it?"

Lucien ignored her sarcasm and opened the door wider. "Please come in. I have a pot of coffee on."

She followed him down the hall and into the sun-drenched kitchen. Dressed in dark jeans, a dark blue crew-neck sweater, and bare feet he oozed casual confidence. His hair was rumpled and his normally perfect five o'clock shadow was unkempt making him look less intimidating than the last time they had met.

"What do I owe the pleasure of your company this morning?"

Sitting on a metal stool beside the kitchen island she tried to ignore the dangerously alluring energy floating around him.

"What are your plans for the old flour mill?"

He shrugged, busying himself with the percolator. "I haven't decided yet. It was just a good investment."

"Mr. Beck, we both know the mill is special, so let's just cut the bull."

His blue eyes flashed, and he raised a brow.

"Please call me Lucien."

He handed her a cup of steaming hot coffee and then poured another for himself. "The mill *is* special. I'm sure you know the energy surrounding it is very active. In the right hands, it could be useful."

"And in the wrong ones, perilous." She rubbed her forehead.

"We can't stop what's coming. The best we can hope for is the ability to wield the prophecy to our advantage."

Lucien came around the counter and sat beside her, leaned in, and lowered his voice. "Do you really want to stop it? I know your destiny, Dane. The burden that's been placed on you. Do you really want to be a savior? Aren't you tired of always being the one who must be strong? The one who others lean on and constantly look to for guidance?"

His seductive energy wrapped itself around her as he spoke. Tenderly he pushed a lock of hair back from her face, his fingers caressing her cheek as he did so.

"Wouldn't it be nice to just let it all go."

Aqua blue eyes stared deep into her own. He smelled clean, like shower soap and laundry detergent. She frowned as her focus blurred, and she rubbed her forehead again as wooziness washed over her. The room spun. As she tried to focus on his words, her mind drifted. Shaking her head, she tried to concentrate on his voice, his face. He grasped her hand and abruptly everything came back into focus, the fog in her mind dissolved.

JACI MILLER

"You keep it bottled up inside, don't you—the anger and pain. Because you're afraid of what you will do if you let it free. Don't you find it exhausting?"

Lulled by the alluring energy surrounding him she closed her eyes. The faint feeling returned, and her thoughts once again became jumbled.

"Dane?"

Eyelids fluttered open and his face came back into focus. A small scar marred the corner of his upper lip. It was mostly hidden by the shadow of his beard. Without thinking, she reached up and ran her finger across it.

He smiled and took her hand, kissing it. Leaning in he pulled her toward him. His lips found hers. The kiss was gentle at first but then deepened. His tongue parted her lips and she moaned softly.

After a few seconds, he pulled back, his blue eyes full of lust. He smiled and kissed her hand again.

"Come to the city with me. I think you will like it there."

She nodded absently as she was overwhelmed by exhaustion. Her mind reeled. A witch, hidden in the shadows and now the burden of her legacy—what had it gotten her?

Heartache.

The world would not accept her, and her friends didn't know her, not really. Hiding her powers, lying to her friends, keeping everyone at arm's length it was exhausting. Now, her future was to be determined by an ancient prophecy—a family legacy that had gotten her mother killed.

Maybe Lucien was right.

Maybe there was something else, something better. She should be the one to determine her own destiny, not one born from another world.

"Let it go," he whispered in her ear as his lips brushed her lobe. "You're safe with me."

A surge of anger raged through her feeding on her thoughts, her perceived betrayals, her frustration. It washed over her in waves, a heated passion that seduced her thoughts. Suddenly, she didn't care anymore about control. She wanted to be free.

The ancient magic in her veins swelled and with it something familiar. The way it reached toward her heart was intimate but before she could identify what it was it disappeared swallowed by the rising tide of anger within.

Lucien saw the black shadow ripple through Dane's green eyes and smiled.

He kissed her forehead. "We will leave for the city this afternoon. Until then, maybe you should lie down. You don't look well."

# CHAPTER 17

I T HAD BEEN YEARS SINCE Nathan Callan visited the underground.

Hidden below a group of multimillion-dollar buildings in Manhattan it was a place where the magical community of New York City conjugated in privacy. Undetected and hidden by the chaotic energy of the city above it, the underground was connected by a network of secret tunnels.

New York was home to one of the oldest and most prominent magical communities in the country and consisted of some of the wealthiest elite in the city. One of the most formidable was Celeste Winslow the woman Nathan had come to meet. A ranking member of the Coven—a body of witch elders who oversee the magical communities' interaction with the mortal world—and a high priestess, her ancestral powers derived from legendary voodoo priestesses of the south.

He hadn't seen her in years and although they were both members of elite divisions of their community, their roles were very different.

Nathan Callan was a Syndicate elder, a foot soldier out in the world cleaning up magical messes. Celeste Winslow on the other hand, as a high-ranking leader of the Coven, directed all undertakings dealing with the magic community. He hoped with her connections she might be able to help because he was running out of time and options.

Entering the World Bank of New York, he headed straight through the marble lobby to a heavy walnut door. It was discreetly positioned under the spiral staircase leading to the upper echelon of the global banking business. Unnoticeable unless you knew of its existence.

He used his iron key to open the lock, closing the heavy door silently behind him.

Inside the small room were two elevators. A small glass pedestal on which sat a rotary dial phone was to the side. Nathan placed his palm down on the electronic pad. The scanner emitted a blue light as it checked his identity and after a few moments, the phone rang. A series of soft beeps came through the receiver, and he waited until he heard the dial tone before hanging up. The sound of the elevator ascending from the underground tunnels broke the silence in the small space.

As the doors slide open, he took a deep breath.

Celeste Winslow was a formidable woman, and he hoped that she would have a way to help him find his wife's killer.

Entering the Syndicate's code on the device inside, the elevator quickly slid to the right before descending into the underground, ten floors under Manhattan's street level. The tunnels had many entrances, but the World Bank elevator was the one that led directly to the Coven's Grand Hall.

A ping indicated his arrival.

The doors opened into a large circular room with a vaulted ceiling. Glass tinkled as the chandelier caught the draft made by the elevator doors. Wrought iron coach lights lined the stone walls. A white flame flickered in each. Nathan walked to the conference table situated in the room's center. He admired the pentacle etched into the high-gloss surface, and the twelve black leather throne chairs surrounding it.

The room was impressive and a bit intimidating.

Besides his anxious breathing, the only sound in the room was the tick of the iron clock hanging on the wall.

He paced the room impatiently until the sound of the elevator descending drew his attention.

Moments later the doors opened, and Celeste Winslow swept in on four-inch stilettos. She was a stunning woman. Dressed in a navy blue pencil skirt and white silk blouse, she oozed confidence and intimidation. A perfect chignon sat at the nape of her long, slender neck and her caramel skin was smooth and tight. Although her graying hair indicated maturity, no one would guess she was in her sixties.

"Nathan," she said, hurrying toward him. "It's been too long."

Taking his hands in her own she gazed at him a look of concern reflected in her amber eyes.

"I'm so sorry about Ella. Please tell me you have news?"

"I do but I'm also hoping you might help me."

"Of course, anything."

They spent the next hour discussing the parameters surrounding Ella Watts' death. What the Syndicate members had found and what Alistair suspected to be the cause and the motive.

Celeste's shoulders slumped and her eyes filled with tears. "It's absolutely barbaric but I'm thankful she didn't suffer. Who could do such a thing?"

Nathan sighed. He felt years older and absolutely defeated because for once, he had no answers.

"Where is Alistair now?"

"Trying to locate where the poison came from. It was a specific mixture of both a sleeping agent and a paralyzing drug concocted so my wife wouldn't feel the desecration of her body or the pain from the poison that killed her. There are very few alchemists who can produce such a precise mixture."

"I assume he's already questioned the ones working for us?"

Nathan nodded. "He's certain it's an alchemist practicing without a license. If he's out there, Alistair will find him."

Checking her watch, she said. "I will look into your requests and get back to you in a day or two." She took his hands in hers and squeezed. "We will find your daughter, Nathan."

"Thank you, Celeste."

"Of course." She walked calmly into the elevator but as the doors closed her amber eyes locked on Nathan's, and he saw a simmering rage reflected in her irises.

"Ella's killer will be found and the punishment severe. You have my word."

Celeste hung up the phone and leaned back in her leather desk chair gazing out the window of her tenth-story office. It had taken her less than twelve hours to track down some answers. There was always someone in New York's extensive magical community who had information or knew someone who did.

After her discussion with Nathan, she'd had her suspicions as to who was involved. The information he provided along with information the other members of the Syndicate had uncovered created a familiar narrative. A highly unusual one that reflected similarities to another matter the Coven was dealing with.

She pressed the intercom on her phone. "Eliza can you bring me the file I requested, please."

"Right away, ma'am," a voice responded.

There'd been a recent uptick in magical crimes, misdemeanors, and strange happenings in the city. It was unusual and there were stirrings within the magical community that a cleansing of some sort was forthcoming—a precursor to a rebirth of magic in the world. Normally, the Coven would ignore such speculations but since the recent discovery by the Coven's alchemist sect, there'd been a shift in thinking. Rumors had long existed within their community that the magic in this world was connected to a dimensional realm long forgotten. But like most stories of old, it was considered a myth, *until recently.*

The office door opened, and her assistant walked in holding a thick file.

"Can I get you anything else, Mrs. Winslow," she asked placing the file on the desk.

"That will be everything, for now, thank you."

After Eliza closed the office door, she opened the file, flipping through the documents.

The Coven alchemists recently discovered a formula, in the basement of one of the oldest buildings in the city. A spell that would allow an individual with magical blood to travel to an alternate reality. It was like an astral projection but instead of the astral body leaving the physical one to travel through this universe, it passed through the veil into another dimension.

Over the past few months, multiple witches had tried it, and all experienced the same thing—a world beyond this one. A universe of magic; a place where ancient civilizations once ruled and elemental magic thrived.

Celeste had been intrigued but skeptical of this discovery until today when Nathan Callan walked into the World Bank of New York and told her of the ancient prophecy, the Five Realms, and his daughter's connection to it all. He referred to it as the Second Coming. A cleansing. A magical rebirth and new world order?

The puzzle pieces had clicked into place and although much remained unclear, she feared her instincts were correct—Lucien Beck was somehow in the middle of it.

Over the past year, Lucien had become distant, secretive. He left most of the day to day business decisions to his executive team while he traveled extensively. She spoke to him on occasion, he never refused her calls, but their conversations were always brief and awkwardly cordial. Then he disappeared—an unscheduled trip to Europe his assistant confirmed after ignoring multiple phone inquiries from Celeste as to his whereabouts.

When he finally returned last month, his stay in the city was brief. He had business elsewhere in the state and left again almost immediately. She tried on multiple occasions to reach him, to tell him of the alchemist's discovery, but he never returned her calls. And now, according to the call she'd just received he was back in the city, and he was not alone—a woman fitting Dane's description was with him.

Finding what she was looking for she pulled the paper from the file. It contained all the names of the witches who'd traveled through the veil. Scanning the list, she noted the names of three coven elders.

She pressed the intercom button.

"Yes, Mrs. Winslow."

"Eliza, please set up a meeting of the council."

"When would you like it scheduled for?"

"Right away."

Sighing Celeste disconnected, picked up her cell phone and tapped out Lucien's number. It rang incessantly until his voice mail connected. Hanging up she glanced at her watch. It was almost seven am, too early to go to his office and too late to cancel any of her meetings. She would have to pay him a visit in the morning.

She sent her scheduler a quick text asking her to clear all her appointments for the following day. An unscheduled visit to Beck Holdings was the one appointment she would be keeping.

Reluctantly she dialed Nathan Callan's number.

After a few rings, he answered. "Celeste? What is it?"

"Nathan, I can't be sure, but I think Dane is here in the city."

There was a pause. "You have seen her?"

"No, but reports lead me to believe it might be her."

"Where is she?"

She hesitated. "With Lucien Beck."

"As in Beck Holdings? Why would she be with him?"

"Nathan, Lucien Beck is one of us." She continued before he had a chance to respond. "He's always preferred to stay in the background for personal reasons, but he's a powerful witch."

*Maybe too powerful.*

Nathan's voice cracked as he spoke. "How does he fit into *this?*"

"The Coven's been following a series of magical incidents, off-book infractions happening across the city in recent months. Our inquiries indicate Lucien Beck may be involved. We've searched tirelessly for him for weeks and today he showed up in the city with a female."

"And you think it's Dane."

"The possibility is high."

"Why?"

"Lucien thinks it's time for magic in this world to become more overt. He's complicated and has never been good at playing by the Coven rules. It's possible he knows about the prophecy and Dane's involvement with it. I've known Lucien Beck for a long time, Nathan and if I had to guess he plans to use her to further his endgame. Whatever that may be."

"But Dane would never let this happen. She's always been a strong, accomplished witch but now as an immortal with the ancient magic of our ancestors coursing through her blood, there's nothing Lucien Beck could do to persuade her to abandon her destiny."

Celeste exhaled knowing she was about to reveal Lucien's secret.

"There's something you don't know about Lucien Beck," she said. "No one does. It may explain how he got Dane to come to the city."

"What is it?"

"Lucien Beck is a glamour witch."

A heavy silence pulsated from the other end of the phone line. It was deafening. Her heart sank as she waited for him to speak.

"I thought glamour witches were extinct."

"He's the only one we know of."

"Glamour witches are dangerous, Celeste. They exist outside the norms of our tolerance and their powers violate everything the Coven and Syndicate believe, what the entire magical community believes. Free will is never to be toyed with. Why did I not know of his existence?"

His voice fluctuated as he tried to control his anger, but she knew it was well-founded.

"I should have told you, Nathan. I'm sorry, but Lucien has never been a threat. He's always been a playboy but never has he used his powers ambiguously or to his advantage. Honestly, he has never had to. He's powerful, good-looking, and extremely charming, women end up in Lucien Beck's bed willingly."

"There is a first time for everything Celeste."

The irritation resonating through the phone was palpable. She didn't blame him. He was right. In an attempt to not betray Lucien, she'd inadvertently betrayed the Syndicate and the Coven by hiding the truth from those who had a right to know.

She exhaled. "I hope you're wrong, Nathan. If he's used his magic to seduce your daughter and coerce her to come to New York, it can only mean one thing."

"Which is?"

Celeste tapped the pen on her desktop as she thought.

"Dane must play a significant part in his plans."

"I can make him forget her."

Her heart clenched. Nathan Callan was no longer angry now he just sounded defeated.

"Using your magic on Lucien is no less of an infraction than him using his on Dane. Let me try to speak with him first before we resort to breaking more rules. I'll go to his office in the morning and see what I can find out. He trusts me, Nathan, let me try. In the meantime, I will have my assistant send you everything we have uncovered regarding the magical infractions. Maybe you can see a pattern that we can't."

She hung up, assuring him she'd call tomorrow after speaking with Lucien.

The remaining days business consumed her attention. It was after eight in the evening before her mind returned to the matter of Lucien Beck.

The lights of the Manhattan skyline shone through the glass wall of her office. She loved being at the office after hours. The night sky always cast a peacefulness over the bustling city, which calmed her mind and her spirit. Unfortunately, it wasn't having the desired effect tonight.

Her fingers tapped rhythmically on her desk as her thoughts went to Lucien Beck. He'd changed over the past few months, and she worried she no longer held any leverage over him. If he'd used his powers on Dane inappropriately, he would have done so knowing he was breaking coven rules and if that was the case, she doubted he cared about the consequences.

Lucien had always been at the forefront of ensuring the magic in this city stay hidden. And those who practice magic do so within the boundaries set by the Protection of the Coven. One of their doctrine's gravest violations is manipulating the free will of an unwilling individual. If Lucien Beck had resorted to such malice, then he was no longer the man she knew. Moreover, if what Nathan Callan says about his daughter is true and her powers are enhanced by ancient magic, then Lucien Beck has a dangerous weapon under his control.

Pulling a bottle from the desk drawer she poured herself a finger of scotch.

The bite of the alcohol soothed her nerves as the amber liquid slid down her throat.

Tomorrow she will find out Lucien's true intentions.

Tonight, she will pray to the goddess that it isn't too late.

# CHAPTER 18

"I'M SORRY MR. BECK, SHE wouldn't listen."

Lucien looked up from his desk to see a very determined Celeste Winslow striding into his office followed by a very flustered Mrs. Ames, his personal assistant.

Lucien's eyes sparked at the unexpected intrusion, but he forced a smile.

"It's fine Mrs. Ames," he said in a dismissive voice.

She nodded curtly, shot Celeste a scornful look, and hurried out of the office closing the door behind her.

"To what do I owe the pleasure of this unannounced visit, Celeste?" he asked, leaning back in the tall-backed leather office chair.

"You haven't been returning my calls and I've been worried. When I heard you were back in town, I thought I would check on you." She gave him her brightest smile.

He stood and rounded the desk buttoning his dark blue suit jacket. "As you can see, I am quite well but regrettably I have plenty of work to catch up on and little time to spare. What can I do for you?"

Celeste's head cocked. The tone of his voice was pleasant enough, but she sensed the irritation behind it he tried to conceal.

The early morning sun silhouetted him in a soft yellowy haze.

There was something different about him. In the few weeks, since she'd last seen Lucien, he'd changed. He was still gorgeous, confident, and intimidatingly charming, but now dark energy seeped from every pore.

"Where have you been?" The question came out harshly and she cringed. She sounded like his mother, accusing him, scolding him for his absence.

His pale blue eyes burned but his face remained a serene mask.

"As my assistant informed you, I was completing a business transaction that needed my personal attention. Now if there is nothing else, I must get back to work."

He moved toward her gesturing to his office door.

Celeste's eyes flashed. He was dismissing her. After all these years, he was treating her like the hired help.

As he came closer a warning sounded in her mind. Her skin prickled, a familiar sensation when her magic detected the spirit of the dead. With lightning reflexes, she reached out and grasped his hand before he could avoid her touch.

Searing pain scorched through her arm, and she dropped his hand. Her amber eyes widened as she stared at him. "Lucien, what have you done?"

A shadow flickered in his pupils and a sneer contorted his handsome face.

"I never could keep anything from you, Celeste."

She rubbed the palm of her hand as burning pain throbbed under the skin. "Your energy, it's no longer that of the living."

Lucien shook his head. "Sometimes, your necromancer powers are a bit bothersome."

"You know I don't like using that term."

"Don't be so sensitive, Celeste." His voice was forceful, and he began to pace. "You have the power to raise the dead, to command the spirits of those who no longer reside in this world. Calling yourself a diviner is so demeaning especially for a witch of your caliber."

A sarcastic tone had crept into his voice.

"Call me what you will Lucien, but it is not I who have done the unspeakable. Your energy is no longer your own. So, I ask again, what have you done?"

"What I had to."

For a moment Celeste thought she detected a hint of regret in his words, but his face remained a mask of superiority.

Her heightened senses reached toward him exploring the dark energy drifting around him. Somewhere deep in her psyche, a memory tugged at her conscious mind—an understanding of why Lucien's energy was so different and why it didn't hold the same composition as the living or the dead. Stained with the scent of death his aura was heavy with dark magic. She stiffened as the reason became clear. The part of his energy that was dead was not his own and sadly, she recognized the magic swirling inside it.

"Lucien, where is Lilith?"

"Dead."

His callous attitude unhinged her. "Did you kill her?"

He lifted his eyes to meet hers. There was a soulless depth reflected in his pupils. "It wasn't like that. Fate chose her. Her sacrifice will be the reason we survive what is to come."

"We?" The person standing before her wasn't the kind, caring, charismatic man, she'd known for the past decade. This man was cold, calculating, and void of empathy.

There was something sinister in the smile that crept across his face. "Those of us with magic."

Celeste's mind wrestled to unravel the meaning behind his words. Lilith's blood and her death stained his energy, which could mean only one thing—Lucien had performed a blood ritual and, she had been his sacrifice. He'd forfeited Lilith's life to gain immortality. Given his soul to a daemon and in return he'd gained dark powers. His energy was neither living nor dead, it was *tainted*—a soul in purgatory existing between two worlds. A wraith forever linked to the daemon to whom this twisted and unholy pact was made.

Blood roared in her ears as she stared at the man before her.

It all made sense now—Lilith's disappearance, the drastic change in Lucien, his unyielding hold over Dane. He wasn't just a glamour witch; he was much more, much worse. The power he'd gained from the blood pact had not only enhanced his natural abilities but also turned him into a predator. She'd encountered one of his kind before many years earlier, but the similarities were undeniable.

Her eyes filled with tears as the realization of what he had become slammed through her mind. *Lucien Beck was an incubus!*

"Why Lucien," she stammered.

"Why what? Why did I kill Lilith? Why did I choose a dark path?" Aqua blue eyes simmered with frustration, and he didn't even try to conceal the fury in his voice. "Because I'm tired of hiding in the shadows. Tired of looking up at a race who is so far beneath us."

"But magic is flourishing, Lucien. It is much more accepted worldwide than ever before."

"Yet we still hide in the recesses of this city, skulking like street dogs. Why? Because humans consider magic fun and games, something to pique their curiosity. They don't know of its depths, its power. To them, it's just people playing at invoking goddesses and casting spells. There is no true understanding of the powers we possess or how deftly we wield them. We would be shunned if they did for their fear always overwhelms logic. It's why the magical community has rules and why we hide our powers from mortals. After all this time, we still don't believe we'll ever be safe from persecution. We're hypocrites."

"Lucien, please." Her voice was quiet as she attempted to reason with him.

His lip trembled but his eyes flared as he shook his head in defiance. "No more will I bow to the sullied masses. Magic will rise again, the earth will experience a reckoning, and those on the right side of history will rule."

Lucien's rhetoric astonished her but thinking back, it shouldn't. He'd approached her almost a year ago concerned about the rumors. There'd been whispers of impending doom rippling through the magical community at the time—talk of an apocalyptic event; a reckoning. Like others who came before him, he had no concrete evidence. Other than some old writings he'd discovered in his family's grimoire there was little else to support his conjecture. She hadn't believed him and dismissed his concerns.

Staring into the stoic face of her old friend she realized how her actions were a betrayal, and most likely resulted in his turn to the dark side to find the truth.

"You can't believe this to be true."

"It's the only thing I believe."

As she looked into his tortured eyes, she recognized the man she knew was gone. This was no longer about coven violations or magical misdeeds and no consequence or reprimand would solve the problem. Lucien

Beck was no longer one of them. He now played by his own rules.

Her mind reeled. "Lucien, where is Dane?"

A slight twitch appeared briefly under his eye.

"She is safe and will not be harmed, you have my word."

"What is your plan?"

He smiled and his handsome face lit up the way it used to.

Seductive magic crept toward her. Her hand reached into the pocket of her pencil skirt fingers brushing over the cold metal of the protection amulet.

She came prepared. He would have no sway over her. Pulling it from her pocket she showed it to him.

He chuckled. "You were always one step ahead of everyone else Celeste. It's why I admire you so." Turning he walked back to his desk. Leaning against the dark mahogany top he crossed his arms eyes sparkling mischievously. "I suppose it won't hurt if I tell you my plans."

Celeste felt ill at the prospect of what he was about to tell her, and she eased herself into a chair in front of him.

"Do you remember a few years back when I showed you the Tierney family grimoire and the notes magically infused onto a few of the pages?"

"Yes," she croaked remembering their conversation and her response. She'd listened intently, thanked him for the information, and then promptly pushed it aside as if it had no importance.

"There was something else I found in the grimoire. Something I didn't share with you," he said a cockiness in his tone. "I knew you didn't believe me. Coven elders are so arrogant you deem yourselves untouchable. The control you think you have over the magic in this city is a delusion and you won't acknowledge your weakness or face the fact that your rules are tyrannical. The Coven has become more of an oppressor of magic than mortals ever were."

Lucien had begun to pace, his face flush as he spoke. "It certainly didn't surprise me that you didn't believe an ancient evil could rise. Something of this magnitude would minimize your power and weaken the Coven in the eyes of the masses. To ignore the possibility was so much better for you."

Celeste's eyes hardened and a film of perspiration made her ebony skin shimmer. "There is no truth to your ramblings, Lucien. The elders did not address your concerns with any conviction because you did not substantiate your claims. Do you know how often there are whispers concerning some impending doom or another? It wasn't until the alchemists discovered the formula six months ago and breached the veil, did I realize your concerns were valid. Unfortunately, by then you were in Europe and not returning my calls."

The last words were a jab, and she forced the words out like daggers.

Lucien walked back to his desk and shrugged. "It wouldn't have mattered anyway Celeste. My destiny, like Dane's, was written long ago."

"What do you mean?"

"Our connection exists because of those worlds as does mine to the daemon. You see my ancestor, Vertigan Tierney, documented in our grimoire how to control the beast. The immortals from his time called it the *ancient dark* an entity like no other possessing immeasurable power."

He leaned against the desk and shoved his hands in his trouser pockets. A dark shadow crossed his features. "Sadly, my ancestor fell victim to its power.

Manipulated through greed and hate to do things he normally would not. When the immortals finally vanquished the beast to a prison under the earth, my ancestor was left with an innate connection to it. He was able to stay inside the beast's mind and because of this he eventually came to understand how it thought, what drove its intentions, but most importantly how to control it."

A shiver crawled up Celeste's spine. "Are you telling me you are controlling an ancient entity?"

"In a manner of speaking."

Lucien walked around his desk. Opening the top drawer, he pulled out a small wooden box its sides intricately carved with runes. Unlatching the lid, he reached in and removed the contents—a small amulet, tarnished and marred, with a black jewel at its center.

Her eyes widened. "Is that a daemon stone?"

"It is. This is the reason I went to Europe. It took me months to track its whereabouts. I, at last, discovered it in a quaint Italian village, in the basement of a small cathedral concealed inside a secret compartment in the cornerstone. It had remained undetected for centuries but the clue to its location was in my family grimoire. For generations, my ancestors had been readying themselves for this day of reckoning. Preparing for the inevitable—the rise of evil dictated by the ancient prophecy."

"And with this stone you have somehow managed to reach this daemon, to control it."

"The daemon stone is just the beginning. You see, the ancient beast gets his strength from magic. It consumes it and feeds off its power but there isn't enough magic on earth, so it adapted. It found a way to thrive off something there *is* an abundance of, *hate.*"

"And what did Lilith have to do with any of this. Why did she have to die?"

"Regrettably Lilith became a means to an end." His voice hitched as he said her name. "I needed a conduit to create a gateway between worlds. A person with magic that the beast could link to. Sadly, it drained her quicker than I anticipated. Her magic was weak, and her body began shutting down. The link made her go mad and brought her to the brink of death. The blood ritual was in fact, merciful. Her sacrifice will restore the family name. You see only a Tierney can initiate the pact and only the blood sacrifice of a Tierney can bind it. It was my destiny and hers."

He lifted his eyes to Celeste. "Lilith was my sister."

Those words hung in the air as if frozen, and she gasped. He hadn't found Lilith on the street by accident, he'd sought her out. He didn't take her in out of the goodness of his heart he needed her magic, and Celeste had gotten it for him. Dormant for so many years Lilith's powers had been difficult to draw out. The process had been physically painful for her and mentally distressing for them both. A tear slid down her cheek as she realized her part in Lilith's life and death—she had readied her for the slaughter.

Her anger surged. "And Dane? What do you need from her?"

"She is the thread joining both worlds together. Ancient magic will free the ancient beast from its confines but only she can truly control it. Her destiny is not to become the savior of this world but to become *wrath*, a source of hatred so powerful it will fuse the ancient magic to this world and create a vortex for the beast to exist within. With Dane by my side, the earth will be cleansed, and we will rule the remains for eternity."

For all his calm confident demeanor Lucien sounded mad.

"Lucien, it's impossible to truly control an evil that dark. Ancient magic is so different from ours. You are dealing with the unknown. There's no way for you to know this beast from notes in your ancestor's grimoire. Through the blood pact you've entered, you will ultimately succumb to its will. This won't end the way you think."

A dark shadow crossed over his handsome features and for a minute she thought she noticed uncertainty flash in his eyes.

Her voice softened. "Please Lucien, listen to yourself, this isn't you. Release Dane and stop this madness before it goes too far."

"The world as we know it will end. Piece by piece, city by city, country by country, the age of humans will soon be over. Magic will flourish and those who wield it will step out from the shadows, free to exist as they once did. Join me, Celeste. The darkness holds so many possibilities and you can unlock them all."

An uncontrollable laugh bubbled up inside her.

"I know what the darkness holds Lucien, the souls of the dead, the lost, the tortured. A shadow world of pain, suffering, and fear—not possibilities. You want me to use my powers to bring *that* darkness to this world knowing it will destroy all that is good and just." Her amber irises flashed, and she shook her head vehemently. "No, I would rather die."

Lucien stood before her resentment twisting his face into a mask of hatred. His calm façade slipped, and he lashed out.

"If that is your decision Celeste then remember this. When you are gasping for your final breath do not forget that I tried to warn you. The prophecy is upon us, Celeste. Eight days until the full moon and then this world will be lost forever. The beast will rise, and mankind will succumb to the darkness that follows. Magic—*dark magic*—will once again rule the earth. If you choose not to accept what is to come, then you shall perish with the others."

"If that is to be my fate, then so be it. But unlike you Lucien Beck, I will go to the afterworld with my soul intact."

She turned abruptly, her anger filling the room with volatile energy. Objects flew from his desk to the floor. Chairs flipped as papers whirled through the air caught in the downdraft that followed her destructive wake. His office door flew open shattering the glass as she strode toward it. Tortured screams echoed all around them as those caught in the underworld were inflicted by her fury.

Lucien's brow furrowed as he observed the spectacle.

Celeste's powers were extraordinary as was her connection to the dead. Her demise would be such a waste.

"It's too late Celeste," he called after her. "No one can stop what is coming. Not even you."

# CHAPTER 19

C ELESTE SPENT THE REST OF the day making calls and sending instructions to the underground. She sifted through documents in the archives looking for anything that may give them a clue, a way to stop the Second Coming and Lucien.

In his boastful rage, Lucien confirmed the timeline she'd received from Nathan, eight days. The Second Coming was set to begin on the eve of the next full moon—March 23rd.

Nathan had called while she was in a late meeting. His message was brief but there was something different in his tone, he no longer sounded defeated but optimistic. She supposed he still had faith in the prophecy and believed that somehow his daughter would find her way back to her true destiny. As she dialed his number Celeste hoped that would be the way things turned out but after seeing the look in Lucien's eyes, she knew he was not a man prepared to lose.

"I'm sending someone to your office," he said after their initial pleasantries.

"Who?"

"Someone who might be able to help. You will understand once you meet her. And Celeste, keep an open mind."

After hanging up she tidied her desk and went to her dinner meeting. An evening of stroking the egos of her biggest stockholders should keep her mind off Lucien Beck.

Three hours later she was back in her office standing by the windows and gazing across the skyline. It had rained for the better part of the afternoon and a light fog shrouded the city in a misty glow.

She glanced at her watch. It was after ten and still no sign of Nathan's friend. Maybe she wasn't coming because maybe she couldn't help.

Celeste walked back to her desk and pulled a bottle from her desk drawer. Leaning back in her chair she took a sip of whiskey straight from the bottle.

*Maybe no one could.*

The drizzling rain finally ceased, and a haze coated the night sky.

From her perch at the top of the Woolworth Building, Gabriella could see the lights of the city as they stretched out for miles. The winter wind swirled ruffling the feathers of her wings. She tugged up the collar of her leather coat and fixed her gaze on the bustling city below.

Closing her eyes, she listened not to the night sounds of the city but the whispering underneath. There was an abundance of magical energy in New York, running through the underground sewers and swirling in the dark recesses of every borough. For there to be this much magic in one place there must be a significant number of individuals who knew how to wield it.

This would be the perfect place for Dane to hide.

She cocked her head, hearing a strange hum beneath the cacophony filtering up from the streets below. Her senses reached out looking for the essence marking those with ancient blood.

The wind picked up breaking her concentration and her eyes fluttered open. If Dane was in the city, she would find her. It was merely a matter of time.

Since leaving Etheriem Gabriella had spent the past two days roaming around Brighton Hill. Dane's essence was faint, but she discovered it lingering here and there. The scent eventually led her to the abandoned flour mill. New padlocks secured the doors and the windows were shrouded with black tarps. Although she didn't enter the mill, she sensed the dark energy saturating its insides and the thrum of the daemon pods. A sharp stench of fresh blood seeped from the building. It was tinged with magic but not with the distinct essence of the ancient bloodlines.

Thankfully it had not been Danes, but the blood did belong to someone born of this world.

After discovering the mill had been sold, and knowing Dane was no longer in Brighton Hill, she had journeyed to the city to investigate Beck Holdings. And now she stood atop the city listening to the nocturnal sounds drifting through the chilly night.

The phone in her pocket vibrated.

"Hello."

A familiar voice came over the line. She stayed silent as he spoke, her eyes flashing as he explained the reason for his call.

"The Woolworth building," she said to the caller. "Yes, I can find it. Broadway, Liberty, Pearl, #120. I will go now."

Gabriella hung up the phone and placed it back in her jacket. Arching her wings, she jumped and soared through the night sky.

Hidden above the ambient glow of the city lights

the wind pushed her toward her destination. Without a sound, she landed on the roof.

The bolt securing the access door broke with ease under the blade of her sword. Entering the building she took the elevator down to the executive floor.

Celeste didn't hear the woman walk into her office, but she felt the magical essence sizzling around her.

It was unfamiliar. Unlike any magic she'd encountered in the past.

Her eyes studied the stranger dressed in black.

A black streak snaked its way down one side of the straight white hair skimming her shoulders. Pale skin, a stark contrast to her rose-red lips, shone under the warm radiant glow cast by the desk lamp. But it was the woman's eyes that commanded Celeste's attention. They flickered with iridescent light; a multitude of colors weaving through her irises that shifted and changed with every blink.

"Nathan said you'd be coming."

The woman nodded. "Celeste, is it? He thought we should meet."

"Why?"

She shrugged. "I believe he feels it necessary. A way for you to truly appreciate the prophecy and its consequences."

Celeste tempered her irritation at the ambiguous and arrogant attitude the woman projected. "I believe I already understand what's at stake."

"Do you?" The stranger unfolded her wings spreading them to their full width. "My name is Gabriella."

"You come from the other world."

The statement required no confirmation or denial.

"You do not seem surprised."

Celeste shook her head. "I have seen much in my time, although admittedly an angel isn't one of them."

Gabriella inhaled sharply. "Celestial."

"Excuse me?"

"My kind are not angels, we are celestials. Angels are a product of man's otherworldly thinking. A way for them to understand things they cannot comprehend. To give your short, insignificant lives merit."

Celeste scowled. "I apologize for my pitiful race offending you by putting yours on a pedestal."

"If mortals knew the truth of our kind they would not be admiring so much as fearing," she stated.

"Well, I'm sure this will be an interesting discussion for another conversation but for now, our time might be better spent on the matters at hand."

Gabriella nodded and folded her wings back inside her coat. She moved closer to Celeste.

"Nathan mentioned you have information about the person I seek—his daughter, Dane."

"She's with Lucien Beck."

"I assume he owns Beck Holdings?"

"You know of him?"

Gabriella's shook her head. "No, but the purchase of the old flour mill in Brighton Hill led me here. His company bought it."

"It recently came to my attention that Lucien purchased a large commercial property in that town. Although I have no idea what he would want with an abandoned flour mill. It's not exactly the type of property he usually invests in."

"From what Nathan has told me about Beck, the old mill in Brighton Hill seems perfect for his needs. It sits alone in a field far away from prying eyes and is saturated with the energy he requires—a dark, tortured force, which has been collecting around the mill for centuries."

Celeste sighed. "I suspected it may."

"You know of Brighton Hill's past?"

"Yes, it has an unfortunate one."

"Over time the veil created a vortex around the mill trapping the imprints of all those who perished violently in the town. Unable to move on, they are fated by their tragic ends to exist within this timeless void. It has resulted in a vast amount of dark energy swirling around the mill. Nathan thinks Beck tapped into this and is using it as a power source to create a portal for the ancient dark."

Celeste chuckled thinking how much Lucien would hate being referred to as Beck. "Lucien calls this entity the beast."

The celestial raised her eyebrows. "Interesting. Tell me, exactly who is this Lucien Beck and what does he want with Dane?"

"Lucien Beck is an incubus."

The fact that she admitted her long-time friend was a daemon wasn't easy, it made her skin crawl. But, the anger at his betrayal of their friendship fueled her conviction to stop him and his insane plan. Her fists clenched as she stared at the celestial's impassive face waiting for a reply.

"I do not know this word *incubus*," she said.

"In our world, incubi are low-level daemons. Their reason for existing is to spread their daemon seed among mortal woman."

"Why would such an inconsequential daemon be interfering with an ancient prophecy?"

She flicked her manicured hand in the air in frustration. "Revenge, a power grab, a sense of family loyalty, twisted justice. I don't know. Whatever Lucien's reasons you can be sure of one thing—he is not a normal incubus nor is he inconsequential. He's been created by ancient magic by invoking a blood pact with this beast, that if I am not mistaken even your kind couldn't defeat."

The celestial glowered at her but remained silent.

"Before he made this pact, he was a glamour witch. His power allows him to get people to do what he wants by manipulating their mind." She sighed. "He's never used his powers to his benefit before, but it must be how he's controlling Dane. To maintain this level of control, especially over another magical being, is extremely difficult and an incubus can only maintain that control over a short period. Just long enough to impregnate. If Dane is not with Lucien of her own volition, then glamour is the only reasonable explanation."

Gabriella walked to the window and stared out at the skyline. "Is there a way to intervene. To break his power over her?"

Celeste pulled an amulet from her pocket and walked to where the celestial stood, holding it up in the space between them. The metal's surface was tarnished and marred with scratches and dents. A blood-red ruby emblazoned one side while crude etchings were carved into the other.

"This has been in my family for generations. It is a protection amulet imbued with the spirits of the dead and provides the possessor with an impenetrable barrier to dark magic. It also provides the bearer with clarity and is how I knew Lucien was an incubus. If we can get this on Dane's person, it may weaken the glamour and allow her to once again think for herself."

Black wings fluttered as the celestial eyed the amulet. She touched the metal, her slender fingers grazing over the strange etchings.

"It is the veve of Baron Samedi," Celeste said, indicating the amulet. "In my culture, he is the loa of the dead. A god. He waits at the crossroads to receive the spirits of those passing into the underworld. But he is also the giver of life. Baron Samedi can block curses, hexes, and dark magic if he chooses. This amulet is said to contain a part of his spirit, trapped in the enchanted ruby on the front. His power maintains a constant wall of protection around whoever has this in their possession."

"And you think it can work on Dane?"

Amber irises flickered as she locked eyes with Gabriella. "Unless you have a better idea."

As if to herself, Gabriella said. "The prophecy did not foretell of this."

Celeste huffed. "Your prophecy doesn't seem to be too accurate. Forgive me for pointing out that it also has another glaring omission."

"Meaning?"

"The race bloodlines of the five realms may be the ones foreseen to stop this ancient evil, but the blood of your world is also what's initiating the passing of the prophecy. Tierney blood, the blood of the betrayed is how the beast will rise—Lucien's blood."

Gabriella's wings rose at the sound of the name and her face was a mask of displeasure.

"You know the Tierney bloodline?"

"A long time ago, yes. The Tierney line of Warlician warriors has always been trouble. In our world, three families of witches ruled the earth realm known as Dywen: Callathian, Morrighann, and Tierney. They were the oldest bloodlines and the most powerful in the Warlician Order. But, unlike the other two bloodlines, the Tierney's were outsiders, rule breakers, and difficult to control. Vertigan Tierney proved to be one of the worse. During the Great War, the darkness of his essence had been manipulated by the ancient dark, and he committed unspeakable atrocities. Stripping him of his magic and vanquishing him to the new world had been, in my opinion, a weak and unjust punishment. I had recommended death but the Warlician sect thought banishment much direr. A cruel way for a supernatural being to live out his days—as a mortal."

Celeste sighed as she finally understood the connection between their two worlds and how their fate was now irrevocably entangled. "Regrettably it seems that fateful decision began the beginning of a new age. The catalyst that would eventually drive the ancestor of Vertigan Tierney, Lucien, to this."

"I must get back to my world at once and find the others."

"What about Dane?" The red gem of the amulet glinted as Celeste held it out to Gabriella. "This might be the only way."

"If what you say about this incubus is true, I will not be able to break the connection alone, but I may know someone who can," she said taking the amulet.

"And what can I do?"

"Are you willing to fight?"

Celeste nodded.

"The Second Coming will commence under the light of the full moon, but it will not begin here in the city. Although the magic here is potent, it is too chaotic making it difficult to focus. Lucien has chosen well; the mill is where the battle will commence. You must go to Brighton Hill."

"If you're sure about the mill, I will gather those willing to fight and meet you there."

"There is no doubt," she replied. "Meet us there on the eve of the twenty-second, no later. Gather the strongest of your kind who are able to fight with magic and force."

She hesitated and her irises flickered. "They must also be willing to die."

"Good luck. I hope you find a way to help your friend."

Gabriella turned the amulet over in her hand. "There is only one person who can get through to her now. Pray the connection between them and between our worlds is strong enough to save her."

Celeste's eyes narrowed as the celestial turn to go. With her wings stretched out behind her and the long leather coat brushing her ankles as she strode toward the door, she was rather an impressive sight.

The sword at her hip shone in the light and Celeste felt a sense of awe as immortal energy swept through the room unimpeded. It was a power; unlike anything she'd encountered before.

The celestial stopped but she did not turn around. Her voice sounded tense as she spoke.

"If we fail and the ancient dark proves to be the victor your world will not be the only one to fall. Thanissia will again feel the ancient dark's wrath only this time it may be lost to us forever."

# CHAPTER 20

THEY ENTERED THE GALENVALE GROVE an hour after leaving Niramyst.

The trek took longer than usual as they often stopped to quiet an increasingly hostile Marlee. Her hands were bound, and a gag secured in her mouth but her feet were free so she could walk and kick at her captors. After the third time she kicked Killenn, this time in the groin, Rafe threw her to the ground, bound her feet and tossed her over his shoulder. He, Brannon, and Killenn took turns carrying her the rest of the way. The humiliation alone seemed to quiet her but during the moments she did act up whoever was carrying her dropped her decisively to the ground.

A twinge of remorse fluttered through Kai as Marlee writhed on the ground cursing at the three warriors.

The Keltie fae had not been seen since the sun rose and Kai assumed, they had disappeared back into their own plane of existence. It was mid-morning and Sebastian said they most likely had until nightfall to find an answer before the Keltie would emerge and try to reacquire Marlee.

The scent of fragrant flowers greeted them as they entered the grove. Long lines of fruit trees as far as the eye could see bloomed. Renewed by the magic flowing freely back into the realm the small flowers exploded on the branches creating a canvas of bright colors.

A dirt path wound its way through the grove leading to the entrance of the Druid Sanctuary. Near the end, the path expanded bordered by stunning white trees on either side.

Kai stood beside one of the trees.

The scent of apple blossoms drifted on the warm breeze, and she inhaled deeply. There were a few crab apple trees on the marina property, but these were nothing like those. These trees had sturdy trunks with smooth white bark unblemished by time or the elements. An umbrella-shaped canopy, which stood about seven feet above the ground dazzled with beautiful rust-hued leaves and white flowers the size of dinner plates.

"What type of trees are these?" Kai asked Sebastian.

"Apple blossoms," Sebastian said. "You have them in your world."

"Not like this." She caressed one of the leaves. Its surface was soft and fuzzy yet prickled her skin.

"Many of the species transferred from our world to yours could not maintain their significant stature without our magic. Stunted versions seemed to be a better fit."

"What else on Earth comes from your world?"

A twinkle reflected in his eye. "Your world was born from this one. There is a little part of everything from ours in yours. While some are significant like the apple blossom, others are more subtle; like the way a warm summer breeze can taste like the ocean or how the full moon's beams ignite a gentle tingle across one's skin."

Kai smiled. Sebastian had a way of making the answer to a simple question so much more. He obviously had an affection for both worlds and an appreciation for the things most took for granted.

"Thank you," she said, tenderly touching his arm.

"For what?"

"For just being you." She winked and followed the others toward the sanctuary leaving Sebastian to trail behind bewildered by her comment.

At the end of the apple blossom corridor, a tall rock face greeted them. It stretched out endlessly in each direction, disappearing into the distant horizon and the clouds above. The stone was smooth with no door or opening, nothing to indicate there was a hidden sanctuary behind its surface.

"How do we get in?" Tauria ran her hand across the warm rock while Diego paced back and forth sniffing the ground.

"There is a door, we just need to find it," Sebastian answered.

"How?"

"For that, I do not have an answer although I believe Rafe may."

His green eyes twinkled with amusement as he grinned at the warrior's shocked face.

Rafe glowered. "Why would you think that?"

"Adaridge thought you might need guidance when the time came. Someone to prod you at the right moment."

"So, he told you of the Druid knowledge he imbued me with."

"He did. And now my friend, it's time for you to draw on that knowledge. Somewhere in your mind is the location of the keyhole. Find it and the door will be revealed."

"But what of the key?"

Sebastian reached under his armor and tunic and

lifted a thick metal chain from around his neck. At its end was a small iron key.

Rafe raised an eyebrow.

"It would be too tempting for one person to have both the knowledge and the key," Sebastian explained. "Adaridge put his trust in the prophecy and in us. Let us not let him down."

With a stern nod, Rafe began to pace the rhythm of his steps matching the tranquility of the grove. The others backed away allowing him to move unencumbered on the ground in front of the rock face.

Kai watched intently as his eyes fluttered closed.

The sun shone on his skin as a light breeze ruffled his hair. His eyes moved rapidly back and forth behind closed lids as if processing information or images only he could see.

The more he paced, the calmer Kai became until she too sensed the elemental magic hovering all around them, old magic, *Druid magic.*

Abruptly Rafe stopped pacing and turned toward the wall of rock striding to a spot near the last apple blossom tree. He slid his hand back and forth across the rock face until his fingers found what they looked for.

"Here," he said.

Sebastian hurried over, iron key in hand. His fingers grazed the stone near Rafe's. He nodded his appreciation as he inserted the key into the invisible keyhole.

"Adaridge chose wisely," he said clapping Rafe on the shoulder. "Come. Let us see what the Druids left us."

The lock screeched as he turned the key and a puff of smoke floated into the air. Resounding clicks echoed somewhere in the belly of the rock face and a portion of the surface, the edges invisible to the naked eye, began to slide sideways.

As they entered the cool, damp passage the rock behind them slid back into place shutting out the sunlight and leaving them in a pressing gloom.

"Does anyone have a light?" Kai asked.

"No need," Sebastian said. "Patience."

Moments later a glow appeared above them. Lines of light scurried across the ceiling bathing the passageway in their soft sparkle.

"This way."

The group followed the lights down the stone corridor and into a small, dimly lit room. It was sparsely furnished. A wooden bench sat against the far wall next to a bookcase, a few dusty old tomes scattered along its shelves. In the room's center sat a rickety table and chairs.

"This, is it? It's not very impressive," Kai murmured surveying the bleak surroundings.

"Oh, this is not the library," Sebastian said. "This is the common area for the Druid's living quarters."

He crossed the small room at a hurried pace and disappeared into the dark of a narrow hallway on the opposite side.

"Keep moving," he called back to the others.

As she walked down the hallway, Kai peered through a door to her left. This room was bigger than the last but just as meagerly furnished. Besides the small desk, wooden bunk beds were the only other fixtures.

Catching up to Sebastian she linked her arm through his. "You're full of surprises, aren't you?"

"I am not sure I understand your inquiry."

"No one knew you had the key to this sacred place.

You didn't think this was information you should share?"

"No one knew Rafe had the information as to where the key goes," he countered.

Kai laughed. "True."

"When the Druid race began to die out six keys were forged by the blacksmiths of Kaizi, so the knowledge kept in the library would never be lost. The Keys of Knowledge were given to the leaders of each race. One key for all time to ensure the knowledge of the Thanissia universe would forever be shared amongst its people. After the Great War when the time of the immortals was coming to an end, all but one key was destroyed. I was given that key as part of my destiny and instructed never to reveal its whereabouts until the time it was needed. The key being in my possession was of no significance to anyone until this day so there was no reason to disclose its whereabouts."

"But why all the secrecy? Evidently, everyone from your world knew of the Druids and their sanctuary. Did they think it lost when the worlds fell during the Great War?"

"I am sure most did not give it much thought. When you are losing your home, the pieces you must leave behind soon become distant memories."

"And the knowledge never came to Earth?"

"The Druids have been documenting our ways for many lifetimes. The knowledge contained in the library pertains to the races of the Five Realms, elemental magic, and the Thanissia Universe among other things. Much of it is of no consequence to your world."

They reached the end of the hallway before Kai could ask more about the Druids. In front of them stood a tall, arched wooden doorway. Slats of metal crisscrossed its surface in several directions. At the center was a small keyhole. Sebastian removed the iron key from his tunic and inserted it, turning the bow in a very specific order—left two turns, right three, back one, forward seven. Each generated a series of whirls and clicks as a mechanism inside the door began to move.

With a groan, the thick door swung open revealing an astonishing sight.

# CHAPTER 21

THE LIBRARY WAS A MASSIVE circular room with a domed, wood-planked roof towering at least fifty feet above the floor. A mammoth iron chandelier, filled with hundreds of candles, hung from its center. The wicks ignited as they entered illuminating the entire library in soft light.

Rows of tables with bench seats lined the middle of the room a wrought-iron candelabra, candle flames flickering, sat atop each.

Bookshelves covered every wall floor to ceiling. Rickety ladders leaned against the lower shelves and catwalks, hung from the rafters above, provided access to the uppers. A circular staircase at the back of the library wound up to a small platform, a nook, where a desk and chair rested. Gangplanks stretched from there to the catwalks providing access to the upper shelves of the library.

"This is extraordinary," Kai said, her eyes full of wonder.

Sebastian nodded in affirmation.

"The Druids were a learned people. Old-world scholars. They believed knowledge was the basis to existence and therefore took nothing for granted. Everything they knew is written in the texts stored on those shelves."

"There must be an extensive amount of information in those pages," she said indicating the bookshelves, which overflowed with dusty leather-bound books, scrolls, and pages of loose parchment.

Sebastian recognized the interest the Library invoked in her. "You have your mother's curiosity. She too was intrigued by the world outside her own."

Kai blushed. "We traveled a lot because of my father's job, all over the world to different navy bases. My mother loved it. The different landscapes, cultures, people. She had a hunger for life and for knowledge."

"I am glad to know your mother was happy in her new world."

"I think she was."

"Well, maybe someday you can learn more about her homeland," he said gesturing to the volumes of books and papers on the shelves. "But for now, we have work to do."

"Rafe, Killenn," he called to the warriors. "Ridding ourselves of one threat would be helpful. See if anything in the Druid texts will provide us a way to close the gateway. The rest of you search for information on the ancient dark. There may be something here that can help us with what is to come when the full moon rises."

He pointed to a wooden box on the far table. "The Druids kept a very simple cataloging system. It should help narrow the search."

Kai scowled. "I thought the Druid bloodlines ended before the Great War."

"Mostly, Adaridge was the only Druid left when the Great War began. He faded into the All Souls before it ended. Because of their extensive lifespans and thirst for knowledge, I am hoping there is text somewhere mentioning this ancient entity or something similar. The Druids often gathered knowledge from planes of existence not their own. It is possible they knew of this entity and therefore there may be something within these pages to assist us in understanding how to defeat it."

The next few hours were spent climbing catwalks, pulling dusty tomes off the shelves, and leafing through pages of text. The one volume they discovered that mentioned the ancient dark was useless and no entries existed prior to its attack on the Thanissia Universe.

In the text, Adaridge had noted the ancient darks use of magic as food, *"the entity consumes magic as substance seemingly providing it energy and strength."* There was also an excerpt about its innate ability to corrupt all but one of the natural elements, *"the entity seems not to rely on the power of one element but many, consuming the magic of each realm equally. It turns fire to ash, water to ice, earth to dust, and thrives on the chaos of the elements. Oddly, air magic appears to be the one element it is unable to manipulate."*

"Look," Elyse said, pulling a tattered scroll from one of the lower shelves. "A map."

She rolled it out flat on one of the tables using the candelabras to hold down the curled edges.

The others gathered at her side.

Although the images were crude and the topography simple, it was clear what the map depicted.

"That's the town of Brighton Hill," Kai stammered.

Elyse agreed. "How would ancient Druids from your time have the ability to draw a map of a town a hundred billion years in the future."

"That is curious," Rafe said.

Sebastian's mouth set in a firm line. "The Druids possessed the ability to access different planes of existence. Although rather unsettling it is not impossible for us to assume them capable of accessing the knowledge of a distant future."

Kai pointed to a spot on the map. "That is the old flour mill, but why does it have those strange symbols beside it?"

Rafe looked closer.

Three small insignias surrounded the mark Kai indicated as the mill. He recognized them at once.

"Those are ancient runes. A lost language. The Druids used it to code documents and text they did not want others to understand."

Drow raised an eyebrow. "Interesting you know that."

Sebastian's eyes softened as he looked at Rafe. "Adaridge was correct in giving you the knowledge he could not pass on to another Druid."

Rafe gave him a sheepish look.

"What do they mean?" Drow asked leaning in closer to the map.

"Destiny, Decimation, Death."

The room went silent.

"Does that mean the old flour mill has been the point of origin since the beginning of time?" Elyse asked.

"It would seem we have discovered the location where the Guardian of Deities entombed the ancient evil, yes," he said.

"It makes sense. People always thought the place was haunted and now—Lilith, the daemon pods, the changing energy." Stevie shrugged. "We already assumed the mill would be the battlefield. So, what does this change?"

Rafe poked at the map with his index finger. "If this is the epicenter and not just a conduit to the other side, ancient powers would be embedded in the earth here. Meaning when the ancient dark rises his strength will be immeasurable."

Stevie groaned. "Could this get any worse?"

"How are we going to defeat him without Dane?" Elyse's eye's filled with tears. "Or Marlee."

At the mention of her name the fae's blue eyes seared with hatred.

"We will figure it out," Rafe said. "We must."

Elyse wiped at a tear trailing down her cheek.

Without hesitation, he changed the subject. "Killenn and I found a way to close the gateway and trap the Keltie on their plane."

He pulled a piece of parchment from his pocket and unfolded it ceremoniously on the table. "Old Druid magic. We are going to manipulate the air to close the gateway."

"How? Only Marlee can manipulate air to that magnitude," said Sebastian.

Rafe knew exactly what the elder Warlician referred to. Elyse's powers were not as physical as the others because for elves the magic derived from the air element was an internal conduit. It made them exceptional in battle for they were quick and agile and had heightened senses, but to manipulate air into destructive formations like tornadoes that ability belonged solely to the fae.

He turned the parchment around, so it faced Sebastian. "It's not elemental magic we will use but an elixir. We are going to create an explosion big enough to cause the air to expand so rapidly and with such violence, it will instantly retract upon itself and seal the gateway for good."

Sebastian glanced at the text. "Where shall we find those ingredients?"

"Already have them," said Killenn lifting a black duffel sack onto the table. "There is a storage area off to the left, in the upper stacks. A small door, not easy to squeeze through mind you but the contents of the room were worth the discomfort."

He untied the satchel.

Inside were powders, glass vials, liquids, and metal containers. A coil of black wire was wrapped around a jar of umber-colored gel that pulsed with light when he shook it.

"It seems one thing may go in our favor—"

He was interrupted by a sound in the hallway, an echo of sorts drifting toward them from the gloom.

Diego growled a low guttural warning.

Rafe pulled his sword. Brannon, Killenn, and Sebastian did the same.

The sound was soft like something sweeping across the stone—a swishing. It continued to get louder as whatever moved through the corridor got closer.

The warriors tensed as the shadows parted.

"I assume those are not for me?" Gabriella said, indicating the drawn weapons as she stepped out of the corridor into the light of the library. "Because you won't stand much of a chance."

Rafe sheathed his blade and chortled. "Good to have you back, Gabriella."

The celestial reached back and wiped the dust from her wings. "That hallway is uncommonly narrow. You would think the Druids did not understand architecture."

"Any word on Dane?" Stevic asked.

Gabriella flashed Rafe a quick look. "Yes. I know her whereabouts. She is in the city. New York."

"What is she doing there?" The shock in Kai's voice was obvious.

"She appears to be under the control of an incubus," she said coolly.

"A what?"

"It is a long story."

Rafe's face went pale, and he flexed his right hand. "Has she been hurt?"

"We don't believe so."

"We?" Sebastian inquired.

"I made a new friend. And she is bringing us a magical army."

# CHAPTER 22

T HE THREE IMMORTALS STOOD AT the edge of the grove, near a small pool surrounded by moss-covered rocks. The water was crystal clear, and you could see the bottom as if no water existed above it. It was neither sand, nor mud, nor rock, but a smooth surface of crystal, which reflected their faces like a mirror.

Rafe tensed as Gabriella's iridescent eyes turned his way.

"At this moment, you are her only hope."

"Are you sure about this?" Sebastian's concern etched his face as he looked at his friend.

Rafe nodded. "Adaridge is the only one who can reach her using the power of the All Souls and I the only one who can reach him."

Moving to the edge of the pool he removed his shirt, lowered himself to the grass, and sat cross-legged, closing his eyes.

Sebastian and Gabby moved back giving him space to concentrate.

The Pool of Sight was a sacred place and if there was anywhere within the grove where Adaridge could cross through to this side it would be here. Hopefully, he had given Rafe the knowledge to make that happen.

Rafe slowed his breathing. His back muscles twitched, and his jaw clenched as his eyes moved back and forth rapidly under his closed lids, searching. His lips began to move as a whisper drifted from them. It was quiet at first barely more than a whisper but as he continued the words became firmer and more forceful.

"What is he saying?" Gabriella said quietly listening to the chant.

Sebastian recognized bits and pieces. "I believe it is a summoning. A way of connecting to imprints who exist behind the veil. Rafe does not have the ability to cross over into another plane, so he's trying to summon a Druid who can."

"Let us hope it is Adaridge who answers."

Rafe's chanting intensified as the surface of the pool began to ripple. Subtle at first, a slight vibration shimmering across the surface. The more Rafe whispered the more intensely the water vibrated until waves pushed out toward the edges.

Something at the pool's center broke through the surface. Moments later, Adaridge, in perfect form, rose from the water's depths. His robes were dry as he waded along the surface and stepped to the grass. He extended a hand toward Rafe and helped the warrior to his feet.

"It has been a long time," he said.

"You look good."

"The All Souls has kept my life essence stable. It is an odd thing being back in this form after all this time. It feels heavy."

He pulled at his long, thick beard. "And uncomfortable."

Rafe laughed. "The brevity of actual existence."

Nodding, Adaridge turned toward Gabriella and Sebastian. "I am glad to see you both well."

The elder warrior clasped the Druid's hand. "It is good to see you too, old friend. You have been missed."

The Druid moved toward Gabriella, stumbling slightly.

Rafe steadied him. "Are you OK?"

He pulled his shoulders back and nodded. "My time in these worlds is long past and my essence no longer belongs here. I am unable to stay in this physical form for long, so we must hurry for soon the All Souls will call me back."

He once again moved toward where she stood. Taking her hands in his he looked deep into her iridescent eyes. "I am sorry your burden has been the most daunting and caused you pain. It was not the intent of the Guardian to have you fall, but under the circumstances, it was the only way. It was I who was to be the one to exist in the new world as a mortal. Alas, I was unable to hold on to my existence long enough to transfer my life essence into the new world. The unexpected arrival of the ancient dark sapped my magic far too soon, and therefore my burden became yours and for that, I am truly sorry."

"But if my true destiny was not to fall and join the other bloodlines then what was it? I carry the blood of the celestial. I am one of the six Arcanists am I not?"

"Yes, but your task was to remain on Etheriem. To wait in stasis like Rafe until the prophecy began to unwind. Dane would find you as she did Rafe. Your paths would have crossed as they were meant to. Your time to descend was when the prophecy came to pass, not before. You were never meant to lead a mortal life."

Gabriella stared at the Druid unable to utter a response. Pushed from her beloved home so abruptly, the Guardian had sacrificed himself, and then he sacrificed her without explanation. She thought back to her last day on Etheriem and how her brother refused to look at her.

He must have known.

Straightening to her full height her iridescent eyes bore into the Druid's. Her pride refused to acknowledge his pity. "If that was the destiny the Guardian chose for me then it was the one, I was meant to have."

She reached into her pocket and pulled out the amulet. "And this is the path you are now meant to walk. You are the one who can reach Dane. She must be given this." Pressing the amulet into Adaridge's palm she continued, "It is the only way to pull her from the darkness this incubus has cocooned her in."

"So, there is still a chance to correct her path," he said closing his fingers around the amulet.

The celestial dipped her head. "Maybe."

Reaching into his robe he produced a small vial. The contents flickered with a purple light and a gauzy substance swirled languidly inside the glass. He handed it to Gabriella. "Then you will need this. She must ingest it."

"What is that?" Rafe asked.

"It is the essence of the All Souls. I am only able to pass through into the natural world using a physical form from this point of origin," he said indicating the Pool of Sight. "For me to help, Dane must come to me. The essence of the All Souls must be consumed so her conscious can pass into another plane. Her dreams will guide her."

"But you already reached out to her before. Why can you not again?"

Adaridge shook his head. "That was different. I projected my mind, not a physical presence. I manipulated time and space in order to contact her. But even then, I was unable to converse with her the way I am with you now."

He lifted the amulet Gabriella had given him.

"In order for me to carry a physical object to her, we must exist on the same plane. The contents in that vial will bring her to me. The essence of the All Souls will always find its way home."

Rafe frowned as he addressed the celestial. "Why can we not just deliver the amulet to her ourselves."

"Celeste worried the incubus would feel its energy long before we could get it on her person. We must take no chances." She put the vial in her coat pocket and looked at Adaridge. "It will be done."

"How will you know when you can reach her," Rafe asked.

The Druid's tanned face wrinkled at the corner of his eyes as he chuckled. "I will know," he said as he walked back into the Pool of Sight.

The water bubbled around him as he began to descend beneath its depths.

"Thank you, Adaridge," Rafe said his voice strained.

Gabriella felt a slight twinge in her heart as the Druid responded.

"I will do what I can for her, but you must understand the darkness is hers alone to conquer. If the ancestor of the Callathian bloodline is to return to her rightful destiny, she must choose which path to take on her own."

As he disappeared beneath the surface of the water his voice echoed through the grove.

"Darkness will not win if she is able to find the light within."

# CHAPTER 23

L ATE AFTERNOON SUN SCORCHED THE sky as the group exited the Druid Sanctuary. Its rays touched the horizon as it sank, crossing paths with the triple moon that rose beside it.

"You must hurry," Sebastian said. "The sun is fading. If you do not destroy the well and close the gateway before the moon rises to its peak the Keltie will be free, and we will have lost our chance. They may not return to their plane once they discover we have captured Marlee."

"We will see it done," Killenn said.

Sebastian glanced to the sky as it roiled and rumbled over the Oberon Fen. "Good luck my friends. We will head to Niramyst and wait for your return."

Inside the Fen a gloomy atmosphere prevailed. Pewter clouds blocked the light of the afternoon sun. No sparkling leaves or babbling brooks waited for them, only death and decay. The air, thick with a caustic stench, dripped with heavy sorrow. These lands, forever scarred, would never see the bright light of any day nor flourish the way the rest of Athir did under the renewed magic.

Both Killenn and Rafe had been young men when

the war between the races broke out, but each remembered the fertile grow lands the way they used to be. The fae took pride in their crops and orchards. Although these lands would never return to their former opulence, the warriors could ensure the rest of Athir did not succumb to the vicious darkness the return of the Keltie would bring.

Rotten vines snagged at their clothes as they weaved their way through the vineyards dilapidated wooden slats. Unfazed, they pushed on. Soon the moon would reach its peak and the Keltie fae would emerge, anxious to find their new fae queen.

Killenn dumped the bag at the base of the well the moment they arrived. His eyes trailed to the top where the breach in the raging sky still throbbed.

The well had flourished under the magic seeping from the other plane. Tendrils of fairy vine twisted up the stone. The emerald green of their stalks contrasted with the dark gray of the well. Tiny pink florets burst outward from their sheaths exuding a heady perfume.

Rafe stood next to Killenn and pulled a paper from his pocket. "You should mix the elixir. Alchemists come from your people."

Killenn shook his head. "But you have the knowledge of the Druids and it's a Druid elixir."

Rafe's eyes tracked to the top of the tower. "I will mix. You can scale the well and set the elixir to light. There will be mere moments to ascend and you are quicker."

"Agreed. I am quicker," Killenn said raising an eyebrow at Rafe.

"For this task," he clarified.

"Of course."

Rafe took the ingredients from the duffel sac. He set

the alchemy burner down and lit it, adjusting the knob until the fiery blue flame turned dark red.

"Maybe we should have brought Stevie," he said as he read the instructions.

"You can do this, but please hurry. The sky above the Fen is darkening, which means the sun of Athir has almost disappeared. We are running out of time."

Nodding, he set the glass carafe on the burner and began adding ingredients, muttering measurements to himself.

The concoction bubbled and the hue turned from putrid green to lilac, and then jet black. A hiss sounded as it boiled, and smoke and sparks erupted from the surface.

Rafe jumped back as the liquid frothed and foamed.

After a few minutes the elixir settled, and the color vanished until a clear fluid was left in the glass carafe.

"Is it done?" Killenn leaned in tentatively.

"Let us hope." Rafe pushed a cork stopper into the carafe and handed it and a piece of parchment to him.

"You must throw this into the gateway as you recite the last line of the incantation for the third time. No sooner. No later. Your timing must be precise."

"Precise got it." He placed both items in a small satchel and began to scale the well, finding footings and handholds hidden among the flourishing foliage. When he reached the top, he looked down plotting his descent so not to waste time later. When the elixir ignited, he did not want to be anywhere near the top of the tower for the force would throw him off.

The fairy vines growing at the top were much longer and thicker than the ones climbing the tower at its base. Their proximity to the ancient magic pulsing from the gateway must be increasing their growth rate. Rain still fell from the opening, but it had diminished and was now more of a mist that covered the vines and the surface of the well in a slick golden sheen.

Killenn stepped over the maze of vines until he stood directly under the gateway. It was lower than it was before, and he reached up toward it. The opening throbbed as his energy moved closer. A sudden ripple coursed through the bright surface and a muffled screech sounded on the other side. Before he could react a deathly white hand with long bony fingers and razor-sharp talons breached the gateway and grabbed his wrist knocking the elixir from his grip.

The Keltie wrenched him upward until just his boot toes touched the tower. He struggled against his captor but dangling as he was, he could not reach the clawed hand that held him.

The ancient fae pushed further through the opening its face a blank mask of white. Soon both its shoulders were visible. It pulled back its thin lips revealing a row of pointed teeth dripping with gel-like saliva. A forked tongue protruded from its mouth. The quivering tips extended toward him.

Killenn struggled against the Keltie's grip. Blood ran down his forearm where the talons pierced his skin. He groped for the sheath strapped to his thigh. Grabbing the hilt of the hunting knife he yanked it from the casing and swung it upward. The sharp blade sliced cleanly into the Keltie's arm and it unleashed an ungodly howl. He fell back to the top of the tower in a crumpled heap.

A chorus of whispers surged above him as the Keltie continued to howl in pain. The gateway quaked as more ripples formed and other fae began to push through its surface.

Ghastly white limbs and faces emerged above him.

He searched for the small satchel containing the

elixir and found it lodged between two thick fairy vines. Unwrapping the parchment, he began to recite the incantation.

*Lavasei ma veritete avadei*
*Broco desella faetelle*

Words flowed from his lips and the elixir started to glow. Above him the trio of Keltie fae screamed, their bodies partially emerged from the gateway thrashed angrily. He repeated the spell a second time and the vial spun wildly in his hand. As he invoked the incantation for the third time, he tossed the ampoule into the air watching as it flew straight into the gateway.

Killenn scrambled to get to his feet.

The Kelties stuck halfway out of the gateway reached for him. A talon slashed his forehead as he tried to avoid the outstretched limbs. The force knocked him sideways, and he tripped. He struggled to stay upright but toppled to the ground as his feet ensnared in fairy vines.

Blood poured into his eyes and blurred his vision.

He wiped at it frantically.

*I must get off this tower.*

He sliced at the vines with his knife until he had freed his feet. Rising on unsteady legs he glanced at the gateway. It began to shake as a strange glow erupted behind it sending shards of light flashing across its surface. The opening shuddered and the Kelties were sucked violently back in.

Killenn ran to the edge of the tower and grabbed the end of a long, thick vine. Hoping it was attached to something at the other end, he jumped. Halfway down the side of the tower, the vine caught. The abrupt force swung him aggressively into the side of the tower. Above him, the elixir exploded deep within the Keltie plane. The force of the blast reverberated outward sending him spinning out of control. He clung to the vine as he swung. Unable to control his momentum he slammed into the side of the well again. The unyielding stone connected with his ribs, and he cried out as a sharp pain rifled through his abdomen. He struggled to stay conscious as he continued to spin wildly at the end of the vine.

The sky above rippled with lightning as the gateway expanded. A white spark scorched through the sky and the opening yawned above him. As it reached its apex the funnel of air began to draw everything back toward it sucking him helplessly upward as it contracted, imploding in on itself.

He flailed desperately searching for a handhold as he was dragged toward the collapsing gateway. If he was pulled through before it closed it would collapse around him, and he would cease to exist, so he clung to the end of the fairy vine determined to not let go.

It was his only hope; a tether to this world.

Glaring light flashed around him as the sky shuddered and fractured. The roar of the wind was a deafening noise. He closed his eyes waiting for the inevitable, waiting for *death*.

"Killenn!" He heard his name in the rushing wind as the vortex roared around him and felt a strong hand wrap around his forearm. He opened his eyes to see Rafe's face staring up at him.

"I've got you," he said pulling Killenn toward him and into the uppermost water bowl where he had anchored himself. They huddled together in the heavy metal basin waiting for the sky to quiet.

Moments later the wind calmed, and the brilliance of the gateway diminished until the dark sky of the Oberon Fen swallowed it entirely.

Wincing, Killenn stood. Blood seeped down the side of his face from the gash on his forehead and the pain in his ribs flared when he took a breath.

"How do you feel?"

"I will be fine."

"You don't look fine. I thought you were fast."

Killenn chuckled then gasped as a sharp pain exploded in his side.

"Can you make it to the bottom?"

He nodded.

Carefully they descended stopping a few times so he could catch his breath.

"How did you manage to get to the top of the tower so quickly?" he asked when they had reached the bottom.

Rafe grinned and clasped Killenn on the shoulder. "I can be fast when I want to be."

Killenn returned the gesture thankful that Rafe had saved him from certain death. "I will be forever in your debt, my friend."

He looked at the surging sky of the Oberon Fen. Lightning flashed, scissoring through the darkness followed by the guttural growl of thunder.

"That may not be as long as you think if we are unable to stop what is coming," Rafe said.

"Let us get back to Niramyst. The others are waiting and there is still much to be done."

"We need to tend to your injuries."

"Don't fuss, I will be fine until we reach the elvish city."

Taking one last look at the well glistening with beauty under the churning sky he followed Rafe.

As they trekked toward the city, Killenn thought about the coming days. The situation was dire. Defeating the ancient dark was an almost impossible task even with all the Arcanists powers at the ready, but without Dane, he was unsure of the future. If Adaridge could not find a way to bring her back, their chances diminished significantly, their future bleak, and if that was the case then he prayed death would find each of them quickly.

# CHAPTER 24

KAI AND ELYSE TENDED TO Killenn's wounds. He'd
sustained a bad gash on both his head and
forearm, but it was the broken ribs that gave
them concern. Breathing proved difficult and the bruising around his torso had Elyse worried there may be
more extensive damage internally.

Kai put a cold washcloth on his head as Elyse mixed
up a thick paste. She'd spoken with the tree spirits who
conveyed instructions for an old herbal earth remedy.

"He's in a lot of pain," Kai said. "I hope this works."

Elyse sighed. "Dane would be so much better at this
than me. Earth remedies work better when the herbalist works within their own element."

Sebastian leaned in. "Your ancestors were exceptional warriors but their connection to the tree spirits
gave them a unique perspective on the natural environment. Earth magic is part of you and your herbalist
skills will be enough."

She looked down at the broken body of Killenn and
his eyes fluttered open.

"This may sting a bit."

He nodded, wincing at the movement.

The thick paste was cool under her fingertips as she
slathered it across his abdomen avoiding the tip of the
broken rib protruding from his skin. He grimaced but

didn't say a word, so she continued working until the entire bowl of paste had been transferred to his skin.

Kai put on a clean dressing and stretched a wool blanket over him.

"Sleep," she commanded as they filed out of the room. "You need your rest."

A fire roared in the hearth making the room warm and cozy. Diego lay snoring on the floor in front of it and Drow sat with Stevie on an overstuffed settee in the corner. He rose as Kai, Elyse, and Sebastian entered.

"How is he?" A thickness cloaked his voice.

Elyse took a deep breath. "If the paste does its job and I mixed it correctly he should be healed in about twenty-four hours."

Drow frowned.

"He will be fine in a day and night," Kai offered, recognizing his confusion with the time reference.

A grunt sounded from the shadowy corner of the room drawing their attention.

Marlee's pale blue eyes glowed ferociously in the gloom.

Gabriella stood beside her a small dagger pressed to her neck.

"What about Marlee?" Kai asked.

Drow walked over to where the others stood. "There may be a remedy. Now the Keltie fae are trapped in the plane beyond and the gateway closed their hold on Marlee should weaken. If her birthright can be manipulated to evolve as her ancestors did then there may still be a way for her to become an Athir fae."

Sebastian glanced at Gabriella; his eyes full of worry.

She shrugged. "Old magic might be a drastic measure, but it is probably the only option. The moon is moving through its phases, we need her."

Marlee struggled against her binds and stared at Elyse her eyes full of contempt.

"Why do I get the feeling this is not a solution any of us will like?"

Sebastian glared at Drow before answering plainly uncomfortable with his suggestion.

"Purging is an old-world practice used by the Dragon Gypsies during archaic times when dragons still roamed their realm. It has not been practiced for generations. It was outlawed when Drow's grandfather took the throne."

"Outlawed! Why?"

Sebastian shifted uneasily.

"Purging requires the subject to drink a very strong tonic. It is laced with a poison created from the poppies grown on Kaizi, which have been mixed with a paste made from dragon bones." He hesitated. "It kills more often than it heals."

"We could kill her!" Kai said glancing at Marlee.

"It is a possibility," Drow acknowledged. "But I do not see another way."

"Nor do I," Sebastian hesitantly agreed. "She is too far gone for any other medicinal intervention. Purging will with any luck change her chemistry, and she will evolve into an Athir fae."

Tears welled up in Elyse's eyes as she bent in front of her best friend. "Marlee, I know you're in there. You must fight this and come back to us."

Marlee's blue eyes seared into Elyse, and she struggled harder against her binds. Gabby's blade dug into her skin and a droplet of blood dripped down her throat. Although the gag muffled her response, her words were still understood.

"*Die, elf.*"

Elyse straightened and walked away her shoulders shaking in anguish.

"Take her back to the new world. The magic is too strong here on Athir and it may help the process if her ancestral power is diluted," Drow said. "I will take Stevie to Kaizi to get the ingredients and supplies we need. As the only alchemist, she will need to prepare the tonic."

Stevie paled. "I don't know how."

"You will when the time comes. Your ancestral knowledge is inside you and will surface when needed."

Turning back to Sebastian he said, "I will harvest enough poppies and gather enough vessels to create elixirs for varying uses. We may not know what is to come, but we can be prepared."

The warrior clasped him on the shoulder.

"Be safe. We will see you back in the new world in a few days."

Drow nodded. "I will check on Killenn before I leave."

"I shall come with you," Killenn said struggling to sit up in bed and flinching as he did.

Drow put his hand on his shoulder pushing him gently back down on the bed. "You must heal."

"I can heal on Kaizi, quicker," he argued.

"Maybe, but the journey through the portal would be excruciating with your injuries. Here is where you must stay until you are well enough to travel."

Drow glanced at Stevie who stood by the door.

He leaned closer to his friend and loyal soldier.

"There is nothing to fear on Kaizi so there is no reason for you to worry. I will meet you in two days' time at the Elder Oak in the new world." He thought about Marlee and how severely affected she was by the Keltie's control and added. "The others will need you more than I."

After a few more minutes of arguing Killenn reluctantly agreed to stay behind.

"Will you watch Diego until I return?"

Stevie stroked the Dragonwolf's head.

"Of course. He will be good company."

"You can take care of each other." She bent down and kissed Killenn on the forehead. "Get better."

"Be safe."

Drow put his hand on the small of Stevie's back. "Come, we must leave at once."

"Stay."

Diego whined as she left, but he didn't follow.

"You will see her soon," Killenn said stroking the animal's thick fur as Stevie and Drow disappear down the shadowy hall.

A warm breeze ruffled Drow's long white hair as they exited the elvish fortress. He took Stevie's hand as they walked along the precarious path up the side of the cliff. The portal was in the gazebo at the top situated on an outcropping overlooking the raging river hundreds of feet below.

A waterfall thundered to their left and its spray made the path slippery. Her boot heel slipped on the slick surface and as she fell back Drow caught her. A chill ran through her skin as his arms folded around her—his lips inches from hers. His cabernet eyes bore into her own and for a moment nothing else seemed to exist.

"Are you well?" he asked breaking the tension.

"I think so," she answered breathlessly removing herself from his embrace with a small smile. "Thank you."

He bowed slightly, and she noticed amusement filling his dark red eyes.

As she turned away and began to trudge up the remainder of the path she wondered if Drow felt the same sparks she did when they were close.

A quiet moan from behind told her he probably did.

# CHAPTER 25

THEY EMERGED FROM THE PORTAL into the courtyard behind the citadel. The bright red sky
swirled above them and the black metal of the
structure glistened.

A warm wind blew haughtily through the revived
lands carrying with it the scent of poppies. The day
was waning, but they still had enough time to harvest
the crops before the sky darkened.

They moved without hesitation through the back
gate and followed the ash path to the fields. A small
metal hut came into view and Drow gestured toward it.

"We will find the vials and equipment we need in
there," he said. Pulling the metal doors open, they entered the hut. Shelves lined the inside walls, and he
handed her a canvas sack and motioned toward the far
wall.

"Fill this with as many vessels as possible. You will
also need cauldrons, pestles, and mortars and anything else you think may help."

"Will it help?"

Drow looked at her his concern deepening. "We are
not just fighting the ancient dark anymore but also a
legion of daemons that will be born from those pods.
It is a first wave threat requiring much more than just
a small group of warriors equipped with ancient magic

and swords to stop it. We got lucky in the Dead Lands when the swarm of daemons emerged from the dark caverns, but luck will not see us through this time. To get an upper hand in the battle we need more and the elixirs you craft might just be it."

He walked to the opposite side of the hut where razor-sharp machetes, scythes, and sickles hung from metal hooks. Grabbing one of the larger sickles he picked up a metal bucket from the floor.

"I will harvest the poppies. I won't be too long."

As he headed to the door Stevie grasped his arm. "Be careful."

He stiffened under her touch. "There is nothing to fear here. I will be fine." He leaned nearer. "But I will honor your request."

They stood for a moment their heads close gazing into the other's eyes. The energy in the small hut intensified and Drow lifted his free hand brushing a stray hair from her cheek.

"I will be back soon."

Stevie gazed after him until he disappeared into the dense poppy fields.

To calm the magic burning inside she inhaled a cleansing breath. Her feelings for him had become very clear. She was attracted to him in a way she hadn't been to anyone before. It wasn't just a physical desire her heart ached when he was near. It was an unfamiliar sensation but one that felt right.

The lush poppy fields swayed in the breeze their potent fragrance drifted with it. This is where she needed to be—with him. The realization made her smile as she gathered the tools she required.

Whatever the future held, good or bad, she would face it with Drow by her side.

It took Drow less than an hour to harvest the poppies and another hour to separate the velvet petals from the crown, pods, and seeds.

"What do you call them?" Stevie indicated the huge velvety poppies scattered across the metal table.

"Besides poppies?" His brow lifted as the edge of his mouth twitched. "Dragon Gypsies do not give frivolous names to insentient objects."

Stevie frowned. Holding a poppy up to the fading light her eyes narrowed as she studied the velvety petals that shimmered with orange, yellow, and red fragments.

"I shall call it the Fire Poppy," she exclaimed.

Drow shook his head, a slight smile coming over his face as he mused her excitement. "Then it shall be so named."

"Is that a royal decree?" she joked.

He bowed his head his eyes never leaving hers. "It is if you wish it to be."

Stevie's heart pounded as their magic essence mingled heating up the small metal hut. "We should finish up. It's getting late."

The sky had turned a dark shade of bloodred so Drow agreed. "We shall take the portal back to earth in the morning. Tonight, let us stay here and get some much-needed rest."

He led her through the courtyard and into the citadel.

After a quick meal, she followed Drow to a part of the citadel she hadn't seen during her previous time here. These quarters were set off from the other floors and accessible by a gated elevator, hidden behind a bookshelf in the citadel's library.

The elevator opened to a small platform where a winding metal staircase led up to the royal quarters. At the top was an open living space full of opulent black metal furniture, deep rich fabrics, and walls lined with leather-clad books. Behind an enormous iron desk and throne-like chair, tall arched windows overlooked the poppy fields.

Drow led her toward the back of the room where two ornate iron doors opened into the bedroom. Through the intricate metal scrolling, the circular room beyond could be seen. As they entered Drow flicked his hand and one after the other candles ignited flooding the room in an amber-hued light.

Stevie gazed at the chamber impressed by its grandiosity.

Small metal tiles covered the walls and hundreds of candles sat on metal shelves around the room. A huge bed covered in black silk linens sat on a raised platform. The headboard, like the entry doors, was made of ornate iron. Thick red velvet weaved around the iron giving the bed a regalness. Long, red velvet drapes cascaded from the ceiling on either side of the patio door. Stepping out on the quaint terrace she was surprised by the view. From here she could see for miles even as night fell. The fiery moon ignited the land in a reddish glow a perfect backdrop for the dark silhouette of the volcano in the distance, orange lava flowing down its sides.

Drow moved in behind her and she quivered.

"Your realm is stunning," she said trying to ignore the electricity that ignited between them.

"It is your realm as well."

Stevie smiled. She supposed that was true.

They stood in silence undeniable energy swirling around them—a sexual tension difficult to ignore. The distant crackle of the flowing lava and the scent of the poppies did nothing to assuage the heady atmosphere wrapping around them.

"I will retire now," Drow said. His voice broke as he spoke, and he clenched his fists as he turned away from her. "If you need anything I will be in the servant's quarters to the left of the library."

*He's such a gentleman.*

"Drow," she purred taking a few steps toward him.

He turned and his deep red eyes locked on hers.

She reached out pulling his face down to hers and kissed him.

A wave of heat rolled through her as their tongues entwined, and he pulled her body closer. She groaned as the kiss deepened and a flaring passion pulsed needy between them.

Breaking the embrace, she pulled him toward the bed without a word.

He studied her face with mild amusement as she undressed him. Her hands explored his pale, hairless chest. Her fingers traced the line of his collarbone, and he groaned under her touch but remained still allowing her to lead their encounter.

She pulled off her own clothes and stood naked next to him, the heat in their skin intensifying wherever it touched the others.

"Take me," she murmured in his ear.

The command was all he needed.

He grasped her buttocks and picked her up. Her legs straddled his waist. The cold metal of the tiles felt good against her back as he pushed her against the wall. Heat flared between them, and she groaned as he entered her. As she moved in unison with him, she wrapped her arms around his shoulders and tangled her fingers in his long hair. Her skin was on fire and her sweat mixed with his. A pungent odor of ash wafted around them. Surging heat rose inside her and she tightened around him as a wave of passion rolled through her. He throbbed in response.

She kissed him hungrily her need for him addicting.

Pulling her from the wall he carried her to the bed and climbed in beside her. This time he never took his lustful eyes from hers bringing her expertly to another explosive end.

Sated, she lay in his arms.

His fingers caressed her skin as the heat from their lovemaking wafted through the room. Her body hummed with satisfaction, and she began to drift off into an exhausted sleep.

Drow's lips moved to her shoulder, tenderly kissing her skin.

For the first time since she initiated their passionate encounter he spoke.

"Sleep, my love."

# CHAPTER 26

TWO DAYS HAD PASSED SINCE Stevie and Drow left for Kaizi. Killenn was almost healed, Marlee had calmed and no longer wanted to slit Elyse's throat, and Brannon and Tauria had left for Dywen to retrieve the weapons from the barrack's armory.

Kai had offered to do the same but the weapons in Viccinius were useless to all but her. Apparently, according to Sebastian, mermaids preferred water warfare as in the ocean they were their most indomitable. Forged to slice through the water at incredible speeds the blades became light and buoyant when submerged without losing their strength. Although usable on land, the blades became weighty and awkward to handle by anyone not governed by the water element, lessening the wielder's swiftness and effectiveness.

She had her blades so if the ones remaining on Viccinius were of no use then she would endeavor to find something else to occupy her time.

Since entering the Thanissia Universe, Kai had been keeping a calendar. As she flipped through it, she tapped the end of her pen against the paper and then scribbled some numbers in the corner.

"If Dane's calculation of time between Thanissia and Earth is correct we only have five days until the full moon."

"Then I suggest we return to your world. Two days

have passed, and the others are sure to be doing the same," Sebastian said.

Brannon and Tauria waited in the clearing when they emerged, three sizable black duffel sacs filled with weapons lay at their feet.

"Tauria enchanted most of them," Brannon said proudly. "They will recognize magical blood, new or ancient. The blades of the swords will not break nor dull and I honed them on a whetstone, so the edges will slice through bone. The arrows too will find their mark and can be effortlessly retrieved with a simple command."

"Good." Sebastian pulled at his goatee. "We hope the witches of this world will come bearing battle magic and weapons but if not, those will suffice."

"And you look better than when we last saw you," said Brannon addressing Killenn who was tying Marlee to one of the trees near the clearing's entrance.

He shrugged. "Elyse's earth magic is commendable. My ribs have healed, and the bruising is fading. Now if I can just get your friend to hold his tongue about saving my life."

Rafe grinned. "Just a little ribbing until yours healed."

Killenn groaned and shook his head. "I have no idea how you put up with him, for centuries no less."

Brannon shrugged. "He grows on you."

"Like an ancient fungus."

The three warriors laughed.

Sebastian observed the younger warriors as they casually interacted. An easy comradery had formed between them as the events of the past months drew them closer. They had each other's backs, a brotherhood born from old customs and new beginnings. He had enjoyed the same friendship with Claaven, and it was something he would always miss.

"The portal," Elyse said and pointed to the Elder Oak.

Cracks in the bark began to glow with a faint red light. Diego barked and circled the tree. The light moved up and down the trunk until a spiral of liquid fell from a gnarled branch and spun idly on the ground. Embers and lava churned upward forming a fiery red portal from Kaizi.

Drow emerged first with Stevie a few steps behind.

He smiled when he saw Killenn. "You are well."

It was a statement of relief more than a question, but the warrior nodded anyway. "I am very well."

They hugged until Killenn pulled away. His brow crumpling as he took a step back and gazed at his old friend. Leaning to the right he looked at Stevie who raised a brow in question.

He straightened trying to stifle a grin. "You have spent your time in Kaizi well."

Drow's face remained passive as he ignored the warrior's inference. "The poppy fields are in full bloom. We managed to harvest enough to make the potions and elixirs we require. Stevie has already started."

He raised a tote and glass tinkled inside.

"This is good news," Sebastian said pulling Killenn aside as the others greeted each other and discussed plans.

He grinned. "You observed it as well."

"What?"

"The change in Drow's aura."

"Because of Stevie, yes."

"I am happy for him. Drow has been so lost and

lonely since the Great War, it is good to see him open his heart again."

"I just hope it does not influence his decisions during the battle." He glanced at Rafe as he said those words.

"You know the royal diplomat, not the fierce Velkia warrior. Trust me when I say Drow will do what he must, to end the ancient dark's rise at all costs. And so will Rafe."

Sebastian clasped the warrior's forearm and then walked back to the middle of the clearing gathering everyone's attention. "Kai confirmed the date on her speaking device." He indicated the cell phone she held in her hand. "It is the morn of the nineteenth and almost daybreak. We have five days until the full moon rises."

Rafe interjected. "We need somewhere to go. A safe place to make our plans,"

"I have a key to Dane's but it's possible Lucien might too." Kai shifted uncomfortably avoiding Rafe's gaze.

"I think Stevie's is the obvious choice," said Gabriella. "It is quiet, private, and close to the old mill, no one should come looking for us there."

"Gabby it's your place as well."

Gabriella lowered her head at Stevie's words.

"The sun will be rising soon. Let us make haste while we still have the cover of darkness," Sebastian said gathering up some bags.

"What of the portal?" Rafe indicated the gnarled Elder Oak. "We must protect Thanissia."

"Agreed. I will lock the portal to the Five Realms, but I am afraid if the night does not go as we hope the ancient dark will find a way through."

Placing his palm against the tree's trunk he murmured an incantation. The white light swirling under the bark dimmed and went dark. The leaves stopped rustling and the Elder Oak quieted.

"It is done."

As the others gathered the remaining satchels and loosened Marlee's binds, Rafe pulled Sebastian and Gabriella aside. "Can you feel her for I cannot?"

"No. Maybe she is not in Brighton Hill yet," said Gabriella. "I will contact Celeste and Nathan when we get back to Stevie's, see what they know. She may still be in the city."

Rafe's shoulders slumped. "I should still be able to feel her and so should you."

Sebastian knew he was right. After the final Druidstone in Athir was reignited, the elemental flow of magic throughout the Thanissia Universe had intensified. As an extension of the ancient realms, a modicum of that power had infused the earth. While the magic here would never rival that of Thanissia, there should be enough to heighten both their senses.

He turned his pale green eyes to Rafe, his voice barely a whisper. "You must be willing to accept the possibility that she is unreachable. That the darkness has taken hold."

Rafe shook his head. "Dane is strong, stronger than many of us. I will not accept that darkness is her true destiny. It must not be for that would mean all we believe and everything we will fight and possibly die for, will be for nothing."

"Then let us hope she finds that inner strength promptly. But if not remember the words Seri left for you."

Rafe's eyes sparked but he nodded anyway.

Sebastian had known Rafe for a very long time and knew how difficult this was for him. It was not in his nature to do nothing. He was a warrior. His vow to The Warlician Order meant laying down his own life in protection of others. Being bound to Dane would intensify those instincts tremendously, yet he may have to defy them in order to save her.

He thought about Seri and Claaven—history must not repeat.

Only Dane can save herself.

As Adaridge said, *Dane must find the light within and conquer the darkness alone.*

# CHAPTER 27

LUCIEN STARED AT THE SLEEPING form of Dane.
His sexual energy swirled around him as his body ignited in desire for the witch. Never had he wanted anyone more or to possess someone so completely. But his unabated desires would have to wait. For now, he required her rage, not her passion. Diluting the anger simmering inside her so that he could fulfill his own innate sexual needs was both selfish and detrimental.

Absently, he rubbed the bulge in his jeans. In five days, he will have her. He'll take her in his bed and stoke the fires of desire until she's a wanton seductress, *his queen*. Sex and power, they'll be consumed by it and together they will rule a world of dark magic. In the meantime, he must find a release—the incubus must be sated.

He turned out the lights and left her sleeping in a dreamscape of his making. Her dreams were dark, violent images feeding the anger and torment. He needed to cleanse her of the good, of the light, so she would not just embrace the darkness but become it. Only then would Dane be wrath and be able to free the beast from its magical confines.

Same as the last few nights he went to the bars in search of sexual prey. He might not be able to have Dane but in the interim, his natural instincts wouldn't allow him celibacy. He'd feed his needs with faceless women until the time came when he could complete his sexual possession of his queen.

The bar was dimly lit when Lucien entered. The interior was thick with the smell of stale beer, cigarettes, and sweat. It was after midnight and a few patrons were left inside, two men playing pool and one at the bar his head on his arm. His eyes scanned the room. The lone female in the place was the bartender, a waif of a girl with hair dyed blue, tattoos, and a nose ring.

She would have to do.

Walking to the bar he caught the girl's eye.

"What can I get you?" she asked leaning over the bar top, her hand resting next to his.

He smiled and ran his fingers over the back of her hand and up the tattooed skin of her arm. His gaze never wavered as he enticed her into a state of acceptance. When the familiar glaze clouded her eyes, he backed away from the bar and without saying a word walked to the bathroom, knowing she would follow.

The moment she walked into the bathroom, he grabbed her and locked the door. Bending her over the sink, he pulled up her short jean skirt and ripped the thin thread of fabric underneath. Undoing the zipper on his jeans with one hand, he held her small body with the other. He pushed himself inside her caring nothing for the flesh he invaded just the release that it would offer. As he thrust himself deeper, he caught sight of himself in the stained dirty mirror. His eyes glowed a bright, fiery red. Small beads of sweat covered his brow, and his muscles rippled under his shirt with each incensed thrust. He wrapped his fingers into her long blue tresses pulling her head back. A satisfied smile played on her lips as she moaned out her pleasure. He sneered at the sight thinking instead of

Dane as he emptied himself inside her. This girl paled in comparison. Disgusted, he removed himself and pulled up his jeans uttering something in her ear. In a few moments, she would remember none of this.

He unlocked the door and walked back through the smoke-filled bar. No one even looked his way as he headed out into the night.

*Weak humans,* he thought. *They don't deserve the power they're about to behold.*

A smile crept over his lips as he walked through the shadows.

The Tierney name would once again be his. He would rule over these worthless humans, a Callathian by his side. Soon he would have his revenge. He would condemn this world to hell and destroy the ancient realms forever.

Fitfully she tossed and turned as her mind careened through a world of hate, prejudice, greed, lies, and deceit. Dark and disturbing dreams haunted her. People were tribal. They didn't care about one another. Humans were programmed to fail, fail in humanity, in empathy, in kindness. There would always be wars, murders, crimes against one another. In the end, they would destroy themselves and this planet. They didn't deserve to be saved for they would neither appreciate it nor change.

Her eyelids flickered as another image exploded in her mind. This time it was of the future. A future where mankind was no longer free, and the world was ruled by those who could wield the magic once again vibrant in this world. It was a place of order. A hierarchy that diminished the need for wealth, power, stature, and greed. Those with magic ruled at the top and those without existed to serve.

Over and over the dreams pummeled these ideas into her mind and slowly she began to acquiesce to the idea that mankind needed the prophecy to fail.

Alistair stood in an alleyway hidden behind a dumpster. He was invisible, just another nameless, faceless, derelict in a large city. Yellow eyes glowed in the dark as they searched the skyscraper across the street his senses pulling his gaze to the top.

*There.*

A corner office drew his attention. The windows were dark, but he knew the man would return.

This is where he felt safe and powerful.

He was patient, he would wait.

It'd taken Alistair awhile, but he was able to track the magic used to incapacitate Ella Watts to an unlicensed alchemist hidden in the sewers of New York City. It was quite easy to extract information from him once he realized the Syndicate did not follow the same rules as the Coven. The alchemist had confirmed his suspicions. Two elixirs were used, one to immobilize and one to sedate. Ella Watts was effectively put into an anesthetic comma before she was eviscerated— thankfully she felt nothing.

It took the alchemist a little longer to reveal who ordered the hit. But after Alistair adjusted his persuasion tactics, he revealed everything. The witch who hired him was hired by another, a man of importance. He received instructions to mix the elixirs in accordance with specific recipes, but the formulas were unusual, and some ingredients had been difficult to find.

What interested Alistair was one of the elixirs was a delicate concoction that wouldn't taint the blood it was injected into. Further, the alchemist had been instructed to hire a magical engineer to design a vessel that could carry a liquid warmed to a specific temperature, and then he was to leave the city never to return.

Fortunately for Alistair, although the witch was a talented alchemist, he was terrible at vanishing.

He had helped him with his shortcomings.

No one would ever see the alchemist again.

His gaze drifted back to the entrance of the building. It was late, but a strange quiet hung over the city. He moved to the edge of the alleyway making sure he kept to the shadows.

Tugging at his hood he pulled it further over his face.

A dark figure approached from the left, and he shrunk back into the darkness. He scrutinized the figure as it entered the building. Minutes later the lights in the corner office illuminated.

Alistair smiled.

*Lucien Beck was back.*

# CHAPTER 28

D AWN BROKE OVER THE HORIZON as Nathan reached the city.

Alistair had resurfaced yesterday and had information, but he refused to discuss anything without Celeste being present. He stressed the importance of a representative of the Coven bearing witness. Nathan had agreed, but something in Alistair's voice made it seem like he wanted Celeste there for a different reason.

He pulled his car into the garage and took the service elevator up to the top using his private key. A hidden door in the back of the elevator opened, allowing him access to the floor reserved for large meetings of the Coven and Syndicate members.

Alistair and Celeste were already in the conference room when he entered.

"Coffee?" Celeste said holding up the pot.

Nathan nodded. "Please."

Alistair hovered in the corner looking uncomfortable.

"It's good to have you back Alistair."

He hadn't seen him since the night of Ella's death. When Alistair hunts, he disappears, only in contact with Nathan or other members of the Syndicate if necessary. Being part daemon, he's become comfortable with solitude even craves it. In a world of magic, Alistair is an outcast.

There are few daemons living above the surface, most choosing to exist below in the realms of the underworld where they'd once been vanquished. A handful of daemons, mostly half-breeds, have assimilated into the magical community but it doesn't make them any less ostracized. Prejudice has a way of weaving its way into the fabric of all societies. Although accepted by the Syndicate and the Coven, Alistair still lives under the stigma his kind evokes, so when he gets the chance to hunt, he does so alone.

He moved toward Nathan. "It's good to see you as well."

His golden eyes flicked to Celeste who nodded.

Sighing he continued. "I found the alchemist who mixed the potions used on your wife, Nathan."

He paused waiting for a reaction, but Nathan kept his expression neutral. "And did he give you any information?"

Alistair turned away subconsciously rubbing his left hand. "More than he would have liked."

"I assume by your tone the alchemist will no longer be breaking the rules of the Coven then." Consequences were harsh and swift when a magical being broke the rules especially if they caused the death of another.

Alistair turned back toward Nathan. "He is no longer a problem. But the one who hired him still is."

Nathan flinched. "Hired him?"

Celeste intervened, her tone soft and caring. "Nathan, Ella was murdered for a very specific reason and the person chose her specifically for what she possessed—a unique item."

"Which is?" Nathan tensed, his jaw rigid.

"Her blood."

Nathan leaned on the conference table as a wave of nausea rushed through him. Sweat beaded on his upper lip, and he rubbed it away with the back of a shaking hand. "He needed a healer's blood."

"Yes."

There was only one reason anyone required a healer's blood—*a blood pact.* Nathan raised his head, his green eyes full of fury. "It was Lucien Beck, wasn't it?"

Alistair shifted his weight but the sorrow in his eyes confirmed Nathan's question.

"Why?" he whispered.

"He required her blood to perform a ritual that enabled him to control the ancient dark. It is an ancient ritual and one that uses dark magic. Without a healer's blood, his soul would have been consumed swiftly. Your wife's blood keeps Lucien Beck on the side of the living, so to speak."

"But why kill her? He could have taken her blood and left her alive."

Celeste glanced at Alistair before speaking. "He required a power source. An emotion so dark it would control the beast. He needed *wrath.* Pushing Dane toward the darkness through anger would consume her and her powers. Ella's death enabled him to get the blood he required and the wrath."

"So, my wife was a sacrifice to enable Lucien Beck to gain control of an ancient evil being. To what end?"

"We believe Lucien wants to bring magic back to this world. Not the way it is now. He no longer wants magical beings to operate within the shadows and tunnels of the city, he wants magic to rule the world."

"And Dane? Is she to be a sacrifice as well?"

Alistair shook his head. "He cannot do this without her. Because of the blood pact, he will forever be connected to the ancient dark. We believe he needs more than your wife's blood to keep him alive he needs the one that can destroy both he and the beast. Killing Dane would mean he would no longer be safe from purgatory."

Nathan Callan ran his hand through his hair as his voice rose. "How do we stop this madman?"

"I'm sorry Nathan, I'm not sure we can. The blood pact has given him the ability to walk on both sides of the veil. We can't kill him, nor can we severe his control over Dane. As a glamour witch, he is formidable, but the transformation to incubus and the power he gained from the blood bond has made him too strong. He's virtually invincible. There's no known magic that can break the pact."

Celeste walked toward him and put her hand lightly on his forearm. "Don't fret yet Nathan. Your daughter is strong, and there is still hope. I gave the celestial my amulet. It can block Lucien's control over her if they can find a way to get it on her person. If anyone can figure this, it's those who've come from another time to help us. Let's not give up yet."

Nathan stood. "You're correct, Celeste. Dane is strong and not easily manipulated and Gabriella is just as determined. If there's a way, she will find it. Where is Lucien Beck now?"

Alistair's raised a brow. "The incubus came home right before dawn. An hour later he left with Dane. They left the city; I believe they're heading to Brighton Hill."

Celeste nodded and clasped her hands together. "Good, then let us begin our own preparations to do the same. We need to be in Brighton Hill in two days to meet with the others. If Lucien thinks he'll be facing only the chosen few on the eve of the twenty-third, he is mistaken. Whatever comes that night it comes to all of us."

Alistair's yellow eyes flashed. "How many do you have?"

"Over a hundred witches, most with physical powers."

He grinned. "It sounds like we will give the incubus and the ancient dark an unexpected welcome indeed."

The daemon grasped Nathan's hands. "For Ella."

# CHAPTER 29

**"I**T'S GETTING LOUDER," KAI SAID to Sebastian, who nodded in confirmation.

Stevie sighed. She was speaking of the shadow of separation, the mystical clock marking their destinies and counting down to a time when a fateful choice must be made. It had been heard intermittently since their return to earth but had grown in intensity since their arrival at her house.

"The time is drawing near when each of you must make a choice. One that will reveal your true destiny and the path to which you will take."

"How will we know what choice to make when the time comes?"

"The shadow of separation is part of you. The decision will be instinctive and most likely not conscious. You will probably not understand that a choice you make will be the one which changes the direction your destiny takes. It may be a choice that simply affects another or one that reaps a far greater result. Fate is a singular entity. Each of your decisions will be as well."

"Not helpful."

Sebastian placed a hand on her shoulder. "Trust in who you are, Kai and the knowledge obtained from your ancestors. If you do the decisions you make, no matter the consequences, are the correct ones. Even small subtle decisions can have an enormous impact. Your destiny is always in your control if you trust in yourself."

The tick-tock of the clock faded, suffocated by the fog descending on this rainy morning.

The cell phone in Stevie's hand buzzed. "Mr. Callan just texted. Lucien Beck has left the city. They believe he's coming here."

"Then it's time to pay him a little visit," Kai said.

Stevie agreed. "Let's deal with the Marlee situation first, and then we can focus on Lucien and Dane."

Drow walked in, a big black satchel across his shoulders. He'd changed from his velvet coats and ruffled shirts into a plain black tunic and pants. His white hair and deep red eyes were vibrant against the dark color of his clothing.

Stevie's stomach fluttered and she smiled to herself. For once, she wasn't afraid of her feelings and no longer wanted to run from them. *I love him,* she thought as he walked over and placed the bag on the kitchen counter.

He kissed the top of her head. "Ready?"

She blushed.

Kai grabbed Sebastian by the arm. "We will leave you to it." She dragged the elder warrior from the kitchen. "Yell if you need anything."

"They are intimate," Sebastian said when they reached the far end of the living room. It wasn't a question but a curious observation.

Kai chuckled. "Apparently destiny has a unique way of moving through time and space."

His brow raised as he smiled. "That it does."

It had taken a few hours for Stevie and Drow to concoct the ancient elixir that when administered would hopefully rid Marlee of the Keltie fae's control. It required three of them to hold her down and force her to swallow the liquid.

They stood at the far side of the bedroom as she writhed on the bed, tugging at her binds. Her blue eyes sparked with fury as she hissed and spat in their direction.

"How long before the elixir begins to work?" Elyse asked.

Drow's shoulders sagged. "It should have taken effect by now."

He looked at Killenn who shrugged. "Maybe she requires a stronger dose."

"If we give her more, it may kill her. She might be gifted with immortality, but she was born a mortal. We have no way of knowing how much she can handle without risking dire consequences."

He turned back to the fae who stopped struggling and shot him a penetrating stare. Tilting her head, she began to speak in tongue. Drow recognized it immediately—the language of the royals and a language only his kin spoke. His body tensed as her eyes and words burned into his very soul.

Stevie grasped his hand. "You understood her, didn't you? What did she say?"

He hesitated, his eyes never leaving Marlee's. "She said the world would burn with a new fire and the flame of the Dragon Gypsy would forever be extinguished."

Unexpectedly, a screech exploded through the room as Marlee began to thrash on the bed. A thick white foam appeared on her lips as it dripped from her screaming mouth. Her eyes bulged in their sockets and blue veins appeared bright against her pale skin.

"It has begun," Killenn acknowledged, moving to the side of the bed to help Rafe ensure her restraints would hold.

Marlee struggled, her body riddled with agony as the poison tortured her being. She pulled at the bindings holding her wrists and ankles trying to free herself. Her body drenched in sweat convulsed as the ancient elixir flowed through her veins. And as the fever rose her face blotched with an angry red rash contorted, and she screamed in rage and pain.

Elyse stood horrified in the corner of the room.

"Let's get her out of here," Stevie said to Kai.

They took their friend by the arm. "There is no reason for us to be in here. Drow will come and get us if anything happens."

Tears sparkled in Elyse's eyes. "What if she dies?"

"She won't," Kai said firmly. "She can't."

Drow sighed as they led Elyse down the hallway toward the kitchen trying their best to distract her from the screams echoing from the bedroom.

A few hours later the house finally became quiet.

Drow leaned toward Sebastian his voice low. "If she makes it through the night, she should be fine."

Sebastian's green eyes flickered as he watched the fae sleep.

Marlee was deathly pale and covered in a shimmering sheen of sweat. Her eyes flicked back and forth under her closed lids and her hands twitched as if she were caught in a dream.

"There is nothing more we can do for her, it's up to fate now. We must focus on what we can control," Drow said.

Sebastian closed the bedroom door softly. "You are

correct. Elyse can check on her throughout the night. We have further business which requires our attention."

They found the others in the kitchen.

Stevie was washing the dishes. "How is she?" Worry etched her forehead and her hands shook as she placed the plate in the drying rack.

Drow's voice softened. "You did well. The elixir calmed her mind. She is resting. Time will tell if it will banish the Keltie instincts and revert them to the more disciplined and mischievous traits of the Athir fae."

She glanced at Kai who reached out and squeezed her hand. "It will work. We can't lose another friend."

Sebastian intervened. "Marlee will be in good hands with Elyse, but we have other matters to attend. This day is far from over."

As the warriors planned their next move Gabriella pulled Kai and Stevie aside.

"You must find a way to get this substance into Dane," she said handing them a vial that flickered with purple iridescent light. "She must consume it so a part of the All Souls is within her." Gabby's voice was firm. "If you don't, she will be unable to release herself from Lucien's control. She will succumb to the darkest part within, and we will have lost her."

Stevie grabbed the vial from Gabby's hand. "I'll find a way."

"Lucien must not suspect anything."

"He won't," Kai said grinning at Stevie. "Let's go. We don't want to keep the incubus waiting."

# CHAPTER 30

L UCIEN PULLED HER CLOSE. THREE days remained until the full moon and Dane's transformation would be complete. He hadn't had a sexual release in days and would be glad when he could take her as his own. Being near her made him constantly aroused and it had become increasingly difficult not to surrender to his needs and desire for her.

The glistening light once so vibrant in her irises had faded. The darkness was taking her. He kissed her passionately his tongue parting her lips. She responded in kind, her body arching toward him as she ran her fingers through his hair. Pushing her away he released her from his embrace. Dane resisted at first but then as his powers dictated, she moved away.

*Only three more days.*

Although he had Dane completely under his control, he had to ensure one more thing. He'd learned a lot about her recently and although he was able to fester the darkness within, he still needed to deal with her innate desire to protect those she loved. Now he needed to curb her instinct to fight evil and mold it into a more targeted response. As well as getting her to accept magic and darkness as the new world order.

Although he couldn't make her forget the others, he could make her think they were in danger if the prophecy comes to pass. He needed her to be firm in her commitment to him and his desires. When the beast rose, he had to be confident she would submit and allow his version of the prophecy to play out.

He lifted her chin.

Her green eyes grew dim a dark emerald replaced the brilliant shimmering jade. The color churned like an angry sea.

Lucien smiled. "I have something to show you."

Dane's reaction remained flat, her apathetic attitude part of the process. Although necessary, he longed for the day when her passion would reign, and she would be hellfire. His body twitched at the notion. He continuously fought every natural and magical instinct he had as both a glamour witch and an incubus when she was near. Sometimes it was torturous. He would be glad for the day when he no longer needed to seek out others for pleasure.

"Dane, it's essential you understand why we are doing this and why the prophecy as foretold is incorrect. There is no way for you and the others to defeat the beast and to save this world. This world has become toxic: the wars, the hate, the killings. Mortals are without guidance or direction. They need to be contained or there will be nothing left but ashes and ruin. What is coming is a much-needed cleansing."

Her reaction remained indifferent.

"What I'm going to show you, will be the state of the world, if we don't intervene and change the prophecy."

He took her hand in his.

"Don't be afraid of what you'll see. It's a mere flicker of the future. It will feel real, but it isn't. Not yet."

Lucien closed his eyes and let the ancient magic stir. He could feel the energy of the beast inside him, building. Fighting to control the power he allowed images to flash through his mind, rapidly at first, and then like a film projector it slowed each frame capturing a fragment in time. A future that hadn't yet come to pass.

He focused his energy allowing the images to transfer through his incubus seduction powers and into Dane. He could feel her tense as the pictures moved through her mind connecting to one another and submerging her within.

Silence pressed down as a thick mist, enshrouded her. The scent of wet earth hung heavy in the air hiding the foul odor caught in its wisps. It clouded her vision, but her other senses intensified instinctively.

Suddenly, the silence broke and a strange wind whistled by. On its wisps, the scent of smoke and ash drifted.

Dane groped into the dense fog her fingers clawing at nothing. A crackling noise drew her attention and as she walked toward it the toe of her boot hit something solid, and she flailed regaining her balance before she tripped. The mist began to dissipate, and images appeared around her as her surroundings were revealed.

She stood at the center of town. But nothing about Brighton Hill looked familiar.

The town had been destroyed. Fires crackled and charred buildings burned. Smoke wafted upward darkening the blue sky. All around her lay ruination and death. A decaying odor soaked the air as it rose from the bodies littering the streets. Some stared vacantly through dead eyes while others had no eyes at all just empty bloody sockets where they used to be.

Rivers of blood ran into the gutters.

A wave of panic surged within her as she searched

the sea of bodies. Her eyes flitted from one face to another until she found them—her friends.

At the top of a pyre with her hands bound to a stake hung Gabby. Her wings were broken, and a sword pierced her heart. Kai's lifeless body, bloody and bruised was being dragged down the street by a withered daemon. Stevie lay face down in the gutter her arm outstretched and her fingers reaching toward the eviscerated body of Drow who lay a few feet away.

Dane's head began to fill with a visceral roar as her eyes found the others—*all dead.*

In the back of her mind she heard it laugh; an ancient death rattle. It goaded her. A prickle crept over her skin as a raspy voice surfaced in her head.

*Behind you.*

Nausea bloomed in her stomach as she turned.

More mutilation and death stretched in front of her, but she forced herself to search the devastation until she found it.

Standing at the end of the street mere yards away stood the beast. Its head was fire, the dark horns twisted and glistening with blood. Its eyes were blazing yellow slits. No longer the smoky entity of old it had transformed into the daemon of nightmares—a devil designed by human imagination. Its body was a hulking mass of withered skin, exposed bone, and raw flesh. It wore nothing but a black hooded cape, tattered and torn and draped casually over its shoulders. Underneath, its naked, genderless body bulged with muscles and sinewy veins. Hairy legs ended in thick black hooves. The beast was hideous and terrifying but what it held in its thick, clawed hands drew her horrified attention—*Rafe.*

The ancient dark had Rafe's long hair clutched in its talons. His exposed throat had the blade of a curved ax pressed against it and his broken body hung limp in the beast's clutch. His green eyes were hardly visible through the blood pouring from a gash in his head, but he was alive!

She moved a few feet closer, closing the gap.

The ancient dark roared and pressed its blade deeper into Rafe's skin.

*Do you want him?* The raspy voice in her head asked.

She nodded. As she looked at Rafe's battered face, her heart thumped painfully in her chest.

*Then he is yours.*

The beast pushed Rafe's body toward her, releasing him. He teetered on his feet too weak to support himself. Through the blood, his bright green irises filled with sadness.

*I'm sorry,* he mouthed closing his eyes.

*No!* She screamed as she began to run toward him.

Her mind roared with anger and fear as she lunged, but every step seemed to push her further away from him.

As if in a dream she could only watch helplessly as the beast, with a speed unworthy of its size, swung its ax outward. The blade hit its mark expertly and sliced Rafe's head from his body in one clean motion. His body toppled to the ground, but his head continued its forward momentum, rolling until it landed at Dane's feet.

A horrified scream bubbled up inside her. A cry filled with rage, terror, and grief echoed through the demolished town as she sank to her knees, defeated.

Lucien was right. There was no way to win and no way to survive. Their fate wasn't to defeat the ancient dark, nor was it to destroy mankind. They were neither savior nor destroyer—they were *nothing*.

Tears streamed down her face as the ancient dark turned and walk away dragging its blood-soaked ax behind. Its rattling laughter filled the air as the smoke from the fires billowed and it disappeared behind the murky tendrils.

They couldn't defeat it.

The prophecy was wrong.

Their world would suffer the same fate as the Five Realms. Mankind would be enslaved, and a new world would emerge.

*A world of dark magic, torture, suffering, and death.*

The world around her began to fade as Lucien pulled her back to the present. She gasped as something inside her broke. The light giving way to the dark. She knew now what she had to do, she needed to survive to ensure they all did.

Lucien held her in his arms for a long time afterward. Showing her the death of all she loved was the final push she needed.

"Do you understand?" he whispered. "There is no other way. If you go against the beast, he will destroy all you love. He will kill every one of them and their deaths will have no meaning. But we can save them, I promise. You just need to do as I say."

She looked into his eyes and nodded obediently.

The dark green of her irises disappeared replaced by an inky black as darkness snuffed out the last remnants of light inside her.

Dane had finally broken.

He kissed her, his lips softly brushing hers.

Soon his queen will emerge, the only one who can keep the beast at bay. The blood pact he made gave him immortality and power, but it also made him vulnerable. She would be his savior. With Dane by his side, the beast will be contained.

He brushed a hand over his tousled hair.

The mortal world would end but from its ashes, a new one will rise, one which he will rule—*the time of magic has returned.*

The doorbell rang jarring him out of his thoughts. He wasn't expecting anyone, and no one knew he and Dane had left the city and were back in Brighton Hill. He had been careful.

"I'll be right back my love."

He reached the door, his bare feet soundless on the hardwood floors, and peered out.

Two females stood on the porch. Although they had never met, he knew who they were. Their distinct energy was unmistakable. It reeked of the ancient worlds.

Without pause, he opened the door.

"Lucien Beck, I assume?"

He nodded and asked with a husky and alluring voice. "What can I do for you lovely ladies?"

"Don't bother," the brunette said. "We know all about your seductive tricks, incubus and came prepared. Your magical charms won't work on us."

Lucien raised a brow. His new powers were no longer a secret. *Celeste,* he thought. "Well, then you must also know your powers won't work on me."

The brunette's eyes narrowed. "I'm Stevie and this is Kai. We're friends of Dane, and we came to see her."

"I'm aware of who you are, but I'm afraid she is not feeling up for visitors today."

"Dane," Kai said. Her gaze shifted from his face to over his shoulder.

He turned to find her standing a few yards behind

him. Her black eyes flashed with anger, but she stayed mute.

Before he could stop her Stevie pushed past him and grabbed Dane in a hug.

Lucien moved toward them, but Kai placed her hands on his chest—a warning. Her blue eyes flashed, and he could feel the icy coolness of her fingertips. He relented. It was too late anyway. Dane had already succumbed to the darkness. Nothing they could say or do would undo it.

He watched Dane prudently. She hadn't returned the hug. Her arms stayed by her side and her face remained passive, void of any emotion.

"Are you OK?" Stevie asked.

No response.

"She's fine," Lucien said, his eyes never leaving them.

"She doesn't look fine," Kai said. The cold in her fingertips increased and he flinched.

Dane's face was ghostly pale and dark circles had formed under her eyes. The brilliant green of her irises had disappeared, and an inky black had appeared in its place. He supposed to them she looked ill but to him she was beautiful.

He smiled arrogantly at the woman in front of him.

Kai wanted to wipe the smug look off his face, but they were here for one reason and Lucien mustn't suspect anything after they leave.

*Distraction.*

Her eyes searched the foyer until she found what she was looking for. On an entry table beside the stairs sat a tall glass vase containing fresh hydrangeas, and water. Keeping her left hand decisively on Lucien's chest she cupped the fingers on her right willing the water in the vase to move toward her. It strained against the side of the impenetrable glass vase. Unable to pass through the barrier, the water began to slosh back and forth. The momentum inched the vase toward the edge until it toppled off and smashed unceremoniously onto the floor.

The sudden impact diverted Lucien's eyes for a moment but that was all Stevie needed to push her lips against Dane's and blow into her mouth. Just before Lucien's gaze tracked back to the two of them, Stevie pulled back.

"That startled me," Kai said, motioning to the shattered vase on the floor. "You must have put it too close to the edge of the table."

Lucien frowned. "I think it is time for you to go. Dane needs her rest."

Like a robot, Dane moved away from Stevie and disappeared back into the depths of the house.

Stevie's cabernet eyes shone with contempt for the man in front of her. "You won't win Lucien. We *will* get her back."

Lucien smiled. His handsome face lit up, but he didn't utter a word.

Kai shook her head. It was disappointing how someone so attractive could be so evil. "Come on Stevie. We've taken up too much of Mr. Beck's time."

As Stevie passed Lucien, she raised her hand. Swirling gray smoke appeared in her palm and sparks of fire spit from its wisps.

"This isn't over Beck," she hissed.

Kai grabbed her wrist pulling her reluctantly out the door.

As they got in the car, she looked at Stevie. "Really. *That* was inconspicuous?"

"I couldn't help it he's so irritatingly smug."

Kai laughed. "I get it. I wanted to wipe that look off his face myself."

Stevie glanced back at the house. "Let's go, there is nothing more we can do. It's up to Adaridge now. Let's hope he can reach her through the portal we just opened inside her."

"Did you get it all in?"

"I think so."

"And did she swallow it?"

Stevie hesitated and glanced at the house. "I hope so, or we're all screwed."

# CHAPTER 31

THE MOON HOVERED LOW IN the night sky—a harbinger of their coming fate. Its spherical size was particularly large for this time of year and in two days it would be full, and the prophecy or some form of it would come to pass.

Stevie's skin prickled as she gazed upon it adding to the foreboding feeling that seemed to hover over Brighton Hill since their return.

The car jerked as the wheels fell into potholes that littered the driveway to the old flour mill. Stevie rolled down her window and turned off the ignition. It was eerily quiet and the air stagnant. The mill was nothing more than a bulky silhouette in the night sky oozing nothing but black shadows from its windows.

"I want to check the pods before we cast the protective dome," she said looking across the car at Kai sitting in the passenger seat.

"OK."

They exited the vehicle just as another set of headlights turned onto the mill's property.

"This should be Mr. Callan."

Stevie opened the trunk and removed a pair of bolt cutters.

A dark sedan pulled up beside them. The tinted windows obscured the occupants' faces, but when the doors opened Mr. Callan, Jon and Alistair emerged.

Kai smiled, hugging Mr. Callan. "It's so good to see you."

"You too Kai." He pulled away and held her by the shoulders at arm's length. Her pale skin shimmered in the moonlight. "A mermaid," he stated. "Unbelievable. Not once in all these years did your father tell me about your mother. I had no idea."

Kai smiled affectionately at her friend's father. "I guess we all kept secrets."

Mr. Callan nodded. "But destiny finds a way to pull those who need each other together."

"My mother used to say that."

His eyes twinkled. "Where do you think I got it from."

Kai's eyes shone with tears as she squeezed Mr. Callan's hand. "I'm sorry about Mrs. Watts."

"Thank you."

His eyes darkened at the mention of his wife, but he turned away quickly and motioned to his companions. "Stevie you remember Jon and Alistair. Kai, meet two members of the Syndicate. Their talents will be useful this evening."

Kai and Stevie nodded their greetings.

"And the others?" Stevie asked.

"The city witches will arrive tomorrow. The eve of the 22nd, as instructed."

"Good," Kai said. "We should have the perimeter up by then and be ready for the wards and magical barriers. If we contain the daemons to this area and defeat the ancient dark and his minions under the cloaked dome, then no one in the town will be the wiser."

Stevie sighed. "If we are unsuccessful, I suppose mortals knowing there are magical beings in the world will be the least of their worries."

Mr. Callan tensed as Alistair moved toward the mill

his golden eyes glowing in the ambient light. A frown wrinkled his brow, his nose twitched, and he flexed his hands. He followed him recognizing the daemon's posturing. "What do you sense Alistair?"

"Death," he said calmly. "There's a fresh scent of death coming from the mill. The imprints trapped within the veil can sense it as well. They're confused. Their energy is erratic" He hesitated as he sniffed the night air. "It comes from the bowels of the structure and is mixed with betrayal and fear. There is something in the mill that shouldn't be."

"You mean besides the daemon pods?" Kai asked raising a brow.

He nodded. "New blood. New death."

Stevie raised the bolt cutters. "Let's take a look."

Mr. Callan nodded. "Jon will begin the cloaking spell and I will prepare the four quarters for the protective dome. It will take us some time so, the three of you find out what you can."

Alistair, Stevie, and Kai entered the mill through the side door after cutting off the massive, new padlock Lucien Beck had installed. The dark interior smelled musty.

Turning on the flashlight, Kai swept the beam across the mill. The pods were dark and silent but as the light found them, they began to pulse.

Stevie placed a hand on the nearest one. She could feel the daemon inside, curious and impatient. They'd be released on the world soon and hundreds of these creatures would need to be contained within the mill's property. The task was daunting.

"Why can't we just burn these pods and kill them before they hatch?" Kai asked.

Stevie removed her hand. "It wouldn't destroy them. These pods are impenetrable. They were created by dark magic and summoned from the depths of a tor- turous hell. Fire will not hurt them. The daemons must be allowed to hatch before they can be destroyed."

Kai's eyes narrowed. "Still freaks me out how you know so much about these creepy things."

Stevie shrugged, giving her friend a small smile. The knowledge they were given through their birthrights was vast and it still surprised her how much she and the others knew about things they previously thought were a myth or didn't know at all.

They moved without pause through the mill to the back staircase. Alistair led the way with his knife drawn. He stopped on the bottom step and tipped his head, listening.

"There's a faint but distinct dripping sound com- ing from somewhere down there." He pointed to a small shadowy hallway off to their left. As they passed through the lower level the smell of sulfur and blood assaulted their nostrils.

"What's that stench?" Kai asked.

Alistair held up his hand to quiet them as he moved toward a thick wooden door. "Dark magic."

He pointed toward the door's surface where a pen- tacle was carved hastily into the wood. As his hand closed around the doorknob, he cast them an uneasy glance.

Kai raised the flashlight as the door swung in and the beam lit up the small room's interior. "What the heck?" she said.

The area had been turned into a shrine.

A marble altar sat in the middle with a few dozen unlit pillar candles surrounding it. Spread on the ground in a circle was a white powder with sigils mark- ing the four quarters. A black cloth covered the marble altar, a corner of which dripped blood onto the stone floor.

Laying on the altar—the skin of her naked body, a pallid blue—was Lilith. Her lifeless eyes stared straight up at the ceiling. The ceremonial athame protruded from her chest where it'd been plunged deep into her heart.

"She's been ritually sacrificed," Alistair said his golden eyes surveying the scene.

Kai nodded. "Gabby said Lucien needed the blood of his own kin to enter the blood pact. She probably had no idea he was her brother."

Turning her dark merlot eyes toward Kai, Stevie said. "Let's see what she knew." Before Kai could object, she grasped Lilith's limp cold hand in her own.

The images came fast and furious as her vision dimmed and Stevie began witnessing everything as it happened.

Fear seeped from Lilith's pores as Lucien lay her on the table. She'd been unable to move but was aware of what was happening. Fear and betrayal were evident in her eyes. The end was near yet in her final moments she experienced a sense of relief, of peace. As the ceremonial knife pierced her skin and the cold blade punctured her heart, a single tear ran down her cheek. No longer would she be in pain, he'd set her free. As her life essence left her body and spiraled upward toward the veil Lucien leaned over and kissed her forehead.

The moment was oddly tender, but it was his final words that surprised her.

Stevie released Lilith's hand and her awareness came back to the moment.

"Lilith is not just Lucien's sister," she said trying to catch her breath. "They were twins."

Alistair raised an eyebrow. "That's the most powerful sacrifice there is. Familial blood is one thing, but to sacrifice the blood of a twin requires also giving of oneself."

"What does this mean for the blood pact?" Kai questioned.

"It means Lucien has essentially created a barrier. One which will be difficult to break. It won't be easy to sever his connection with the ancient dark nor will he be easy to kill. It was what I feared after my conversation with the alchemist. With the blood of a twin and the blood of a healer, Lucien Beck might just be invincible."

Lucien put her to bed and kissed her forehead.

"Goodnight my love," he said in a hushed voice.

Turning out the light he closed the door.

Dane would drift off soon and her mind would take her to places dark and sinister. It would feed the darkness within her and help create the weapon he required to change the course of the prophecy.

Blood surged through his body. His power strengthened the closer they came to the full moon, and in two days when the beast rose to cleanse the earth, magic would return to its rightful place and his family name would once again be restored to its former glory. He would be indomitable.

His thoughts drifted to Lilith, her body lying on the marble slab in the basement of the old mill. When the world was his, he'd build her a crypt. A final resting place worthy of the sacrifice she'd unwittingly made— worthy of a Tierney.

*His twin sister deserved at least that.*

An endless soothing darkness shrouded Dane in its dark embrace. The violent images had faded a few days before leaving her alone in this dark abyss. Its aching silence had become a part of her, and she relished its company and the solitude of the pitch-black nothingness.

Somewhere off in the distance, a noise drifted toward her interrupting the cocoon's visceral silence. At first, the sound was indistinguishable but as it continued it became recognizable—the sound of fabric tearing. As she floated aimlessly her senses searched for the source.

A pinhole of light flashed.

Then another.

It beckoned her toward it and as she moved closer the tear expanded and a searing brightness came from the other side.

As the rip grew the darkness vanished, and she was pulled through the void into another time and place.

# CHAPTER 32

A MAN STOOD BEFORE HER DRESSED in brown wool robes. Thick wooden toggles closed the fabric at his neck. The sleeves were bell-shaped and hid his hands as his arms sat folded across his chest. Long hair peeked out one side of the deep hood covering his head and a scraggly, unkempt beard covered his chin.

His amber eyes held a heavy sadness as they stared at her.

"Adaridge?" Dane asked.

The last Druid of Thanissia bowed his head. "At last we meet."

With fluid and unencumbered movements as if he were gliding, he came toward her. The wool robes swayed noiselessly around him and as he moved the energy of the All Souls rippled outward like water in a pond.

"Where am I?" she asked, her eyes scanning the small rocky landmass they stood on. It was surrounded by water and in the distance stood another rocky land-mass, a tree at its center, its branches empty. Nothing else seemed to exist in this place just them and the tree. The sky above stretched upward into endlessness and everything in this environment was an analogous shade of deep purple. Adaridge, in his brown robes, looked oddly out of place. Only the brown bark of the dead tree offered him any parallel.

A warm wind blew around them, but she noticed everything remained still. Her eyes flicked back to his strong face as she waited for his answer.

"The All Souls."

Her nose wrinkled. "How?"

"An ancient form of astral projection used by the Druid sect of olde. I was able to call your spirit through time and space by calling home the energy of the All Souls, which your friends were able to get you to ingest."

Dane's mind was fuzzy but somewhere deep in her memory the name Stevie surfaced. "Why am I here?"

"It is the only way to release you from the binds of the daemon who holds you in his otherworldly grip. The one you know as Lucien."

"Daemon?" She rubbed her head. "Lucien Beck?" She laughed and her voice echoed through the strange place. "He's not a daemon, he's a businessman."

"He is so much more than that." Adaridge reached into his pocket and pulled out a small glass vial handing it to her. "Drink this. It will help clear your mind."

She took it and without hesitation drank its contents. Almost instantly, the fog cleared taking the confusion with it. Her mind once again her own.

"It's a temporary fix, so we must hurry. There is much you need to know."

"Tell me about Lucien."

"Lucien Beck has been involved in the magical community in your world for a long time. He is what is known as a glamour witch and possesses the power to make people succumb to his wishes. Like your father, he is the only one of his kind."

"I've never heard of a glamour witch," Dane said.

"They have always been a rare breed, even in my time for their powers go against the belief that one should never use their magic to manipulate another's free will."

*The code,* she thought.

Adaridge's face paled. "The only other glamour witch I knew was Lucien's ancestor—Vertigan Tierney's wife."

Her mind raced. All the feelings erupting inside her when Lucien was near weren't real? She found him intoxicating, desirable and longed for the taste of his mouth and his touch constantly but it was all a lie. "Are you saying I'm under his spell?!"

"Yes, but there is more. His powers are linked to the ancient dark now because he freely gave his soul and the life of another to gain dark magic. Lucien Beck is no longer just a glamour witch, he is a daemon—an incubus."

Dane felt sick. "Who did he sacrifice?"

Adaridge knew to whom she referred but could not provide her with the answers she sought. Lucien had killed her mother to invoke Dane's wrath, to unleash the darkness within. But wrath was bedlam and un-predictable and Adaridge required her focus. He could not chance the fate of her world on a twisted desire for revenge. Lucien Beck must not see his death coming.

Thankfully, the truth was not that, and he an-swered without remorse.

"Lucien had a sister."

Something in her cloudy memory shook loose. "Lilith."

Adaridge nodded.

"He killed her?"

"The ancient dark required a blood sacrifice to initi-ate the pact, but not any blood would do. It must be the sacrifice of someone from the Tierney line. A sacri-fice worthy of immortality."

Her mind reeled. *Lilith was dead.*

Even though she'd wanted the same, she couldn't help feeling empathy toward the woman. She too had been betrayed.

"What does Lucien want with me?"

His amber eyes darkened. "That is a complex answer and that hearkens back to a different time. You see Lucien's ancestor, Vertigan Tierney was not the first, nor only, in his lineage to fall to darkness. Their souls succumbed long ago to pure evil and its tainted the bloodline for centuries, damning those who carried the Tierney blood to fall to their own weakness and desires."

"And what was his weakness."

"For Vertigan, it was your family."

The temple on her left side began to throb, and she rubbed it softly with her fingers as Adaridge continued.

"You may suppose he had remorse for how things ended after the Great War, but you would be mistaken. His treacherous acts against the Order, Rafe, and Claaven became his undoing, but in his mind, everything he did was justified. Justified by the festering hatred he felt toward your ancestor which he aptly concealed from everyone. You see, Vertigan's jealousy had no bounds. He desired Seri, the celestial Claaven was bound too. He envied his status within the Warlician Order and the respect of those who served under him. Even his trusted position as sentry leader was not enough because he knew he would never ascend beyond that rank. The Order would never be his. Rafe's father was Claaven's second in command and Vertigan knew one day Rafe would succeed him in power. The authority and prestige he so badly desired, Claaven had. Vertigan Tierney was easily corruptible by the ancient dark because he already lived within the darkness."

"And because of their lineage, Lucien and Lilith carry the same darkness."

"Yes. She succumbed to hers, but Lucien has found a way to harness it for his own gain. He seeks revenge for his lineage and for the treatment of his ancestor. But unlike Lilith, he does not desire to end your life. Lucien Beck does not hate you, quite the opposite, he desires you. He wants you to rule beside him in the new world where magic will once again exist without fear or consequence. He wants you to be his lover, his confidant, his queen. And that gives you the upper hand."

"How."

"He has crafted his seduction of you for a very long time and for good reason. Once the ancient dark is released from the depths of the earth, it becomes unpredictable. Although Lucien has power over it now, he knows it is fleeting. His powers come directly from his connection to it. Yours come from the ancient realms, the elements, and the ether. Your power is infinite. Without you, he is unable to control the ancient dark. With you, he becomes unstoppable. You are the only one who can change the prophecy, Dane. He needs you."

Lucien's words echoed through her mind. *"You just need to pull the right thread and the whole thing will unravel."*

The purple environment flickered.

"The magic is fading we must hurry. As the night of the full moon approaches and the prophecy nears Lucien Beck's powers will grow. The stronger the ancient dark gets; the more powerful Lucien will become. The blood pact bound his inner darkness to the ancient dark and in turn, has disrupted the ancient prophecy. If the pact is not severed, then the future of your world is bleak. Anarchy will rule as darkness spreads out across the lands and all those born without magic will be enslaved or perish."

Dane thought of the images Lucien had shown her. A world of devastation and death. Was that the result of the prophecy coming to pass or was it in fact, the world's fate if it didn't? Lucien's handsome face floated through her mind. Could he really be so cruel, so cold?

Adaridge touched her arm. "You are blessed with the gift to see light within the darkness but do not be fooled—not all light is good nor is it always true. Lucien cannot be saved. For the pact to be severed, and the ancient prophecy realized—Lucien Beck must *die*."

He reached inside his robes and pulled out a knife.

The handle was carved from a white substance. *Bone?* The ebony blade glinted as runes embedded into its matte surface reflected the subdued light. It was the size of a ceremonial athame, and archaic energy pulsed from it.

As if reading her mind Adaridge explained. "This athame is the one thing that can kill the daemon. You must plunge the blade straight into Lucien's heart. It is essential that the handle touch skin, so it must be pushed in up to the hilt. The magic bound to this knife is primordial; older than time and space. The bone of the handle comes from the first Druid and the blade is forged from dragonscale. Magic from the four natural elements imbue the runes. Only this knife can sever the pact and release the Tierney soul from its unhallowed binds."

Reaching out she took the knife from Adaridge.

"Dane you must remember one thing. Because of his connection to the ancient dark, Lucien will recognize this blade. You must not let him see it until the moment you plunge it through his heart. If he knows you possess this weapon, you will not get the chance. Killing the incubus and ending the pact will weaken the ancient dark, and in turn, its connection to the new world will become precarious. That will be your time to attack. Without severing the pact there will be no chance to defeat the incubus or the ancient dark. Your world will fall, and all will be lost."

Dane's mind was whirling. She'd been under Lucien's spell for weeks and much of her memory was still foggy. "But how do I succeed when I'm under his control?"

Adaridge smiled. "Your friends have not forsaken you."

He again reached into his wool robe and pulled out another metal object—an amulet.

"Gabriella has acquired a token from your time."

He held the amulet up.

"It stores potent magic called voodoo, magic able to break the hold the incubus has over you. But it too must remain hidden—always in your possession. If the daemon finds it you will not recover, and the prophecy will find a new path, a darker path."

Dane took the amulet he offered. "How did you get this from Gabby? How is that even possible?"

"I provided someone long ago with the knowledge of the Druids. Not everything can be written down, some things must pass verbally to those who require specific knowledge."

"Rafe," she sighed, thinking about their conversation and how Adaridge chose him as the vessel for the Druid knowledge.

He nodded. "I knew one day you and Rafe would be bound. The Pool of Sight showed me your destinies.

You were destined to connect our worlds and make them stronger, but he would be the bridge back when your path forked, and darkness beckoned. I needed to give him the seeds of knowledge to be able to access the All Souls, so when the time came, he would know what to do. Rafe has been my conduit to you, allowing me to communicate across time and space and to connect the All Souls to your plane of existence so that this moment in time would exist. Druid knowledge is magic and Rafe has kept it alive. Your destinies are linked in more ways than you know."

Dane glanced down at the amulet in her palm. "This will release me from Lucien's control and steer my destiny back to Rafe?"

The All Souls flickered as it began to fade, and the Druid's physical form ebbed.

"There is darkness in all of us and, if allowed, it becomes all-consuming. That amulet will save you from the daemon's darkness but only you can conquer your own and decide which path you wish to walk."

His amber eyes closed, and he began to fade. "I must go."

The warm wind swirled around her as his essence returned to its maker and the All Souls turned to black.

As she was pulled back through time and space to her own world, a faint whisper drifted through her mind.

*"Remember to use the darkness, do not become it."*

# CHAPTER 33

A MASS OF ANGRY GRAY CLOUDS clustered in the early morning sky as Lucien stared out the bedroom window. It rained yesterday and most of the remaining snow had disappeared. Spring wasn't too far away but mortals wouldn't see another. After tomorrow, they would know nothing but darkness and misery. The sun would be cast aside, and the warmth of its rays would fade into memory. The world would be lit by fire and brimstone as the skies churned with anger and the lands leeched blood. In time, magic would once again rule the earth and those without its power would submit to a new hierarchy.

He smiled as he watched Dane sleep.

*Tomorrow a new king and queen would rise from the ashes as a new era came forth. The earth cleansed of its sins would start anew and mankind would no longer exist as it does now.*

They arrived at the mill a few hours later.

The surrounding field still held the moisture from the rainstorm and the driveway was thick with muddy puddles. Trees drooped under a menacing gray as drops of water fell from their leaves. A gloomy atmosphere shrouded the mill in its embrace but one that aptly reflected what was to come.

Lucien exited the vehicle and sniffed the damp air. A faint essence of magic tinged its wisps. Someone had been here. Glancing around the property he saw nothing out of the ordinary, but magic had a way of hiding in plain sight. He grinned, maybe the immortals would make this more interesting.

He sauntered around the car and opened the passenger door for her. He was dressed all in black: a black turtleneck sweater, dark jeans, combat boots, and a leather bomber jacket.

His bright blue eyes looked at her with affection as he extended his hand.

"Come, my love. We have one more thing to do before tomorrow evening."

Together they walked into the musty old mill. The interior began to hum as hundreds of pods recognized their presence and pulsed a sickly yellow light.

Soon their time to open would come.

Lucien walked without hesitation through the crowded space and disappeared into the basement. Dane stood for a moment surrounded by the daemon pods. A faint pulse throbbed from each one like the thump of a heartbeat. Reaching out she touched the nearest one. Her fingers tingled as the dark magic ignited her skin. A soft whisper drifted on the stale air, and her dark eyes flashed in recognition.

Smiling she walked to the stairs.

"There you are," Lucien said.

They were in the small storage unit at the back of the basement. The room was still the same as when she was last here. Burlap flour bags stamped with a black Gristmill Flour Co. were piled in the corners and pulley wheels, machinery parts, and other tools lined the old rickety shelves. The difference was now the dirt floor contained a sizable crack stretching from one side of the room to the other. Yellow light glowed from its depths and the current of magic throbbing within filled the entire room in a ghastly glow.

Lucien took a small knife from his pocket. The handle was black with three runes etched into the surface and the thick metal blade glinted in the light from the candle. He stood beside the open fissure and drew the edge of the blade across the skin of his palm. A line of crimson appeared, and he clenched his fist holding it over the crack in the floor. Blood dripped from his hand. As it fell into the chasm, it sparked the yellow light into blazing flames that licked at the edges.

Closing his eyes, he began to chant.

*Sever the light*
*Sever the day*
*Sever the weak*
*Rise beast of darkness*
*Lord of realms*
*And cleanser of earth*

The fire flashed upward sending bright yellow sparks toward the ceiling. Flickering shadows danced across his handsome face as he turned to face her. "It has been done. Our future belongs to the beast now. It will rise when the full moon is at its peak bringing with it a prophecy of our making."

Dane reached up and placed her hands on either side of his face drawing him close. She pressed her lips to his and then said. "Tomorrow your life will forever change."

Elyse knocked softly on the bedroom door. "May I come in?"

There was no response, so she turned the knob. Marlee sat upright in bed. A pink tinge softened her pale skin and her eyes shone. The bindings had been removed, and she seemed much better, yet she looked defeated.

"How are you feeling."

"Empty."

"Are you hungry? I can make you something," Elyse asked and walked further into the bedroom.

She shook her head. "I feel like something is missing. Like a part of me has been torn out from the inside."

Elyse sat down on the edge of the bed. "There is nothing missing, just different. You need to trust your instincts and in who you are now. You are still Marlee, my friend."

"We are not friends," she spat. "Our ancestors tolerated one another. Don't pretend it was anything more than that."

Elyse placed a delicate necklace in Marlee's palm and closed her fingers around it. "I want you to have this and remember what it meant."

Placid clear blue eyes assessed her. "That is in the past. We are of two different worlds now; worlds that exist in defiance of one another. We can never be what we once were."

"Then we will be what we can."

Marlee turned away. "Why do you not hate me? I tried to kill you."

"Because I choose to forgive."

"I do not want nor deserve your forgiveness."

"Maybe not, but you shall have it anyway."

Elyse rose from where she sat. "We may carry the blood of our ancestors Marlee, but we don't have to carry their fear and hate. That choice is ours."

Before Marlee could respond, Elyse left the room and an aching quiet filled the space she'd vacated. She looked down at the pendant she'd given her. It was a small silver compass, a gift Marlee had given Elyse on her twenty-fifth birthday, to remind her that no matter where they journeyed, they would always find their way back to one another.

She sighed as she twisted the delicate silver chain around her finger. Tomorrow the prophecy would come to pass, and fate would decide if their journeys would continue or end forever.

# CHAPTER 34

NATHAN AND CELESTE RODE IN silence.
It was almost eleven when they entered the town. Brighton Hill looked as charming and unassuming as it always did. People were out with their dogs for late-night walks in the park and warm inviting light lit up the house windows. Cars wound their way through the streets oblivious to the evil about to descend on their little world.

They circled the town once before heading to a small motel located on its outskirts. Nathan had used his powers to convince the motel owner to allow them, and only them, lodging for the evening. Although he'd hesitated at first, Celeste reminded him it was in their best interest and breaking Coven rules at this point, was the least of their concerns.

The motel was inconspicuous. It sat far off the main road a few miles from the flour mill making it an ideal spot for a hundred plus out-of-towners to congregate.

The New York witches of both the Coven and the Syndicate got out of their cars.

Celeste had done well. She'd gathered the strongest and most experienced Coven members, all of which had some sort of physical power—kinetics, pyromancers, and windwitches. She'd also brought a handful of healers. Although he was appreciative of their help, the mortal witches were a mere distraction against the ancient powers of the incubus and the ancient dark. And if Dane was still in their clutches there would be nothing that could stop her from destroying them all.

His heart ached as he thought about his daughter. The loss of her mother had been such a devastating blow that she'd been easily manipulated by a darker power. He should've been the one to find Ella. If he'd been in town, maybe things would be different.

Celeste walked over to him and placed a hand on his forearm.

"You can't blame yourself, Nathan. Fate has a way of making its own path whether we intervene or not. Dane's destiny is her own as is the darkness that was fated to find her. We must pray to the goddess that her inner strength can defeat it."

Her uncanny ability to read him had always slightly unnerved him. "You need to stay out of my head, Celeste."

"That was not necessary. You have been carrying this guilt with you ever since Dane disappeared and it's shifted your aura tremendously. Now we're here and you're about to come face to face. You are not that difficult to read, my dear friend."

Nathan straightened. "I'll be fine."

"I know you will, and so will she. Have faith."

Celeste squeezed his arm again before turning to the others. "Take a room and get some sleep. Tomorrow you will need all your strength, courage, and determination."

As the witches bustled around unpacking the cars she turned back to Nathan. "What time are we to meet the celestial."

"Midnight." He checked his watch. "We should leave soon. Her store is in the shopping district in the center of town. It will take about twenty minutes to get there."

"I'll be right back, and then we can go."

Nathan watched Celeste as she walked over to a tall, Asian witch with long, sleek, black hair. He leaned in, listened intently, and then walked away.

Returning to Nathan she said. "Kiro will ensure the readiness of the plans we discussed while we're gone. Every witch will know their task by sunrise. Nothing will be left to chance."

Nathan knew Kiro, but only from Coven meetings and reputation. He was an influential seer with the ability to assess future outcomes and scenarios. It made him a superb tactician. While it was difficult to lay plans for a scenario where the opponents were unpredictable and the future changed by the minute, Nathan knew he would evaluate every scenario he observed to the fullest, factoring in as many variations as possible.

The witches would be ready.

They pulled up to Gabby's shop at ten minutes to midnight. The storefront was dark, but Nathan noticed a small light flickered in one of the back windows.

He knocked three times and waited.

A few moments later the lock clicked, and Gabby opened the door.

"Come in, quickly," she urged stepping back and allowing them access. The bolt slid back into place as she locked the door behind them, and then led them to the supply room in the rear of the store.

An array of weapons was laid out on a long table.

Nathan whistled in appreciation.

"Take what you like. These come from the armories of Etheriem and Dywen. They have been enchanted to recognize any type of magical blood, making them easier to wield by a mortal. Unfortunately, without the blood of each witch in your party to enchant the weapons specifically too, the spell is wide-ranging. If any of these weapons are seized by a daemon, it will shift its power to the new blood."

"Understood. Most of our elite witches are trained in hand-to-hand combat and will use the swords effectively. I have also brought a half-dozen sharpshooters who will engage from the perimeter. The bullets have been manufactured to specific specifications by our alchemists and engineers. We are hoping this design will take down a daemon with one bullet to the head."

"And the elixirs you mentioned," Nathan asked.

The celestial pulled a small vial from her coat pocket. A bright red liquid sloshed inside as she placed it on the table. "This is made from the poppies of Kaizi. It is a deadly tonic and can be used in multiple ways. I suggest for any who can shoot a bow, they dip the tips of their arrows. There are crates of them on their way to the mill as we speak."

"I will spread the word," Celeste said. "The Coven witches are the strongest New York City has. They won't disappoint."

"I have full confidence in them," Gabriella responded. Her eyes flicked to Nathan. "Are you prepared to stay near town."

He locked eyes with the celestial his mouth set in a grim line. He knew what she referred too. They'd decided he would stay with many of the witches on the outskirts of Brighton Hill as a second line of defense. He'd initially protested the idea but Gabby, in no uncertain terms, reminded him he was too close to the situation and if Dane did not come back to them, her future was dire. He'd reluctantly agreed because deep

250

down he knew his presence there could complicate matters. If his daughter could not be saved, she would need to die.

"I am."

Gabriella pulled a tightly rolled piece of paper from a cabinet and spread it out on another table. "These are the battle plans. We have already set the protective dome, the concealment spell, and marked the quarters with magical altars. These plans will show you how we are dividing up the elemental powers so you can decide where your people with be most effective."

Nathan moved closer ready for a long night of preparation. Tomorrow the prophecy would pass, and they would either be victorious, or they'd watch the world fall into darkness.

# CHAPTER 35

March 23, 2016, *eve of the full moon*

*And from the ashes of the old world, chaos, destruction, sickness, and death will rise. Time will stand still, and the world will cease to breathe. At that moment only the fate of one will matter.*

–The final entry in The Book of Realms

R AFE STOOD ON THE BACK deck watching what may be the final sunset disappear behind the horizon. After tonight, the world could exist in endless darkness. A river of pain and suffering washing over those unlucky enough not to have died.

He thought about Dane.

Had Adaridge reached her?

He could not let himself believe her destiny was one of darkness. She would find a way back to the light and come back to him.

His mind shifted to Lucien Beck and his hands began to tremble. The incubus needed to die at Dane's hand or another's it did not matter for he deserved nothing less than death. If Dane failed, Rafe would find a way to seal his fate.

Sebastian's voice interrupted his thoughts. "We have mere hours before the moon is at its peak and the prophecy either comes to pass or a new day will be born upon this earth. Let us prepare."

As he entered the kitchen, he found the others waiting. They stood around the large table, a rough blueprint of the old flour mill and its surrounding property, laid out on top.

"We must contain the daemons and the battle to the mill's property. A protective dome surrounds the perimeter indicated by the red circle." Sebastian pointed to the map.

"The dome encircles about seven acres of property including a portion of the lake," Stevie interjected glancing at Kai.

The elder warrior continued. "Stone altars have been built at the quarters. These altars control the dome, and each will contain one of the portal stones. The stones will act as a conduit for the elemental magic of the Thanissia Universe. Your powers are effective on earth but as there is no elemental magic contained within this world, they may weaken over time. Using the portal stones to infuse the dome with ancient elemental energy from the ether will sustain the strength of your powers."

They spent the next hour going over their battle plan, formations, tactics, and use of magic.

"Everyone knows their task, yes?" Sebastian asked.

Gabriella spread her wings. Her iridescent eyes sparkled in the light of the rising moon. "This night will be our last stand. Pray we do not fail otherwise tomorrow will be bleak and our future unbearable."

"Well, that was encouraging, Gabby," Stevie said, shaking her head.

Kai agreed. "Not sure you should be giving the pep talks anymore."

Her feathers ruffled. "We have battled the ancient dark before and lost. You must not underestimate the task ahead. It is dire."

"Understood," Elyse said, redirecting the building tension. "Shall we go? It will take time to prepare the site."

The others agreed.

"The Book of Realms. Where is it?" said Sebastian. "We need to ensure its safety. If the prophecy fails and this world succumbs to evil, it must be destroyed. The book cannot fall into the hands of the ancient dark or his minions."

"Hidden. In the forest," said Stevie pointing toward the back yard. "We thought it best not to leave it lying around. I'll retrieve it and meet you at the mill."

Sebastian nodded. "Hurry, we will need all the powers of the ancients but most definitely yours."

"I will be there long before midnight with the book," Stevie said running from the house. Like a wisp of smoke in the wind, she faded into the darkness.

Deep within the woods behind her house was a small pond. It was surrounded by a dense grove of pine trees and therefore hidden from view and not easily accessible. Not many knew of its existence. A few years ago, Stevie discovered the trees grew in a specific formation around the pond and if you moved in the correct direction you would find a small path winding through their trunks like a maze.

The pond's surface lay still, frozen by a thin sheet of ice. Its breathtaking serenity still captivated her even after all this time. The water had a magical way of sparkling under both the sunlight and moonlight even on cloudy days or when it was ice-covered as it is now.

It was her secret spot and the perfect place to hide the Book of Realms.

Snow crystals crunched underfoot as she walked to the edge. It was colder here, deep in the woods, and she shivered. Somewhere under the muddy snow-dusted shoreline, the Book of Realms called to her, its magic reaching forth luring her toward it. She crouched down. Placing her palm on top of the muddy earth she moved it back and forth until she felt the magical energy pulsing underneath.

Using a small garden tool hidden behind a rock, Stevie dug up the ancient tome. Pulling it from its hiding place she brushed off the mud and debris and unwrapped it from the plastic bag protecting it.

The book felt warm to the touch and the moonlight cascading through the pines ignited the leather in a spectral light.

In her haste to exit the clearing, she stumbled on a tree root. The Book of Realms sailed from her grasp as she landed face down on the cold soil. Picking herself up she walked to where the book lay, open. Wind swirled through the trees ruffling the sheets of paper and flipping them back and forth. The light of the rising moon caught the pages, and they quieted. Squatting, she ran her fingers lightly over the words the moonlight had revealed. She studied them for a moment before picking up the book and running as fast as she could back through the woods.

༄ঌৎৡৣ

The abandoned flour mill was silhouetted against the full moon and the fields were awash with its silvery light.

Stevie checked her watch as she climbed from her vehicle.

It was almost eleven.

Diego ran ahead, nose to the ground as she glanced around at the hectic scene before her. The others were busy setting up traps and barriers to both contain and destroy the daemons, which would certainly emerge from the pods at any time.

She grabbed the Book of Realms and walked over to Sebastian.

"Here," she said handing the heavy tome to him.

His eyes narrowed as he took it from her and placed it atop a pile of rocks, covering it with a white cloth. From his tunic, he pulled an ampoule of clear liquid and placed it atop the book.

"If we cannot defeat the ancient dark this vial must be broken, and the book set on fire. The liquid it contains is the one thing that can destroy the magic contained within."

Stevie nodded. "About the book. There was something—"

She was interrupted by a group arriving from the darkness.

A tall, mocha-skinned woman cloaked in dark green walked to where they stood. Holding out her hand she smiled. "I'm Celeste."

Sebastian took it in both his own. "A pleasure. Nathan told us of your arrival. Thank you for your assistance. I am Sebastian and this is Stevie."

Celeste's eyes flicked between the two immortals.

"While this may not be our fight one of our own has affected the prophecy's course. For this, we are responsible and will stand with you until the end."

His green eyes crinkled at the corners as he squinted at the small delegation of witches behind Celeste. "And the others?"

"There are over a hundred more on the outskirts of town. Nathan is with them and will ensure the town's defense should we fail to contain them here. Whatever may come, we won't falter. Not while at least one witch stands."

"Good. I will be just a moment and then I will show you the grounds and the battle plan."

He returned to the task of covering the pile of rocks with boughs of greenery, camouflaging the Book of Realms from sight.

"Remember where this is Stevie for you are the only one with the power to ignite it from afar."

A brazier stood a few feet away, and he lit the kindling inside setting it ablaze.

As the fire ignited a line in the dirt a trench of flames snaked toward the next brazier, which in turn lit another until the entire perimeter was ablaze in a ring of fire.

"This will make it easier to contain the daemons. It will also give you fuel for your elemental magic."

"And the dragons?"

Sebastian glanced at her as a haunting memory passed over his eyes.

"Let them reign down destruction on the mill itself. We must destroy the portal Lucien has created for the ancient dark. Once it rises, the dragons might be our most effective weapon against it, especially if we cannot access the power Dane holds."

Sebastian walked away leading the witches of New York across the expanse of the mill's grounds.

She stood with Diego at the edge of the property watching as immortals, witches, and her friends scurried around, turning the abandoned mill into a battleground. There would be no time to tell any of them what she'd seen in the book—the strange words that revealed themselves to her under the light of the full moon.

Nor was there time to decipher their meaning.

# CHAPTER 36

THE TIME WAS ALMOST UPON *them.*

Each immortal took a group of modern witches and prepared each quadrant for the fight ahead. The initial battle plan was designed to thin the herd of daemons which would surely flood the mill's grounds once their pods broke. If they could minimize the early threat, they might have a chance.

Celeste, Jon, and Alistair were key to this succeeding.

Using her necromancer powers and a reverse incantation Celeste would fell as many as she could while Jon cloaked her from the daemons' sight. As both their powers required total concentration, Alistair would protect them from any threats.

Currently, the three of them were stationed near the loading dock hidden by a row of old dumpsters. Behind them and to the right of the mill, Kai and Tauria had taken refuge by the water's edge near an old oak tree. Three witches from the New York Coven were with them.

Stevie and Rafe were positioned near the Book of Realms at the back of the property closest to the road. The pyromancers surrounded the outer edges ready to manipulate the fire in the braziers as necessary. Together, Brannon, Sebastian, and Killenn stood ready for battle. Drow had taken up the left flank with Marlee and Elyse and the windwitches.

The kinetics stood at different points around the mill ready to fling sharpened sticks, heavy boulders, and vials of a toxic flammable elixir Stevie had created from the Kaizi poppies. With their minds, these witches could direct their weapons wherever they wanted with impressive precision.

Kiro moved among them, his eyes glazed to white and his hands shifting as if moving unseen chess pieces across a board.

The full moon ebbed in and out as gray clouds sprinted through the night sky. The air was tinged with late winter crispness and a light dusting of snow covered the open field.

In the distance, across the lake, a rumble could be heard echoing through the dark.

*Is it supposed to rain?* Stevie thought to herself as the late-night sky shifted and rolled above her. Her reaction to something so mundane and normal as the weather surprised her but as she looked around the field at the others, she supposed it may be an involuntary reaction to the fact that nothing about this night was normal or mundane.

The brightness of the moon had a calming effect by veiling the approaching evil. Her eyes followed the subtle shimmer that rippled across the dome as the cloaking spell invoked by Jon was infused with ancient magic. The braziers burned brightly and the altars, set at each quarter, glowed with the light of the portal stones.

Everything seemed serene but the shifting feet of the witches and the anxious energy surrounding them said otherwise.

Two shadowy figures emerged from the side of the mill both wrapped in long black cloaks.

The hackles on Diego's back raised as he emitted a warning growl.

"Dane," whispered Stevie as they left the shadows and moonlight illuminated their faces.

The incubus clutched Dane firmly around the waist as he walked her toward a makeshift altar at the front of the mill.

Beside her Rafe swore under his breath but remained stationary his hand on the grip of his sword, his eyes never leaving Lucien.

They watched as he released Dane, walked to the altar, and lit the candles, four white and one red. He pulled the hood of his long dark cloak over his head doing the same to Dane's. A large tome sat on a raised pedestal at the center of the altar, and he flipped through the pages until he found the one, he wanted.

His firm voice echoed across the open field, carried on the quiet night air as he recited an incantation. He spoke in a tongue Stevie did not understand.

"Why can't we just go stop him?" she asked Rafe.

The warrior flexed his hands and through clenched teeth, he said. "It is futile to try to impede an ancient prophecy. Any attempt to do so will shift its course temporarily but in the end, it will find its way to a conclusion. Prophecies, especially those seen by the ancient Druids, must come to pass it is the way of our world. Until midnight, we remain observers."

Stevie glanced back at Dane. Her eyes were barely visible under the hooded cloak. *I hope Adaridge was able to reach you.*

A deep bellowing noise filled the air interrupting her silent thoughts.

"What was that?" she asked searching the sky for the source.

Rafe moved in closer and his eyes lifted skyward. "It can't be."

"Can't be what?"

Another throaty blast ripped through the dark sky.

"A battle horn," Rafe said as he looked across the field to where Gabriella stood. Her wings were flexed straight out, and her iridescent eyes scanned the sky above.

The horn crescendo again, its deep bellow reverberating ominously through the clouds, a haunting din heralding in the unexpected. Gabriella recognized it at once. Turning her attention skyward her eyes flicked back and forth until she located the bright light hurtling toward earth.

The sky cracked and flashed as the light broke through the atmosphere and the protective dome around them rippled as the ancient power moved toward it.

"Open the dome!" she screamed at Alistair who'd assigned witches to ensure the quarter altars were protected.

Alistair looked at the bright light hurtling through the sky. "What is that?"

"Quickly," she shouted over her shoulder as she ran toward the southern altar.

Without hesitation, Alistair sprinted to the altar in the east.

Pure white light shimmered through the dome as the light plunging down from above got closer.

"NOW!" yelled Gabriella, as she closed the altar's

connection to the magic infusing the dome. Alistair did the same and the dome between the altars began to crack. Small fractures appeared and pieces slid away leaving holes in its surface. The fractures enlarged and soon a quarter of the dome had disappeared leaving a vulnerable entrance point in the protective shield.

The bright light was almost upon them.

She ran to a spot in between the altars where the opening was right above her. Raising her sword, she muttered a few words. Iridescent light sparkled under her skin and flowed upward through her hand and into the sword, bursting out the blade's tip into the night sky.

*A beacon.*

The light hurtling toward them shifted course heading straight for Gabriella as the horn bellowed again. A bright light burst through the dome's opening and crashed into the ground yards from where she stood. The earth shook from the impact as the last of the horn's deep roar faded in the distance.

Gabriella sheathed her sword and scowled at the Seraph standing yards away.

"Gabriel what are you doing here. I thought you were forbidden to come?"

He rose to his full height, two heads above every other man on the field. His gray armor gleamed enhanced by the iridescent glow of the ether ebbing under his skin. The tips of his enormous wings brushed the cold earth as he came toward her.

"You had no choice in your destiny sister, but I do in mine."

She looked at her brother in shock. "You are betraying the Guardian of Deities."

He shook his head. "The Guardian knows of my decision. He does not condone it, but he understands and accepts it. If this world perishes and the ancient bloodlines are tainted with darkness, then there will be nothing left for us to rebuild. The ether will become stagnant and us with it. Mortals knowing of our existence will be irrelevant if we fail."

He walked toward her and placed his hand on her shoulder. "Fate has joined our worlds, Gabriella. This battle is not for me to watch from afar."

The dome above them crackled as Alistair and another witch resealed it.

"There is no leaving now brother, even if you wished to."

"Then it is a good thing I have chosen this as my destiny as well."

His solemn face lit up as yellow light exploded across the field from inside the mill. The entire dome was cast in its eerie glow, and she raised her hand to shield her eyes from the blinding flash.

"You came just in time, Gabriel," she said as the loading dock door began to open. It squealed as the metal wheels grated in their tracks heaving the door upward. The darkness encompassing the mill echoed an unnerving silence until a hollow shuffling sound penetrated the night air.

Across the field, Stevie and Rafe covered their eyes as the blinding glow burst from the mill's interior. When it receded moments later, Dane and Lucien were gone, the altar was bare, and only the candles were left flickering on its surface.

Stevie's eyes searched the area. "They must be inside the mill."

The ground beneath them shook as the shuffling sound grew louder.

Rafe drew his sword and turned to look at her. "It is time."

She checked her watch.

*11.59 pm.*

*The witching hour was upon them.*

A shudder ran through the dome as the full moon peaked. Crackles of lilac hued energy snaked across its surface as the ancient magic flowing through the portal stones ignited. The perimeter fires hissed and flared. The water in the lake surged upward as white-caps formed on the surface. A ripple beneath the earth caused the grass to sway and small tufts of air funneled in circles.

As the ancient prophecy came to pass like a ripple carried through time, the sky darkened. Gabriella felt the static in the air as it breached the atmosphere. The energy surrounding them was ancient. Magic, she had been born from and which the others were tied by blood and destiny.

The static surged, ruffling the feathers of her wings as it passed. She glanced at Gabriel whose eyes locked with her own. He felt the same thing—the ancient ether and the magic of their realms were at full power.

Stasis was over.

The Thanissia Universe, their home was once again as it had been.

Her eyes flicked to the altars. The glow of the portal stones no longer pulsed but emitted a steady, strong beam of light upward. The magic of the ether swirled inside the dome as midnight came, the prophecy passed, and all their destinies collided.

"For Etheriem," Gabriel said, drawing his sword.

"For the Five Realms," Gabriella echoed, as a wave of daemons poured from the bowels of the abandoned mill.

The first wave hit the spell Celeste had cast. A type of reverse necromancy that pulled the dark magic animating the corpses from within. The sickly yellow light throbbing under their skin extinguished and their decomposed corpses crumpled to the ground until they were nothing more than piles of bone and ash. The spell was not as strong when the second wave of daemons encountered it and although it slowed them considerably, it didn't fully remove the dark magic.

"It will be a few minutes before I can re-cast," Celeste said looking at Alistair and Jon.

They both nodded and drew their swords.

"We will take out this side of the flank," Alistair said. "You stay here. Jon has cloaked this area. If you don't move, you will remain undetected."

Celeste removed the fabric doll and the black powder from her coat pocket. "I will begin at once. Be careful."

An echo of gunfire followed her words as the Coven's sharpshooters opened fire from their perches in the trees along the left side. Daemon heads exploded as the bullets tore through their skulls.

As Jon fought the daemons heading toward the water, Alistair signaled to Rafe.

"They are adapting to the frontal attack," Alistair said as he met them near the back of the east quadrant. "Moving away from the middle and heading toward the outer flanks. Celeste's spell will be useless if the daemons go around it. If the dragons can circle the boundary inside the outer fire barrier, maybe we can keep the battle away from the edges of the protective dome."

"And give us less ground to cover,"

"Yes"

Stevie held her hands in front of her. Soon, a gray mist spun upward. As it rose it expanded until the smoke dragon hovered menacingly in the night sky, its red eyes glowing. Twisting her hands around one another she compacted the smoke until it began to spark. The sparks ignited a flame which funneled like a beam toward the sky, swirling ferociously until the fire dragon was born.

The fire dragon was substantially bigger than the other and its charcoal black eyes shone like empty pools as they reflected the flames. Long tendrils of fire streamed behind its wings as it twisted and turned in the air above her and when it inhaled its entire body flared.

It was magnificent.

The two dragons circled overhead waiting for direction from the dragon gypsy they served. Stevie muttered her command sending them to the outer edges of the dome where they blasted the daemons with their fire breath.

Daemons squealed as they burned their deathly screech echoing through the night.

The three Warlician warriors watched as the daemons collapsed under the necromancer's spell. Hundreds more poured from the belly of the mill clambering over their fallen brethren.

Like the ones that emerged from the depths of the caverns in the Dead Lands, these too were macabre skeletons of rotting flesh, broken bones, and death. They shuffled and lumbered; their eyes lit with the sickly yellow glow of dark magic. Translucent skin hung in strips from their bodies, and they moved as if they were ghastly marionettes controlled by an unseen puppet master.

Brannon unsheathed his sword as the daemons surged toward them. His green eyes sparkled as he turned toward the other two warriors and raised his blade.

"May this night see The Order victorious," he said laying his free arm across his chest so that his hand rested on the medallion on his right shoulder.

Sebastian, his black armor gleaming, lifted his sword and placed the blade across Brannon's. "The Order."

Killenn repeated the motion—three blades laying across one another. He smiled at the two Warlicians. "May the fate of this night smile kindly on our paths. And may the power of earth and fire fuel our swords to victory."

The three warriors pulled their swords back, turned, and ran toward the oncoming daemons. As they slashed through the corpses of the risen dead, the steel of their swords gleamed under the full moon.

The battle for mankind had begun.

# CHAPTER 37

L UCIEN STOOD IN THE GLOOM to the left of the mill,
hidden behind a stack of old flour crates. He
clasped tight to Dane's hand as the battle raged
before him. It had been an hour since he'd performed
the ritual, which released the daemons from their
pods, but the humans and immortals still fought. Their
perseverance would be admirable if not so annoying.
Some had fallen under the onslaught but those who
remained seemed more determined than ever.

His face twitched as his eyes scanned the bodies
of the daemons littered across the property. He'd underestimated the power of his enemies. Even without
Dane's magic, they were organized and formidable.

His gaze landed on the winged Seraph just as he
mowed down three daemons with one violent swing of
his massive sword.

Lucien scowled. *Another thing he hadn't anticipated.*

Glancing skyward he saw the dragons coming toward them. Streams of fire billowed from their mouths
and scorched trenches in the earth. The fire dragon careened toward the right side of the mill and blasted the
loading dock area followed by the smoke dragon who
destroyed the back corner of the mill. It crumbled under their wrath sending stone, glass, and timber flying
in all directions. When the dragons circled over the lake
gaining momentum for another attack, he searched the

grounds for the dragon gypsy until he found her near the back of the property. She was trying to destroy the mill, but it was a futile attempt to obstruct the beast's rise to the surface.

The other immortals had been pushed to the far edges of the field and most were separated by raging fires and advancing daemons.

"It is time for you to work your magic," he said taking Dane's hand. "Remember, they must be divided."

Her black irises reflected the horror of the battlefield, but her face remained an emotionless mask as she followed Lucien. They moved from the shadows along the front wall careful to avoid the sides of the mill the dragons were destroying.

"Those who possess ancient magic must be contained until the beast has surfaced. The prophecy isn't theirs to guide, but ours."

His searched the destruction for Rafe. Locating him he pulled Dane across the smoky battlefield in his direction just as the dragons attacked the mill again sending debris showering over them.

Through the chaos, they ran. He wanted to see the look in the warrior's eyes when he realized Dane was no longer his. To see him suffer as those around him perished. Rafe, along with Claaven Callathian had stolen his legacy, taken his home, and cursed his family to mortal life. His revenge would not come in the form of death but in the endless suffering, the warrior would endure. There would be no place for a Morrighann in the new world, no magic for him to control, only an endless life of anguish as he was forced to feel Dane's dark and sensual emotions for eternity.

*In time he would wish for death.*

"Now," he instructed as they reached the center of the field. Dane bent down and placed her hands on the cold ground. The snow melted under her touch as she began to mutter. Rafe battled a group of daemons a few hundred feet away oblivious to her presence. Her darkness cloaked her emotions and altered their binding.

With growing excitement, Lucien watched as the fighting intensified. The daemons spread across the field, mindless corpses, hunting, searching, drawn to the warm blood of their enemies.

Lilith had made him proud. She'd created these ghoulish specimens without even knowing she was doing it. Even while succumbing to the madness brought on by the beast, she'd produced an army of darkness unlike any this world has ever seen.

The ground shuddered beneath his feet as Dane's murmuring increased. He took a step back, so he was closer to where she crouched. The earth beneath her hands began to crack. Snow, soil, and dormant grass flew as a fissure formed. The crack enlarged, racing out along the ground until a yawning gap opened from the right side of the mill diagonally across the property.

He watched with fascination as she turned the other way, placed her hands on the earth and repeated the process. Another crack split the ground, this one running transversely back toward the left side of the mill and trapping another group of her friends near the western altar.

Lucien admired Dane's handiwork.

The cracks in the ground had cut off access to them and the mill. There was no way for any of the immortals to traverse the fissures without falling to certain death. Dane had cut the field in three and now Lucien, her and the mill stood alone on one piece of the property.

"You have done well, my love. Now the beast can come forth without hindrance. The dragons may destroy the structure, but their magic can't penetrate the portal to hell."

He glanced down at Dane who remained in a crouched position. Her eyes were shadowed by the hood of her cloak but for a moment he thought a flash of bright green flickered in the black abyss of her irises.

*Soon.* He thought as he took her hand and helped her to her feet.

*When all this is over, she will emerge as the queen of darkness ready to rule by my side.*

# CHAPTER 38

T HICK SMOKE BILLOWED INTO THE dark night as the bodies of the dead fueled the fires burning around the property. The horrid stench of burnt flesh and decay mingled with the blood-soaked earth and saturated the air.

*They were trapped.*

The altar hummed behind them as the dome began to shudder.

"I can't hold it," yelled the witch who was manning the altar. "The others must have failed." Her ashen face was marred with worry as her eyes locked on Drow.

He sliced down another daemon, its rotting body collapsing in a pile at his feet. "Do whatever you can," he said, his voice barely audible over the rushing wind the others stirred up around them.

Above him, the dome started to crack.

Fissures of glowing light rippled through the invisible field and small pieces of its surface began to slide away. Holes appeared in the protective shield as the entire dome began to crumble around them.

Drow swung his sword again as another daemon surged forward. They were trapped by the fissure which had opened in the earth and there was nowhere to flee, at least not until the dome collapsed. Bodies lay piled up around him, mostly daemons but also the corpses of those who had fought bravely beside him.

He looked around counting those still standing.

Besides the witch managing the altar there were five left including himself.

To his left, Marlee created small tornadoes that picked up the corpses of fallen daemons and flung them at those still attacking. Elyse and a New York witch were near the far edge of the breach battling a squat, rotund daemon whose bulbous eye made a squishing pop when the witch stabbed it with a saber.

The remaining windwitch used the billowing smoke to push back the horde of daemons trapped on this side of the breach. He knew what the witch was trying to do. The cavernous crack was deep and if she could push them back far enough the daemons would fall to their deaths or at the very least be trapped at the bottom.

As she created a wall of wind and smoke in front of them her powers began to falter.

The altars infused the dome with an abundance of ancient magic but as the dome fractured, the magic escaped into the night sky leaving the witches of the earth without the added boost to their natural-born powers.

Fighting two daemons, Drow watched helplessly as the windwitch's magic ebbed. The wall of thick, blustery smoke vanished allowing the horde of daemons to surge and overpower her before she could react. Her scream pierced the darkness for an excruciating moment before she was silenced by death.

After finishing off the daemons in front of him he ran toward the ones that had killed the witch. From his peripheral vision, he saw Marlee and Elyse do the same.

As the distance closed between them and the remaining daemons Marlee drew her weapon. With the magic contained within the dome weakening, they could no longer rely on their physical powers. Earth did not sustain enough elemental power to create an abundant source to fuel their magic. Without the dome's protection and the altars' connection to the ether, their only defense was their fighting abilities. In order to survive this night, they would have to defeat the remaining daemons on this side of the fissure and hope no others found their way across.

The daemons surged toward them at an awkward gait but with uncanny speed. The yellow light glowing behind their hollow eyes forced the rotting corpses to move in impossible ways.

They were the ultimate weapon created by dark magic.

Elyse swung her polearm back and forth cutting through withered skin. Black blood sprayed from the wounds and covered her in a thick, dripping, rancid sludge. She didn't care. Anger coursed through her veins, and she thought of Cal, her husband, who was in Britain unaware of what was happening here at home.

*I will see him again,* she thought as she used the heel of her boot to push the head of a daemon from the tip of her weapon.

She thought of Marlee who stood feet away, her arrows drifting noiselessly through the night air until they found their mark. Nothing would ever be the same between them. Their paths had been irreparably altered and their friendship changed forever by an ancient feud. Whatever their fate, one thing was certain, she and Marlee would co-exist, nothing more.

As she sliced through the face of a horribly deformed daemon one thing was clear, because of her
true destiny she'd lost a friend.

Marlee kicked a few of the daemon bodies into the
chasm. A thud echoed back up to her as the decaying corpses found the bottom. Thick smoke stung her
eyes, and she wiped at the tears. Her mind reeled at
the horrors of the night, so much violence and death
but at least her mind and magic were her own. Her
power felt different from when she was first reborn, but
it still ached of ancient betrayal, loss, and revenge. She
was glad for the separation from her Keltie ancestry,
but she knew somewhere in her blood and magic the
ancestral race would always exist.

They'd dispatched all the daemons on this side of
the breach, vanquishing them back to whatever hell
spawned them in the first place.

*Good riddance*, she said, wiping the blade of her
knife on her sleeve. Movement in the smoke caught her
attention, and she turned her knife at the ready, but it
was just the elf, pulling her weapon from the head of a
corpse. No matter their mortal past Elyse would forever
make her blood simmer with a deep-seated hatred. She
wished it could be different, but she was no longer the
same person. In fact, she'd become the one thing she
most feared—

Before she could finish her thought, a shadow in
the thick smoke behind Elyse moved.

She yelled out a warning just as the daemon
emerged but the screams and sounds echoing through
the field drowned out her words.

In its rotting, deformed hands it held a long blood-soaked pike, the sharp blade pointed at her back. It lumbered forward. Marlee ran, her excessive speed propelling her quickly to Elyse, and pushed her out of the way with moments to spare.

The blade of the pike pierced her chest.

The daemons momentum and otherworldly strength pushed the razor-sharp blade clean through her until the tip protruded from her back. She gasped as a red-hot pain seared through her torso as the sting of dark magic flooded into her blood. Fighting against the foreign object which severed it in half her heart struggled to beat. Air evaded her and a black haze flooded across her vision as all ambient sound disappeared.

The cold night clutched her in its chilly embrace, but she welcomed its sweet sting.

Powerless, Elyse watched from where she fell as Drow swung his sword and lopped the head off the daemon. As its body tumbled to the ground, the weight of the pike's handle pulled Marlee forward. Her hands feebly grasped the handle trying to dislodge it from her chest. But the end jammed into the damp, soggy earth acting as a wedge and holding her at an obscene angle.

"No," Elyse cried as she scrambled to her feet, rushed to her friend, and pushed her upright.

Blood poured from the wound in her chest and dripped from the corners of her mouth. Her eyes were glazed and when she coughed the blood sprayed.

"I'm sorry," Elyse whimpered as she grasped the handle and pulled with all her might.

Marlee screamed as the pike's double-sided blade cut deeper into her flesh as it retreated from her body. Elyse tried to hold her upright, but she staggered and collapsed to the ground. Her blue eyes shone with tears as she gasped for air, the wound bubbling blood with every breath.

Elyse threw the pike aside and sank to the ground beside her, pulling her close. "You're going to be fine, Marlee, I just need to find a healer." Tears streamed down her blood-stained face. "Hold on."

Marlee heaved in her arms gasping for a breath that would never find her lungs.

She could feel Drow's eyes on her as she rocked back and forth, Marlee's head cradled in her arms. Her gaze drifted to his sword. The blade was thick with black blood, yet the sheen of the steel still glimmered beneath. The contrast mimicked the dark and light colliding this night.

"I thought we couldn't die," she sobbed, her eyes begging Drow for an answer. Tears flowed and the mark on her face cooled. In her sorrow, the magic of the Elves of the Wood faded.

Drow shook his head and his shoulders slumped. "There was no way of knowing how our magic would affect your mortal lives. Whether you would endure an immortal existence or still have a fragile life as is the way of mortals. The effects of dark magic are even more unpredictable."

He hesitated for a moment, trying to find the correct words to comfort her.

"Even immortals die, Elyse. Sooner or later all life comes to an end."

As she cradled Marlee in her arms, her chest stopped heaving. Blue eyes stared, unblinking into the night sky. Elyse crumpled over her body as her agonizing wails drifted across the open field.

Guilt and grief engulfed her.

Marlee had given her own life—to save an elf.

# CHAPTER 39

THE ENDLESS BATTLE CONTINUED UNDER the ethereal glow of the prophesied full moon. Smoke from the braziers turned black as blood and flesh filled the metal cauldrons and the moans of the dying echoed through the night air.

Rafe drove the blade of his sword through the rib cage of a daemon.

*There were so many.*

Withered and decaying bodies surrounded them—an army of death. Their eyes glowed with malice as they lumbered through the battlefield, using weapons infused by ancient magic to kill the ones who once wielded them.

They were outnumbered and hopelessly trapped by the sudden appearance of vast fissures that carved the property into islands.

A splitting sound resonated through the sky.

Over the last hour, fractures had appeared in the dome as one by one the altars failed. The ancient magic weakened as did those fighting inside the protective structure.

It would not be long before the dome collapsed entirely and released the horde of daemons on the unsuspecting town of Brighton Hill. The remaining witches waiting on the outskirts would be overrun and those inside the dome would not add enough strength nor magic to help defeat them, even if they could get to them in time.

*They were losing.*

The smoke and fire dragons Stevie had conjured circled the area aimlessly, seemingly no longer under her control.

Rafe eyed the bloody battlefield, searching for her. Through the smoke, he spotted her standing with her back to Killenn's, swords swinging as they fought to stay upright among the horde of daemons surrounding them. Across the fissure to his right was Gabriella. Her wings spread out as her dual blades found the neck of a daemon sending its head sailing into the sky as she sliced it cleanly from its body. Beside her, Gabriel swung his mace knocking three daemons back in a single blow while ramming his sword through the eye of another.

But even the mighty Seraph was waning. As the portal stones went cold, the ancient magic of the ether disappeared taking with it the vitality of their magic.

The fissure behind him hissed as another fire sprang up from its depths. His eyes searched the waterline for Tauria finding her in the upper branches of the towering oak that stood on the banks of the lake. Her arrows flew, each one hitting their mark with precision. But it was futile for she would run out of arrows before she ran out of targets.

His eyes drifted to the base of the tree where Kai attempt to keep the daemons from overwhelming them. She pulled water from the lake and sent waves crashing across the earth, but she too was losing ground as her magic diminished. Soon she would be unable to manipulate the water element to the extreme she was now, and the daemons would swarm the tree.

Rafe scanned the field looking for the others

but could not see Elyse, Marlee, Brannon, Drow, or Sebastian. He knew others were still alive for he could hear shouts and the clash of metal somewhere in the smoke-filled distance. If they couldn't defeat the horde, eventually they would all perish and there would be no one left to halt the ascent of the ancient dark.

The prophecy that would come to pass would not be the one foretold and the Second Coming would ensure mankind's downfall.

He attempted to lift his sword as another daemon approached, but he was too late. The forceful impact sent him sprawling. His back hit the edge of the breach and his shoulders and head hung precariously over the fiery fissure.

Instantly, the daemon was on him.

Broken and chipped fangs gnashed at his face, but he managed to hold it off with his sword. His muscles ached as he struggled with the daemon. Throwing its decaying body aside he scrambled to his feet just as the daemon jumped again, but this time he was not distracted. It landed on the tip of his sword and the sharp blade slid through its decaying body without resistance. As he kicked the screeching daemon off the edge and into the raging inferno consuming the fissure, a deafening roar exploded from the mill.

The ground shook as the building broke apart. Bricks and mortar crumbled as the structure collapsed, sucked into the yawning cavern opening under its foundation.

The portal to hell had opened and the ancient dark was ascending.

From the depths of the fiery canyon, an earthshattering roar echoed upward.

Some daemons retreated toward the crumbled ruins of the mill heeding the call of their master.

Rafe felt a twinge, something he hadn't felt since Dane disappeared. It pulled his attention away from the odd behavior of the daemons and toward the other side of the fissure.

The smoke thinned, and she appeared standing across from him with Lucien Beck. The incubus returned Rafe's gaze and smiled, pulling Dane into his arms in victory. Rafe called out to her but the fierce roar of the ancient dark as it rose from the fragmented ruins swallowed his pleas.

Lucien's eyes were full of glee at Rafe being confined to the other side of the gaping chasm. *It will not be long now, warrior. Dane will forget you, and she will be forever mine.*

His eyes left the warrior as he surveyed the surrounding devastation.

Daemons climbed from the chasm, clawing their way to the surface and away from the raging fires. Bodies lay strewn across the battlefield. Swords clashed in the distance and arrows flew through the smoke-filled air.

Lucien breathed in.

This world is forsaken and those that don't rise with the new one will be cast aside or enslaved for eternity. He glanced around at those who continued to fight valiantly. The ones whose blood surged with ancient magic—her friends.

When the beast rose, they would be the first to *die.*

Lucien pulled Dane to him, his arms encircling her waist. "You chose the right side," he said, kissing the top of her head and pulling her in tight.

As their skin touched, he stiffened. Something wasn't right.

He took a step back as she lifted her face.

The full moon cast its beams across her skin and lit her eyes with its glimmer. Her irises were no longer a dark black instead, a gleaming light jade stared back at him.

Her lips curved at the sides as a look of confusion darkened his features. For a moment he seemed in disbelief unable to grasp the fact she was no longer under his control.

"Dane?"

Breaking his embrace her hand gripped the athame and her eyes lit up with a quiet fury. "Yes," she whispered. "I did pick the right side but unfortunately you did not."

Before he could react, she swung the knife upward and plunged it through his chest piercing the center of his heart. His handsome face contorted as he staggered backward. Desperate hands reached for the knife, but as instructed Dane had pushed the blade in up to the hilt, and he couldn't pull the athame out—the Druid's bone had fused to his chest.

White light flooded from the blade and seeped into the wound. His face registered uncertainty, disbelief, betrayal, anger, and then fear as his mind realized what was happening.

He dropped to his knees as bright crimson stains appeared on his shirt and blood dripped from his lips. Frantically, he clawed at the hilt trying to dislodge it from his chest as the white light snaked its way through his body. Sweat covered his pale skin, and he howled in pain and rage as the dragonscale blade infused his blood with ancient Druid magic.

Frightened eyes locked on Dane's.

*Why?* He mouthed as his body began to shake violently. White light exploded from within as the ancient clock unwound, and the dark magic was cleansed from his body.

Dane raised her hand blocking her eyes from the searing light as it swirled upward and disappeared into the night. She lowered her arm just as Lucien crumpled to the ground, blue eyes drenched in panic. He looked so vulnerable as he lay dying surrounded by the chaos of his making.

Kneeling beside him she lifted his head into her lap and stroked his forehead. His breath became raspy and shallow and his skin, a sickly pallor, was cold and clammy to her touch. The blood pact had been broken and the darkness that enthralled him was gone.

"I'm sorry," he gasped, taking her hand in his. "I really did love you."

His eyes drifted to the sky and he coughed. Blood bubbled from his throat covering his lips and chin. She held him until his body went limp and his heartbeat slowed.

As the last of his life essence dwindled from his eyes a tear fell from hers.

She sat for a moment staring into his lifeless face as the battle raged around her. The stench of burning flesh seared her nostrils, but she didn't move. Incoherent yells drifted on the wind and the sound of metal clashing with metal echoed closer, but she stayed with Lucien. Minutes ticked by before she closed his eyes and lifted his head from her lap laying it tenderly on the blood-soaked earth.

A thunderous growl erupted from the rubble that

was once the old flour mill and Adaridge's words surfaced in her mind, *"killing the incubus and ending the pact will weaken the ancient dark."*

Dane stood and pulled the athame effortlessly from Lucien's chest. The blood on the blade had turned black. It was thick and congealed, and she wiped it on the sleeve of her cloak.

Her heart clenched as Lucien's beautiful face drew her attention once more. He looked so peaceful under the light of the full moon, and she felt a surge of empathy for the man he used to be, not the one he'd become.

Unclasping her cloak, she laid it over his body.

*"Goodbye, Lucien."*

# CHAPTER 40

A TREMOR RIPPLED THROUGH THE GROUND under her feet as another deafening roar erupted from the cavernous hole. She steadied herself until the quake subsided.

*The ancient dark must be near the surface.*

Fires burned on the other side of the breach sending thick, sooty smoke curling upward. She couldn't see far in any direction and feared for her friends.

*Were any of them still alive?*

The pods had obviously borne the daemons Lilith had unwittingly created, and they swarmed everywhere.

She scrutinized her surroundings. Deep and cavernous fissures cut her off in every direction leaving her with only one option and one way to go—back toward the mill.

Without warning a searing pain rifled through her arm, and she dropped to her knees. Her forearm was on fire. Tears streamed down her face but through the blur, she could make out a fresh scorch mark on the inside of her wrist. The skin was bright pink and raw, but she recognized the shape of the symbol. It was one she'd become all too familiar with.

The mark of death—*burnt in flesh.*

Surrounded by death and destruction a moment of clarity came to her. She'd assumed the mark of death was a harbinger signaling the end times—*first in fire, then in blood, and finally in flesh.* A symbol marking the resurrection of the ancient dark and the destruction of the world by either it or the Arcanists. But what if instead of a sign of death it was one of hope.

A rebirth of life through sacrifice.

A mark symbolizing a destiny written for only one.

Her fingers grazed the seared flesh and she winced.

She knew now what she must do.

As she pulled herself upright a voice which had been silent for weeks, sprang up in her mind.

*Dane. Don't.*

Rafe stood on the other side of the flame-laden fissure his green eyes full of love and desperation. She walked to the edge ignoring the heat from the flames. Through the fire, she smiled at him and her eyes filled with tears.

His voice was soft in her mind. *You can't.*

*I have to.*

*There must be another way.*

Dane shook her head.

Her heart thumped eagerly in her chest as it yearned for the one it was bound to. *You must let me go. It's the only way.* Closing her eyes, she envisioned his face and pulled him close in her mind pressing her lips against his. She could taste his sweat and hear the way his heart pounded rhythmically in his chest, matching her own. They would always be one half of the other. Through time and space, they were one.

*Dane, please!*

Opening her eyes, she stared at him across the fissure the light from the flames danced across his handsome face and for a moment

*I love you.*

His face crumpled. *Please don't leave me.*

She smiled at him and placed her hand over her heart. *I will always be with you.*

Without a backward glance, she ran toward the remnants of the old mill burning in the distance. Her heart ached for him the further away she got, but she kept moving toward her destiny.

As she neared the edge of the chasm the earth beneath her feet trembled and tossed her to the ground.

The roar that followed was deafening.

Daemon shrieks filled the air, and she covered her ears as the crescendo of the chorus became unbearable.

There was little left of the mill besides a pile of rubble teetering on the edge of a gaping hole. Smoke filled her lungs as she struggled to her feet and wiped the sweat from her brow. The fire was excruciatingly hot.

There was a shift in the energy around her and the ancient magic in her blood responded, throbbing out a warning.

Something was coming. Something dark and ancient and born from the pits of hell.

Moments later the fires of the chasm separated as something moved within them.

Taking a step back she observed as the prophecy came to pass and the ancient dark, trapped for billions of centuries under the earth's core, appeared.

First, clawed hands the size of tables grasped the edge. Curved horns embedded into both sides of a hairless head appeared next. Two yellow slits where the eyes should be, shone in the firelight as they peered over the edge. Its face was a plain mask without a nose and its mouth was sewn together by pieces of thick skin.

Dane backed up further as the ancient dark dragged its body over the edge. Thick decaying skin stretched taut over a muscular human frame. It wore nothing but a black cloak tied loosely over its shoulders and its manhood was non-existent. A genderless entity and the last of its kind with no way to produce another. *Its only instinct was survival.*

It stood at the edge of the chasm on strong bent legs ending in curved black hooves and looked down on Dane. Thick saliva dripped from its mouth. Although its face did not reflect any expression, Dane sensed it mocked her.

An unexpected pain rifled through her head, and she clutched her temples.

The beast's voice reared up in her mind.

*You have betrayed the one who is bound to me.*

She struggled to stay conscious as waves of pain ripped through her. Stumbling back, she bent over and wretched. Her eyes closed as waves of nausea rolled through her. Through the pain, she searched her mind for the ancient magic that would stifle the connection and allow her to control her interaction with the creature.

A white wave of ancient energy swelled and coursed through her blood. As it rose the pain ransacking her body subsided, and she opened her eyes with a renewed clarity.

*You both underestimated me and assumed my weakness, my anger, would be enough to pull me into your darkness. But you were wrong.*

Its rattling laughter filled her mind.

*Wrong? You are nothing to me, nothing more than a lingering reminder of a long-dead bloodline. I do not seek to understand your kind, nor do I grieve for the death of the one I bore. He was weak as all humans are, a species unable to function without emotions, ambitions, and betrayal. Like those who tried to defeat me before, you too will perish under my wrath. Your kind took my freedom and destroyed my world and for that, I will take yours.*

Stretching its arms wide it pulled the ax from where it was strapped to its back. Heaving the heavy blade up it advanced toward where she stood.

Black, sinister clouds rolled overhead as a thunderclap tore through the sky and the moon disappeared. Sheets of water cascaded from the dark heavens as the storm unleashed its fury. The air was filled with the hiss from the flames as they were doused, and a sooty fog rolled from the ashes.

As the beast drew near Dane's warrior magic erupted, and she attacked with fury throwing energy balls at its massive size. Her intention, *death.*

The sky flashed with green light as the elemental energy seared through its skin opening gashes that streamed black blood. The ancient dark's face contorted, and it lumbered faster toward her.

She pulled her family sword from the sheath, the blade singing with the power of her ancestors. The green energy pulsed up and down its blade as she raised it high and swung it toward the beast.

Their blades met and the sound of clashing metal rang out.

Green sparks flew from her sword.

The ancient magic gave the weapon strength and swiftness, and she moved the blade deftly. Avoiding the ax blade, she swung her sword in a graceful arc and connected with the soft, decaying flesh of the beast's arm. It howled and staggered backward as the blade singed its skin.

Its ax swung again, and she moved promptly to the left, but while the blade missed the handle of the ax caught her neatly in the side. The force of the blow sent her flying, and she slammed into the wet ground gasping for breath.

The ancient dark, its yellow eyes ablaze, roared.

Wiping the rain from her eyes she searched for her sword. The mud created by the downpour was thick and it pulled her into its grasp as she slogged through it toward her weapon. The ground trembled as the beast thundered toward her. Grasping the hilt, she rolled sideways just as the ancient dark's ax sliced down. The blade just missed her head, and she scrambled to her feet. Dodging the backswing she sliced at the ancient dark's hoofed feet as she passed.

The surrounding battle raged on.

Shouts echoed in the dark.

The rain had diminished, and the moon peeked out from behind the thick cloudbank.

She ran back toward the edge of the burning crevasse with the ancient dark in pursuit. Her hand grasped for the athame in her belt, but it wasn't there. Desperately she looked for it.

A beam of silver light glistened from the moon and glinted off something stuck in the mud. The white bone handle of the athame protruded from the dirt just feet from where the ancient dark now stood. Its body heaved as it stomped its hooves in the soggy ground and shook the rain from its ax blade.

Something behind the beast drew her attention. It was Rafe. Somehow, he'd managed to get to this side of the breach, but daemons swarmed him, and he was trapped.

His blade dripped with blood as he swung it toward two daemons, severing their heads in succession.

As if sensing her eyes upon him, he turned.

Suddenly, she could hear Adaridge's voice echoing in her mind.

*Use the darkness, do not become it.*

Moonbeams cascaded over her as the clouds parted and a strange enchanting peace cocooned her in its tranquility. A chorus of voices sang softly in her head— voices of those long forgotten. Through the chorus, she heard one voice stronger and clearer than the others.

*It is time.* Adaridge whispered.

The ancient dark bellowed.

And Dane knew. Their power and blood were a part of her. This was her destiny. With a renewed furor she spun in a circle as the ancient dark charged. Her sword cut deep through the flesh and into the sinew of his thighs. An enraged roar erupted as he floundered, unsteady on his legs. The ax swung, but she avoided the blow and the blade buried itself deep into the soaking wet ground.

Using her momentum and trusting her instincts she dropped the sword and darted forward. She rolled onto the ground and seized the athame from where it was lodged into the earth and turned to face the ancient dark. Hooves pounded the wet earth and its eyes glowed with what could only be described as the dregs of hell. Reflections of the prison that had caged this evil entity for billions of centuries.

Its voice reared up in her mind. *It is time to die.*

*You first,* she thought.

And then she ran.

Her legs throbbed as she sprinted. The muddy ground grasped at her boots, but she kept moving, ignoring the pain. She ran to the edge of the void where the old flour mill used to sit and from where the ancient dark had emerged.

Its laughter rang in her head as it lurched toward her.

She stood with her back to the gaping hole and lowered her stance.

The ancient dark bent so its horns were low. Like a bull and matador all in one, the black cape flew gracefully behind him as its massive hooves churned up the soft, wet ground. It charged and just as it reached her, she flipped to one side. Her body skimmed the entity as it thundered past, and she plunged the athame into its shoulder, pushing the blade in up to the hilt.

The beast howled in rage as white light exploded from the blade. Its hooves dug into the sodden earth as it tried to stop its momentum, but the wet soil crumbled underfoot.

The ancient dark plummeted over the edge carrying Dane with it, her hand clutched tight to the handle of the athame.

# CHAPTER 41

A s Dane and the ancient dark disappeared over the edge of the chasm, an explosion rocked its depths. Debris tumbled as the remaining rubble of the old mill was swallowed by the expanding sinkhole.

A chorus of unholy screams pierced the night sky and Rafe sank to his knees and covered his ears as the cacophony reverberated over the field. The daemons surrounding him fell, one by one as the evil light filling their hollow eye sockets extinguished. Like a macabre wave, they collapsed until only a pile of bones, sinew, and black blood littered the ground.

An eerie silence draped over the field.

Wiping blood and sweat from his eyes he stood. His head reeled as the first light of day escaped over the horizon. A shadowy figure came toward him through the heavy smoke furling from the rain-drenched fires. Its movement was slow and unsteady, and he raised his blade in defense.

"Rafe?"

Recognizing the voice, he lowered his sword.

Stevie appeared from the haze followed by Gabriella. Both were covered in black soot and ash, their hair matted, and faces splattered with blood.

"Are you hurt?" Rafe asked.

Both shook their heads.

Stevie's eyes searched desperately around the area, panic rising in her voice. "Where is she, Rafe? Where is Dane? I saw her fighting the ancient dark."

His shoulders sagged as his eyes drifted toward the vast crater that had consumed the mill. An enormous fire blazed from its dark depths and black smoke billowed up hundreds of feet into the early morning dawn.

He waited for what seemed like an eternity his heart pounding in his chest—waiting for that familiar connection. But no matter how hard he tried he couldn't feel her anymore. Instead, an emptiness took the place of the emotional bond they shared, a deep void that filled him with a haunting ache.

"She's gone," he choked out.

"What do you mean—*gone?*" Stevie's voice cracked.

"I can't feel her anymore."

"Try again!"

His energy reached toward the chasm as his heart searched for her but there was nothing, just emptiness. The heaviness inside became suffocating as he realized what that meant.

"Anything?" Stevie said moving in closer.

The intense smell of blood and ash swirled around her and his stomach lurched. Ignoring her question, he stared back at the fiery chasm as the ache in his heart grew heavier. He so badly wanted this nightmare to be just a bad dream and for Dane to be standing safely beside him.

The scent and sounds of death and decay, of burnt flesh, wafted all around them. A macabre requiem for the dead.

"Rafe?"

"No," he said quietly. "Nothing."

Stevie glanced over to Gabby who stood a few feet

away. Her eyes implored the celestial for a different answer.

She folded her enormous wings back as her iridescent eyes searched the area. A shadow passed over her face as she too shook her head. "I can't sense her anymore nor can I feel the ancient dark."

Rafe couldn't speak. The emotions washing through him were torturous. Beside him, Stevie's eyes filled with tears, and she began to tremble. Exhausted and grief-stricken, they continued to stare at the billowing fire in solemn silence.

The smoke rising from the ruins attempted to block out the coming dawn, but the new day stubbornly cast an array of purple, orange, and blue hues across the early morning sky. The medley of color was a stark contrast to the bleak landscape surrounding them.

Soon, others emerged from the smoke.

Witches and immortals, the wounded and the lucky. They stood in proximity to one another staring at the raging fire, each lost in their own thoughts and mourning the loss of their own.

The prophecy had come to pass, and its end realized. The Arcanists had defeated the ancient dark but at a devastating cost. Many had lost their lives, but thankfully mankind would remain oblivious to tonight's events. Those who carried the blood of the ancient races had prevailed.

Rafe surveyed the grounds.

The old mill was destroyed leaving nothing but a yawning blazing pit and a pile of rubble. Nothing remained to reveal its existence prior to this evening except an old concrete pillar with a brass plate inscribed with the mill's name and the year of its founding. His eyes locked on it as it methodically swung back and forth from the one bolt still holding it in place. The sound of metal scratching on the concrete was deafening and, he closed his eyes willing it to stop, to disappear from his mind with the rest of this nightmare.

Dane had defeated the ancient dark but in turn, had given the utmost sacrifice—*her life*.

As that realization embedded itself in his very being blood began to roar in his ears, and the aching thump of his heart blocked out all the awful sounds around him, encasing him in its agonizing rhythm. Sweat ran down his blood-soaked skin stinging as it seeped into the wounds on his arms. Unforgiving reminders that he was still alive and still breathing alone without her.

Rooted in his misery and as the pain overwhelmed him, he hung his head, shut his eyes, and wordlessly begged the gods to release him from this suffocating prison.

An eternity seemed to pass before he felt someone squeeze his shoulder, and he heard Stevie's voice in his ear.

"Rafe, look."

There was an unexpected excitement in her voice, and he opened his eyes. Tears blurred his vision but when they cleared, he saw what she did, and he stared in disbelief and awe.

The fire blazing in the crater was changing.

The red flames, their scorching tendrils reaching in all directions, began to turn *green* as the crackling transformed to a concordant hum.

*The fire was morphing into something else, something otherworldly as the green energy of the Warlicians consumed it.*

As the scorching flames of destruction disappeared a calmness seeped from the enormous crater and spread over the scorched earth of the property. The black smoke curling from its depths disappeared, replaced by a thick green mist that created a curtain between them and the dark abyss.

Rafe squinted into the dense fog.

His heart pounded as he sensed a presence in the swirling fog, and he tightened his grip on his sword. The strange essence came closer until a shadow emerged into the light of dawn.

The figure was familiar. Long dark hair flowed behind her as she strode with purpose toward them but there was something different about her presence. Her movements were languid and effortless, and her bright green eyes held a wisdom that had been lost to the ages.

He blinked several times unsure if what he was seeing was real?

Was Dane *alive?!*

She reached the battle-scarred ground where they stood before any of them could utter a word.

Every eye was transfixed on her in disbelief.

When she smiled, her jade eyes twinkled with an iridescent light. A faint lilac hue shimmered on her unblemished skin—there wasn't a mark on her, no blood or dirt, no ash or scars.

"How?" Elyse asked, finding her voice.

Dane arched an eyebrow and tilted her head in Elyse's direction. Without saying a word, she lifted her right arm out in front of her and opened her clenched fist.

Gabby gasped and took a step back her wings lifting into the air. Blood-soaked feathers quivered and splattered droplets on the ground around her.

"The ether," she said softly, gazing at the iridescent purple substance that flickered and floated in Dane's palm. She lifted her eyes. "Impossible. Even those of us born from the ether cannot wield its power directly.

The ether is not a malleable substance and therefore cannot be manipulated or contained." Gabby faltered. "How?"

Dane closed her hand around the ether and let her arm drop to her side.

"Something happened after I fell into the abyss with the ancient dark. As I plummeted, time and space seemed to shift around me, and the worlds collided—this one and the ancient realms. Magic flared, some I recognized, much I didn't, elemental magic flowing through the ages and fusing to me. The further I plunged into the void the stronger the magic became, and I could sense a change in myself. Suddenly I knew I could defeat the beast. Not just entomb him back into a dark prison but destroy him forever."

Her eyes flashed with the iridescent light of the ether.

"All the elements were at my command and I harnessed their combined power to destroy the ancient dark."

Roused from his shock Rafe said, "You can control all the elements."

With a nod of acknowledgment, her gaze shifted to Gabby as she spoke.

"The energy infused in your aura has long been absent from any of the Five Realms and the magic you wield is primordial, as old as the Thanissia universe itself," Gabby said.

"Now it makes sense," Stevie squeaked, the awe in her tone elevating its pitch.

Sebastian looked at her quizzically, "What does?"

"There was a passage in the very back of the ancient tome. It was hidden on the inside of the back cover infused into the pages by some type of magic. When I dropped the book, it fell open and the full moon's light illuminated the ancient script that was written there."

"What did the inscription say?" asked Sebastian as the others drew closer to Dane their astonishment at her escape from death turning to morbid curiosity.

Stevie shifted uncomfortably as she recited the words. *"And from the ashes will rise the Arcana—the one who wields the magic of time, the one who controls them all."*

As Stevie's words echoed through the early morning air, Rafe thought about what had transpired here this night. They had battled tirelessly and against all odds—witches, immortals, friends, and strangers—and sacrificed much to save the future of not just this world, but the worlds lost long-ago to time.

The crackling of the green fire rising from the crater began to diminish and the morning sky turned into a brilliant blue, shedding its kaleidoscope of dawn colors.

His eyes turned to Dane and a surge of emotion ran through him as she gazed lovingly back at him. He walked over and took her in his arms. A sense of relief flooded through him as she melted into his embrace and their hearts once again beat in unison.

Fatigued eyes stared at the others as he held her close.

*She was the reason they fought and the reason they survived, and she will be the reason this world and his will thrive.*

*Dane was the past, the present, and the future.*

*She was the very essence of the ETHER.*

# END OF BOOK 3

# ACKNOWLEDGMENTS

It is bittersweet coming to the end of something that has delightfully consumed years of your life, but I have left a few portals open to these worlds just in case I wish to return someday. But for now, it's time to move on and experience the joy of creating something new.

Writing might be a solitary endeavor but creating a book is not and I would like to thank all those who have been involved in bringing The Scrying Trilogy to life, from cover designers and critique partners to editors and beta readers. Without you, these books would just be words on a page.

To all those who are emotionally invested. You persevered through this journey with me and your love, support, and dedication are what gives me wings to follow my dreams.

Most of all I would like to thank the readers who have loved my characters and their stories and immersed themselves in my worlds without fail. You are the heart of what I do.

# ABOUT THE AUTHOR

Jaci Miller was born in Ontario, Canada and moved to the United States at thirty-four when she married her husband. She received a Bachelor of Arts in English from the University of Phoenix, developing her writing skills in multiple creative writing classes. During her studies The Scrying Trilogy evolved, beginning with a storyboard that claimed one of her basement walls for over a year. *The Arcana* is the third book in the trilogy.

When she is not playing with her imaginary friends and writing down their stories, Jaci enjoys reading, cooking, home décor and DIY projects, paddleboarding and yoga. She currently resides in Vermont with her husband and their Jack Russell Terrier, Ike (aka The Grumps).

You can find Jaci on Instagram and
Facebook @jacimillerauthor

www.jacimiller.com
www.solitarypenpress.com

Made in the USA
San Bernardino, CA
25 June 2020